LOVE'S KNIFE

LOVE'S KNIFE

TROBAIRITZ SLEUTH
BOOK ONE

TRACEY WARR

❀ Created with Vellum

For my grandfather, William John Warr (1905–1968),
who went deaf working as an artist in a printing works,
and who was my childhood inspiration for becoming an
avid reader and writer.

'Such others go around talking and talking big of love,
  But we have a morsel of its bread, and a knife.'

—Guillaume IX of Aquitaine, the *trobador* duke, 'Ab
la dolchor del temps novel', early twelfth century

CONTENTS

GLOSSARY

Occitan spellings are used for personal names and place names (e.g., Tolosa for Toulouse) within Occitania. Occitan was the language of troubadour poetry. See the Historical Note for more on Occitania and the Occitan culture.

- Aquamanile - water jug for washing hands
- Garrigue - low scrubland on southern French limestone soils, often composed of kermes oak, lavender, thyme, white cistus and a few isolated trees
- Hypocras - medieval spiced wine, considered an aphrodisiac
- Jograresa - female performer of song, dance, juggling, acrobatics
- Oud - short-necked, lute-type, pear-shaped, fretless stringed instrument, like a guitar
- Portarius - gatekeeper
- Razo - introduction to a *trobador*'s song

- Trobar - to find and invent poetry
- Trobador - composer of poetry and song in the Occitan language
- Trobairitz - female *trobador*
- Vectuari - merchant
- Vicar - nobleman or woman acting as the chief administrator for the count (a secular role)
- Vida - the life of a *trobador*, often told in performance as an introduction to songs
- Vielle - stringed instrument similar to a violin

PROLOGUE

Around Midnight, Easter Monday 1093, Chateau
Narbonnais, Tolosa

*T*he undercroft swam woozily back into view.
His head was pounding. Huge, dark barrels
stacked on their sides loomed around and above him. He
was propped askew against a barrel, with his legs splayed
in front of him. Another cask to his right dripped wine
from its spigot. On the edge of his vision, he could just see
a dark red, misshapen stain from the drips pooling on the
earth floor, but... Pain. Terrible pain on the right side of
his neck. He groaned aloud.

Something was lodged above his collarbone. If he
turned his head even slightly, it set off a searing pain. He
swivelled his eyes back to straight ahead and held his head
still, desperate to reduce the agony. His vision began to
focus in the gloom. How did he come here?

Not a heavy drinking session. A struggle. Someone hit him on the head and rammed this knife into his neck that he was feeling now like a lump of hard bread stuck in his gullet, a solid, unyielding intrusion in his flesh, agonising his every breath. His head was angled slightly downwards and he could see a long, dark stain spilled down the front of his tunic. His blood, not wine. He breathed out on the pain.

With his left hand, he tried to reach for the thing jammed in his neck, but his arm dropped back weakly onto the floor beside his hip, palm splayed upwards, jarring the injury. Even if he could pull the blade from the wound, would his life's blood gush out?

He tensed the muscles in his left thigh to see if he could stand but could barely lift his leg at all before it collapsed back down, enfeebled. He was pinned. Could not move any part. He panted with the heavy ache of the knife, trying to regather himself. Had to keep his eyes from closing. 'He-lp!' he croaked. A rat in a dim corner ahead of him froze on its hindquarters, two paws held together in front of its chest.

There was rustling to his left. Too noisy, too big for a rat. He was still here! Someone was riffling through the parchments in his satchel. Someone who had stuck this dagger into him. Panic rose to meet the pain.

Legs came into view in front of him. Yellow hose. Muscled legs. He could just see the edge of a green tunic, but couldn't lift his head to see who stood there. The legs came closer, green shoes stepping delicately between and over his calves, moving to his right. His throbbing neck was immobile, but his eyes swivelled, straining to see what the legs were doing.

Had he gone? 'Help!' he croaked tentatively. Nothing happened. 'Help! Help!' he tried again, a little louder. Suddenly, the man was behind him, wedging a leg between his back and the barrel, a knee pushing him forward to bend at the waist. He screamed at the torment of his neck. Taken into an embrace, a filament flashing past his eyes, a necklace dropping round his damaged throat. He should try to slip his fingers between the desperate pulse of his artery and the cruel garrotte, but he had no power. He clung feebly to the man's arm and watched his feet scrabble in the dirt in front of him, raising dust.

PART I

January–April 1093

HOLY LOTS

18 January 1093, Chateau Narbonnais, Tolosa

eatriz woke to the sound of heavy rain on the roof tiles immediately above her bedchamber, although 'bedchamber' was an exaggeration for this tiny, cold sliver of attic in the Galliarde Tower. Still, it was private, and nobody knew she was here. The tower room was preferable to sleeping with the snoring soldiers and visitors in the Great Hall, even though she was missing the warmth of the hearth. It was also preferable to sleeping on a mattress in Imbert's chamber.

She sat up. Her breath came in small, white clouds around her face. Imbert and Count Raimon would be away in Dijon for a few more weeks. She had taken the opportunity of Imbert's absence to bring her few possessions up the ladder into this forgotten space. She looked with longing at the sleek curves of her *vielle* where it leant against the wall. The room was cold but dry, which the *vielle* appreciated. She had been up for several hours in the night, starting to compose the new song, and she was impatient to get on with it, but Lady Philippa insisted Beatriz come to her first thing. The bells of Saint Etienne Cathedral had woken her some time ago calling the monks to Prime, but she had fallen back to sleep. Light was slipping around the edges of the heavy green cloth slung across the window.

Braving the chill for a moment, she stood and pulled her night shift over her head. After the nest-warmth of her bed, the January air was like a shard of ice held against her naked skin. She wrestled on a brown undertunic and green overtunic and bent to lace her boots. Wrapping her cloak around herself, she nestled her chin into its high fur collar. It was only rabbit fur, not the ermine on Lady Philippa's cloak, but it kept her throat warm. She could not afford to take ill and risk her voice. She lifted her long black curls free from the collar. Anna would comb the sleep tangles out for her later.

Perhaps there would be a few moments to snatch to herself for composition. She picked up the *vielle* and bow and fitted them into the sling Anna had stitched for her with a band across her shoulder and chest so that her instrument could sit safely on her back. She made her way down the three short ladders that joined her attic to the fourth, third and second floors. An arched doorway on the second floor let out onto the arcaded walkway above the massive Narbonnais Gate, the main southern portal to the city of Tolosa, built into its Roman wall. She threaded her way along the stone passage, with its windows overlooking the circular courtyard on her left and the countryside, ditch and palisade protecting the gate on her right. Lady Philippa's chambers were in the east tower, the Tour de Sire Claude. The two towers – the Galliarde and the Sire Claude – stood either side of the gateway, forming the Chateau Narbonnais, the fortified palace of the count of Tolosa.

Roger and his tattoos stood guard just inside Philippa's door. Roger was Lady Philippa's huge Norman bodyguard who had come from Sicily. The snaking tattoos on his neck and lower face made him look permanently ferocious. He nodded a greeting to Beatriz as she entered. Lady Philippa's accommodation consisted of four rooms on the second floor. In the first ante-chamber, Beatriz saw Philippa and Anna sitting at a table with a pile of parchments and inkpots before them. Their uncovered blonde heads were bowed close together – the rich gold of Anna's hair contrasting with Philippa's silvery yellow. Anna's mother had been Philippa's wetnurse, and they were inseparable. They and Beatriz were of an age, in their seventeenth years.

The ante-chamber was lavishly decorated with textiles, cushions, tapestries, finely carved chests, shelves holding books and parchments, great vases of flowers. Beatriz luxuriated in the colours – blues, purples, yellow, green – and the sweet scents of the bouquets. This was where Lady Philippa received her guests and carried on her business as the daughter of the count of Tolosa. She owned several properties and had tenants, stewards, merchants and clerics to correspond with, accounts to look over. A fire was burning well in the large hearth.

Beyond this room was the smaller bedroom with a fine canopied bed and a chest holding Philippa's tunics. There were two small rooms off the bedchamber: on the window-side, a *garde de robe* with a chute emptying directly into the ditch around the chateau, and on the other side of the chamber, a tiny room where Anna slept.

Anna looked up at Beatriz's entry.

'How did you know I was approaching?' Beatriz asked, enunciating the words clearly, looking Anna squarely in the face, since Anna was deaf.

'I felt the vibrations of your steps through my feet.' She pointed at her bare feet on the floorboards. Anna's voice was thick. Her phrases came in short bursts. Beatriz tried and failed to imagine the experience of a silent world.

'What are you doing?' Beatriz looked at the papers on the table, frustrated as always that she could not read them herself.

'Preparing the menu for the Saint Valentine's day feast,' Anna said.

'And looking over my correspondence,' Philippa added. 'Still nothing from my mother. I should have received a reply by now, surely!' Philippa tapped Anna on the arm as she said it. Anna could read the words on your lips by watching your mouth, seeing the formation of the words. She had not always been deaf. It had come on her suddenly in childhood, after an illness. Philippa repeated her question. 'I should have received a reply from my mother, don't you think?'

'Perhaps, lady,' Anna answered hesitantly, looking around the chamber at Beatriz and Roger for support. Philippa's cat, Tibers, had squeezed herself in alongside

Anna's thigh, taking what warmth she could find there. Anna fended her curious claws away from her quill.

'How long has it been?' Beatriz asked, to help Anna out. Lady Philippa's demands could be difficult to manage sometimes.

'Near a month,' Philippa said. 'I sent the letter just before Christmas.'

'That's less than a month, Lady Philippa. You have to be patient,' Beatriz said impatiently. She was keen to get back to her song and having to humour Philippa's girlish anxieties today was wasting precious time. Philippa's mother, Countess Emma, was at the court of Jaca in Aragon, where she was negotiating a marriage for Philippa to the ageing king, Sancho Ramírez. Philippa's letter had argued against the marriage, even though it would make her a queen. She had informed her mother that she needed a young husband from the local Occitan nobility, or perhaps from her mother's Norman kin to the north or in Sicily. Philippa had read the letter to Beatriz and Anna before sending it. Beatriz judged Philippa's address to her mother to be a rather high-handed harangue, but she had kept her opinion to herself.

'There must be a reason for your mother's silence,' Beatriz said. 'Perhaps she is away and hasn't read the letter yet.'

'At least we have a respite, Beatriz. My uncle Raimon and Imbert will be absent a while yet at the court of Burgundy. Although that journey is just another of the prison bars hemming me in,' Philippa declared dramatically.

'What do you mean?' Beatriz asked, as she was meant to.

'My uncle is negotiating a marriage for my cousin Bertrand with the duke of Burgundy's daughter.' With both her mother and father away, Lady Philippa was in the guardianship of her uncle, Count Raimon of Saint-Gilles. Philippa's father was on pilgrimage to Jerusalem, hoping for a cure for a festering war wound he had taken and begging God to let his last remaining son live. Her father had been gone for over a year already.

'How does Bertrand's proposed marriage hem you in?'

'It is just another confirmation that I am discarded, sent far away and my cousin regards himself as the heir to Tolosa in my place.'

Beatriz held her tongue. She had been an audience for Philippa's complaining for long enough this morning.

'Try Saint Agatha,' Roger said abruptly. The three young women turned to stare at him in surprise. Roger rarely spoke. Despite his silence, you could never forget, however, that he was in the room.

'What do you mean, Roger, try Saint Agatha?' Beatriz asked testily.

Roger sighed, reluctant to have to say more. 'Divination,' he conceded.

Beatriz rolled her eyes. With Roger's usual locution of one-word answers, gaining his meaning was going to be a slow process.

'Do you know what he means?' Philippa asked Beatriz. She often spoke about Roger in front of him.

'Princess chest,' said Roger cryptically, pointing at the marriage chest of Princess Mafalda, which he had carried himself, hefting it on and off his muscled shoulder, on Mafalda's long voyage from Sicily to marry Philippa's uncle Raimon. The oak chest had short legs and spiralling patterns carved into its front side. It had iron hinges and silver latches decorated with roses. When Count Raimon had repudiated the princess and banished her to a convent, Roger had, without being asked, transferred his services to Lady Philippa. She had inherited the chest along with Roger himself.

'Ah!' said Beatriz. She crossed the room and lifted the lid to peer down at the carefully packed contents of the chest. Whenever Philippa riffled through the various clothes and objects in the chest, Roger would refold, reorganise, and repack them in their original state. Beatriz supposed it was an homage to his lost mistress. Roger stood alongside Beatriz (the top of her head was on a level with his armpit) and they looked down into the chest together. He pointed to a large cloth pouch. Beatriz fished it out.

Philippa and Anna had followed them across the room and were peering over Beatriz's shoulders, curious to know what Roger had indicated. With their blonde heads and if they were seated together, Philippa and Anna could be taken for sisters, but when they stood alongside each other, the contrast between them was pronounced. Where Philippa was tall and slender, her body almost without curves, flat and narrow in all directions, Anna was short and plump. Philippa's eyes were almond-shaped and a vivid green, set in a long, thin face, while Anna's face was small and round and her dark grey eyes within it were like two currants. Beatriz glanced with envy at Philippa's blue dress with its silver edgings. It hugged her angular figure and bloomed into enormous sleeve-cuffs in the new fashion. Anna, like Beatriz, was dressed in the plainer, old-fashioned style, in a brown tunic showing the tight red sleeves of her undertunic.

Beatriz took the pouch to the table, and the girls resumed their seats. They were always careful to position themselves so that Anna could see their mouths when they spoke. Anna pushed the inkpots to one side, and Beatriz untied the ribboned neck of the pouch. The objects she drew out of the pouch were a candle with a picture of a female saint pasted to its side, three bone dice, and a small, old book bound in dark green leather. On the cover, the words *Sortes Sanctorum* were inscribed in gold leaf. 'Holy Lots,' said Anna, translating the Latin and looking up at Roger. He nodded blithely, his mute expression suggesting he had provided them with the meaning of life, and that was all they were going to get out of him.

'Well, how does it work?' Philippa demanded, turning the dice over curiously in her hand.

'I know,' Anna said. 'The feast of Saint Agatha is especially effective for divination.' She picked up the candle and studied the picture. 'See, this is the saint with her breasts in a dish. Saint Agatha is a Sicilian saint.' She looked to Roger, who made no acknowledgement of his homeland. She turned the candle so that Philippa and Beatriz could study the picture.

Beatriz grimaced at the depiction of a young woman carrying her own breasts, severed in the Roman torture of a Christian. 'Hideous,' she said.

'Beatriz!' Philippa exclaimed. 'Saint Agatha suffered for her faith and should be venerated by us for that.'

Beatriz cocked an eyebrow by way of disagreement. She frequently found herself at odds with Philippa's extreme piety. Anna glanced at Beatriz, amused, and returned to studying the book. Beatriz listened to its old parchment pages whispering and creaking as Anna carefully turned them.

'You ask a question,' Anna announced, 'throw the dice, and use the numbers to find the answer in this book.'

Roger nodded.

'Lady Mafalda used this, did she?' asked Philippa, but Roger clearly felt he had completed his exposition and had nothing more to say.

'Saint Agatha's feast is in three days' time,' said Anna. 'Time enough to fast in preparation for the divination.'

Beatriz rolled her eyes to the ceiling beams again. Not *another* fast! As she rushed along the passage to Philippa's chamber this morning, she had glimpsed the cook's boy in the courtyard below. He had been carrying a succulent-looking chicken towards the kitchen.

'Yes,' said Philippa, pleased to have found a solution to her marriage dilemma. 'We will fast – no meat or cheese – for the next three days, and you and I, Beatriz, will ask the book our questions on Saint Agatha's day.'

'I don't need to ask it anything,' Beatriz objected.

'Yes, you do,' asserted Philippa. 'I have to ask if I will marry a young, handsome lord and you have to ask if you will have to marry Imbert.'

Beatriz frowned. 'I would rather not be reminded of that.'

'Perhaps you should ask if you will marry Lluis,' Anna said, laughing.

Beatriz frowned some more. 'I don't need to ask a dusty old book anything.'

'We will do it,' said Philippa with a snap of finality.

Beatriz looked at her sourly, but Philippa's gaze was fixed on the pages of the *Sortes Sanctorum* book, while Anna returned to her sewing. Beatriz shivered at a sudden cold draught in the room. Two large tapestries clad the walls to either side of the chamber, and their edges lifted slightly here and there. The tapestries depicted the four seasons – spring and summer with greens and blooms to one side, and autumn and winter with glimmering leaf colours and the white of snow and ice to the other. Beatriz longed for the light and heat of summer, still far off. 'May I leave you now, my lady? I need to complete my songs for the return of your uncle.'

'And the return of Imbert,' Philippa reminded her unhelpfully.

2

THE PATH THROUGH THE
FOREST

21 January 1093, Chateau Narbonnais

*B*eatriz opened her eyes again on the *vielle*, where it waited patiently for her. Her stomach growled. Thank goodness the Saint Agatha's fast ended today. She was sick of beans and vegetables. She rose and threw her cape around her nightdress.

She pulled herself up onto the stone sill of the long window of her eyrie, pushing aside the curtain. Gingerly, holding fast to the bevelled edge, she inched as far forward as she dared to take a view of the city of Tolosa with the morning mist and rain just clearing. The opening was designed for an archer, but was fairly wide, as it was so high up. She liked to look out from her perch in Chateau Narbonnais to watch the city waking and setting about its daily business.

Directly below her was the old Roman road that led

out from the courtyard into the city. Looking right, she could see the tall bell tower of Saint Etienne Cathedral and beyond was the Saracen Wall, separating the old city of Tolosa from the new bourg where she could just glimpse Saint-Sernin. The new basilica was rising rapidly in a chaos of scaffolding and stone dust. The distant chink of hammers and shouts were perceptible on the cold air. Work had already started this morning and Lluis would be labouring in the sculptors' workshop.

Movement on the road coming from the bridge on the left caught her eye. A large group of pilgrims were heading for Saint-Sernin. Even though the basilica was only part-built, it was already holding masses, when the hammering would fall silent and the Augustinian canons in their white cassocks for holy days would brave the dust with bells and incense. Saint-Sernin was a draw for the pilgrims on their road to the shrine of Saint James in distant Compostela. Below her, to the left, were the red roof tiles of the Mint, which was striking silver coins showing the likeness of Philippa's father, but those coins were all destined for the coffers of Philippa's uncle Raimon now.

Was this finally home, she wondered. This wealthy court of Tolosa at the crossroads of the trade routes from the Mediterranean Sea to the east to the Atlantic Ocean to the west, from the Iberian kingdoms in the south to the cities of Poitiers, Dijon and Paris to the north? She had travelled widely with Imbert in the last four years, performing at many courts – earning their crust, as Imbert said – although he gambled away most of what they earned as soon as they earned it.

Lady Philippa intended to ask Count Raimon if she could take Beatriz into her household as her official *trobairitz*. If that failed to thwart Imbert's marriage plans, Beatriz would have to run away again. She would lose the comfort and stimulation of this court. She would lose everything she had built here: the patronage of Philippa, the friendship of Anna and Lluis. If Philippa's plan succeeded, Beatriz might find herself on the road to Aragon, where Philippa would become the new queen. Saint Etienne's bell rang for Terce, reminding Beatriz she was late again. Hastily, she stepped down from the windowsill.

She picked up her *vielle*. It was a simple design, an oval with two capital Bs cut into the sounding box, back-to-back, either side of the four strings. The strings were raised up on the bridge positioned between the two Bs. Imbert had given the instrument to her last year as a Christmas gift. If Philippa were officially her patron, perhaps she could buy a more elaborate instrument with the kind of beautiful, wood inlay that Imbert had on his *oud* but, for now, she loved the simple lines of the *vielle*. She had already composed five of her own songs on it.

Beatriz positioned the wide bottom of the *vielle* under her chin, against her collarbone, and the body and neck rested along her arm. She drew the bow across the four strings experimentally, tightening the pegs at the neck until she was happy with the tone of each string. One she set to drone. She listened to the tones amplified by the hollow box. That was another advantage of her attic room. No one could hear her practising unless they advanced a long way up the ladders from floor to floor.

The rooms below were used for storage and nobody slept there. Finding protected, hidden places was a skill she had learnt when she had lived on the streets as a beggar, before Imbert found her.

She was struggling with the melody for the last stanza of this new song, which she would perform at the Easter feast. A text without music is a mill without water, Imbert had told her. Pushing the worry of Imbert from her mind, she tried to focus on sound instead. She used the ridged frets on the *vielle*'s neck to help her fix the position of her fingers and ran through the song as far as she had got it. The sound soared in the room and she closed her eyes, hearing it fill the space, ripple in the four corners, tug at her heartstrings, shiver the hairs on the back of her neck.

Beatriz stopped and held the instrument at her side, trying to ignore the guilt buzzing at her head like a mosquito. She did not feel compunction about her resolve to refuse Imbert as a husband. She had to do it. But she felt a little guilty that she would take the fruits of Imbert's labours in tutoring her and turn them against him, to free herself from him.

She looked at her battered travelling chest, which she had set up as a portable desk. It held Lluis' small sketch of her home village of Farrera in the Catalan Pyrenees. The sketch was propped against the wall and showed Beatriz's father at work in his forge. Beatriz had described her memory of Farrera, and Lluis had magically captured it on the parchment. Her five songs with their melodies were stored in a leather pouch on the chest. Beatriz had to rely on Anna for her scribing. If Anna did not have needlework in her lap, you could be sure to find a parchment there instead. Anna was trying to teach Beatriz to write words and musical notation, but she was still a beginner and sometimes felt she would never master it.

Beatriz moved to the desk, bending her neck carefully to avoid braining herself on the sloping beams of the attic. She slid the five parchments out of the pouch and looked them over. Anna had shown her how to write her name at the bottom, and Beatriz had gazed intently at Anna's long fingers as they worked to paint a beautiful illustration of Beatriz playing the *vielle* to one side of the signature. She placed the parchments carefully back in the pouch and positioned it with satisfaction on her desk, weighting it down with a shiny brown stone she had found on the riverbank. A strong gust of wind might penetrate the unglazed window of the high tower room.

Philippa was Beatriz's best hope and defence against Imbert, so she could not afford to displease the lady and must hurry now. Inside Lady Philippa's chamber, Beatriz nodded to Roger. Her stomach rumbled again at the sight of a tray of cakes on a side table. They were bell shaped, decorated with white icing and topped with a cherry. 'They are for afterwards,' Philippa told her. Beatriz realised with a rush of revulsion that the cakes signified Saint Agatha's severed breasts.

'Now our destinies are waiting for us,' Philippa declared.

Anna cleared away the writing materials on the table and set out the Saint Agatha candle, the *Sortes Sanctorum* book and the three dice.

'Sit here, Beatriz,' Philippa instructed. 'We are ready to begin.'

Beatriz suppressed a sigh and took her seat. That old book better have something palatable to say to her about Imbert. There was a knock on the door and Philippa looked to Roger. 'Viscount Ademar requests entry, my lady,' Roger told her from the doorway. Philippa nodded her assent. The viscount was a favourite with the three girls. He was an intelligent and kind man in his fifties. Bertrand's scribe, Gauzlin, entered the room behind him.

'Please, Viscount, will you take a seat? Roger, bring the wine jug.'

The viscount bent his long, slender form to sit on the low chair opposite Philippa. Gauzlin took a stool that Roger set for him. Beatriz turned her eyes away from the sight of Gauzlin's pale scalp protruding from his tonsure. One side of the monk's scalp sported a large, discoloured lump. Roger offered Philippa's ornate *aquamanile* with its fish mouth for the viscount and monk to wash their hands, set five beakers on the table for the three girls and the guests and poured the wine. Philippa reached for her beaker, but Roger held up a hand to stay her. He poured a small amount into a beaker for himself, tasted it, waited, and then nodded to Philippa. Beatriz rolled her eyes. Since Roger had himself decanted and poured this wine, it seemed rather overly dramatic to be tasting it for poison, but he insisted on his ritual every time something was due to pass Philippa's lips. Gauzlin refused wine and Roger filled his beaker with water.

'I have a few papers in need of your consent and signature, Lady Philippa,' the viscount began. Philippa moved the *Sortes Sanctorum* book and Saint Agatha candle to one side to make room for two scrolls that Gauzlin set on the table. 'Your cousin has drawn up a charter regarding the tolls associated with his new castle at Najac,' the viscount said. He pushed one scroll towards Philippa, who read it over, nodded, and added her signature to the witness list at the bottom. Beatriz enviously watched the rolling shape and flourishes of the lady's signature. *Philippa Matilde de Tolosa, filha de comte Guilhem IV de Tolosa.* With her father and uncle away, Philippa and her cousin Bertrand were acting for the counts in all matters of business for the moment. 'There is a second document pertaining to the canons of Saint-Sernin.' The viscount passed the second document to Lady Philippa.

Gauzlin squirmed on his stool at the mention of Saint-Sernin. Until recently, he had been one of the Cluniac monks at Saint-Sernin and had looked likely to rise to prior, but Pope Urban had intervened in the dispute between the Augustinian canons of the basilica who had been ousted and the Cluniac monks who had taken it over. The basilica was a vital link on the pilgrim route and in receipt of many offerings. The pope had weighed the arguments and decided in favour of the canons. The monks, including Gauzlin, had been ejected from their comfortable berth at the great church. Instead of returning to the abbey of Moissac, Gauzlin had opted to work as clerk for Philippa's cousin Bertrand.

Philippa finished reading over the document, dipped her quill in the inkpot, and signed her name. Gauzlin fussed at the document, blotting the ink dry and carefully rolling and tying up both parchments.

'Thank you, lady,' the viscount said. 'And there is the end of work. Now play!' They smiled at each other. 'I bring you this manuscript as a gift from my wife. We know you like poetry.' He nodded at Beatriz. 'It is a poem by Baudri of Bourgueil.'

Philippa took the manuscript, beaming at Ademar. 'Oh, how kind, how marvellous! I have read several of his poems before and love his work. I am very excited to read it. Would you like a cake, Viscount?' She nodded to Roger, who held the tray to the viscount and then to the clerk.

'Ah! Saint Agatha cakes!' said Gauzlin. 'Delightful! Your piety adorns you, Lady Philippa.' Beatriz screwed up her nose as she watched him bite down on the severed breast cake.

'Anna made the cakes,' Philippa said.

'Delicious,' observed the viscount, nodding to Anna. 'You don't eat them yourselves?'

'We will later,' Philippa told him. 'We three have been fasting for Saint Agatha's day. We will break our fast in a while.'

'Won't you play something for us, Beatriz?' Viscount Ademar asked, nodding at her *vielle* where it leant against the princess chest.

'Yes, do, Beatriz!' Philippa said in a tone of command.

'Well, I have been working on my *vida* and *razo*,' Beatriz said. 'I could sing that for you all?'

'We would be very glad to hear it,' Philippa said.

Beatriz stood and positioned her *vielle*. She strummed a few notes as she declaimed, lilting her speech melodiously and projecting her voice,

> *Ladies and lords, charge your goblets with*
> hypocras *as we play the game of* trobar –

composing and finding poetry, singing tales
of beautiful lovers, such as yourselves, talking
of joy and bliss and kisses.

Beatriz glanced at her audience and saw they were smiling, apart from Gauzlin, who was frowning, and no doubt disapproved of lovers, kisses and *trobar* altogether. Even Roger was smiling.

Born in the high mountains of Catalonia, the
song of Beatriz de Farrera tripped the hillside
with the jangling bells of the flocks, trickled
with the slipping brooks, soared with the
circling eagle. She wandered the world in
search of a true friend for her wild poetry.
Fortune found her, led her to the trobador
Imbert of Uzès, whose renown sounds in the
proud courts of Tolosa, Poitiers and Dijon,
and even so far as Barcelona and Benevento.

Imbert nurtured her song and, true to her name,
Beatriz's music brings joy to lords and ladies
in the palaces of Narbonne, Montpellier,
Orange and Carcassona. She knows well how
to invent poetry, how to compose sirventes
and planhs. *She reproaches false clerics,*
sings of spring and birds, love and slander.
She sings better than anyone else in the
world.

Courtly Beatriz is beloved by artists. Will she

compose songs of happiness? Or, oh!, spurned, must she leave the court, wander more, live in pain and sadness, take ill aboard ship, be carried to the silence of a nunnery, die from the pangs of love? She composes many good melodies for this bold love. Oh, will her lover come to her bedside, take her in his strong arms and sustain her?

Because of her wit and courtesy, Beatriz is esteemed, lavished with the gifts of a beautiful and generous lady. Wise Philippa of Tolosa, daughter of the count, bestows great honour upon her verse. In the game of trobar, *I* Beatriz, trobairitz, *composed these poems and sing for you now, Toulousains!*

Her audience clapped with enthusiasm, apart from Gauzlin, who merely touched his fingertips together a few times. Beatriz savoured her phrase, 'reproaches false clerics', which no doubt had angered him.

'Better than anyone else in the world? ... well, it is wonderfully dramatic!' Philippa declared.

'Thank you. What do you think, Anna?'

'I could not get all the words – you will tell me more slowly later?'

Beatriz nodded.

'Thank you, Beatriz. I'm looking forward to your new songs at Easter,' the viscount declared, rising from his seat.

Gauzlin followed suit, gathering up the signed documents. As he did so, he noticed the *Sortes Sanctorum* book at the side of Philippa's table and the Saint Agatha's candle. 'What's this?' he asked.

'Something we found in Princess Mafalda's old wedding chest,' Philippa said.

'*Sortes Sanctorum*,' Gauzlin said in a tone of great disapproval. 'You are using the book for divination, lady?'

'It's a harmless tradition, Brother Gauzlin,' the viscount told him, saving Philippa from having to defend herself. 'We have work to do below.' Taking Gauzlin's shoulders, he turned him around towards the door, cocking an amused eyebrow to Philippa as he did so.

'Thank you, Lord Ademar, and for the wonderful gift.'

Roger closed the door behind the two men and returned to stand beside the girls. Philippa moved the candle, book and dice back to the centre of the table.

'Who are these artists you are beloved by?' Anna asked Beatriz. 'Might Imbert take offence?'

'Of course not. It's just part of the convention and invention of *trobar*. I have to sound love lorn.'

'You are not lorn at all, I think!' exclaimed Philippa.

'Imbert might imagine he is one of these loving artists,' Anna said.

'Yes, he can think that.'

'Lluis might think so too,' Philippa smiled.

'He can think what he likes.'

'I don't believe any nunnery would take you, Beatriz, by the way,' Philippa told her, still smiling.

Beatriz shrugged.

'I will write the *razo* and *vida* down for you later,' Anna said.

Philippa lit the candle and looked at Beatriz and then Anna with excitement. 'Will I receive a favourable reply from my mother and marry a handsome, young lord?' she pronounced, laying emphasis on the words 'handsome' and 'young'. She threw the dice.

'You take the numbers in descending order,' said Anna.

'Five, four, one,' Philippa said.

Anna lifted the book and searched for the corresponding text. It took her a while and Philippa gripped Beatriz's hand in her suspense. 'Here we are,' said Anna. 'You want to seize the horns of a running stag while it is lingering in the woods; as soon as it returns to its lair, you will be able to catch it, and what you are doubtful of will come into your hands.'

Beatriz looked up at Roger looming over them, nodding his shaggy head sagely as Anna read. Philippa clapped her hands gently together, smiling. 'He will come into my hands,' she said to Beatriz, her eyes shining. 'You were right – my mother must be away and not able to reply to my letter yet. She will send a response soon and it will be positive. What I am doubtful about will come into my hands!' She released Beatriz and opened her hands like a book, looking at her palms as if she could see the face of her beloved there. 'Now you do it.'

'It's nonsense,' Beatriz protested.

Philippa scooped up the dice and clapped them into Beatriz's palm. 'Ask your question!'

'Er ... can I avoid marrying a fat old man?'

'Beatriz!' Philippa hissed with disapproval.

Beatriz huffed and threw the dice. 'Six, six, two,' she read out to Anna, who searched through the pages.

Philippa took Beatriz's hand again and pumped their two hands up and down against Beatriz's thigh.

Anna frowned and cleared her throat. 'You seek to be put in a forest where you will find no path, and many powerful serpents hide there to harm you. Therefore, give up this plan – just when you think you go safely, you will be deceived by your faults.'

'I have no idea what that means,' Beatriz said. 'Apart from the serpents part,' she added in a sour tone.

'Yes, it is less clear than my answer.' Philippa looked puzzled. 'What plan does it want you to give up? Are you intending to run away again?'

'No,' Beatriz said slowly. 'But I won't be marrying Imbert.'

'Don't ignore what it says about your faults,' Philippa told her primly. Beatriz controlled a scowl as best she could. 'Now you, Anna,' Philippa said, holding out the dice to her.

'No, no. Not me!' Anna pushed the dice away and turned her face away so that Philippa could not speak to her.

Roger lifted the tray of breast cakes and presented them to the three girls. Beatriz selected a large cake and, closing her eyes on the severed breast association, she bit down on the sweet cherry and icing.

3

DISINHERITED

Mid-February 1093, Saint-Pons-de-Thomières Abbey

*B*eatriz looked down into the open grave. It was smaller than the usual. Lady Philippa's brother Pons had seen only eleven summers. A thin worm, piebald red, pink, brown and translucent, bored its way out of the freshly sliced earth at the head of the pit and dangled, half in, half out. Another squirm and it flopped out onto the boy's shrouded face. Beatriz pulled her hood closer about her frozen ears. The wind carried off the thin sound of the priest intoning the burial prayer. Beside her, Philippa gasped on an involuntary sob, and Beatriz watched a tear meander down the lady's blanched cheek to the corner of her mouth.

Philippa had carried clothes and jewels for her brother from Tolosa to this place of his internment at Saint-Pons-de-Thomières Abbey. Beatriz had helped Anna wash and clothe the thin body for burial. Beneath the pale shroud, Pons was dressed as a prince of Tolosa. His dark blue tunic was hemmed with a red band embroidered with tiny pearls. His belt held a fine sword that reached as far as his ankle. Anna had adjusted an emerald ring to stay on Pons' dead finger. His brown and gold mantle was a half-circle with a high collar, pinned at his shoulder with a gold and garnet brooch. Anna had added Pons' name and title in fine stitch to the cloak hem so the angels would know him when he arrived in heaven.

Beatriz looked across the grave to where Abbot Frotard stood alongside Philippa's cousin Bertrand. Next to Bertrand was his father and Philippa's uncle and guardian, Count Raimon of Saint-Gilles. Raimon's long red cape whipped around his tall frame in the wind, resonating like a ship's sail in a storm. His head was bared to the elements, and he frowned up at the sky as if commanding it to desist with its antics. His blond-grey hair lashed at his face. Bertrand stared down into the pit, and Beatriz could not see his face. Only the top of his head was visible with its mop of thick, black hair. His hands were clenched before him in embroidered grey gauntlets. Abbot Frotard was wearing a rope-tied black habit and open sandals and could only be distinguished from the other clerics at the graveside by the very large ruby cross nestling on his chest. Despite his advanced age and lack of any other clothing, he did not seem to register the rawness of the morning.

The early light tried feebly to bring colour – slivers of dim yellow and blue – to the grey of the sky, which looked loaded with more snow. All around them were the gloomy monuments of Lady Philippa's ancestors in the cemetery of Saint-Pons-de-Thomières. Philippa's great-great-great-grandfather, Count Raimon-Pons of Tolosa, who had founded the abbey, leant in lichened stone on his blunted sword and glared at them. Yes, Beatriz said to him in her head, you are dead, and I am not.

She turned to Philippa and said gently, 'Come away now, lady.' Anna added her own quiet encouragement. The three young women made their way between the tombstones towards the anticipated warmth of the abbey refectory, gripping each other's arms and hands for balance on the uneven, ungiving ground. Here and there, first spring buds pushed their fragile way up, impossibly, through the frozen sod. Philippa paused at a grave with a sculpture of a woman with a baby in her arms. 'My other half-brother,' she gestured, 'and my father's first wife.' Beatriz swallowed. Philippa's father had lost two sons now. The gloom and doom was making her feel the familiar need to break out somehow: dance, shout, drink too much, sleep with someone she shouldn't.

The long tables of the abbey refectory shone with strenuous polishing. The iron candle-holder suspended from the ceiling was empty. Abbot Frotard maintained a strict frugality (apart from in his own quarters). Pale light filtered through the many arched windows. Beatriz smiled at the welcome sight of Lluis as he came strutting down the centre of the refectory towards them.

Lluis was a Catalan, like her. He had grown friendly with Bertrand and accompanied him as part of his entourage. 'Come and sit by the fire and warm yourself, my lady,' he said to Philippa, setting wine and a freshly baked loaf on the table closest to the hearth. He held out a brass bowl filled with water and a towel. While Philippa washed her hands, Beatriz studied Lluis. He had a wide mouth and nose, grey eyes. His hair was fair and rumpled. He had pronounced cheek bones and the smooth planes of his face cut down towards the V of his chin. It was not a conventionally handsome face, like Bertrand's, but Beatriz found him mesmerising, though she was loath to admit it to herself.

Abbey servants were clearing away the remains of the monks' breakfast on the other side of the refectory, clattering goblets and serving jugs together. The hearth was tiny for the vast, high space and gave out a meagre heat. It was a good deal warmer, though, than the graveside. The three young women huddled together, blowing on their fingers. The claws of Philippa's white hound clicked smartly on the stone floor slabs, and the dog wrapped herself around Philippa's ankles in a bid to garner warmth.

'I'm so sorry, Lady Philippa,' Beatriz said.

Philippa tried to smile. 'It has been coming for a while. He is out of his suffering,' she said, but her mouth crumpled and she wept. Philippa's parents had sent her brother to the care of the hospital here at Saint-Pons-de-Thomières Abbey when he was small, but he had never been well enough to return home. He had suffered with a constant bloody cough and fevers. 'I hoped our prayers would save him.'

'I'm so sorry,' Beatriz repeated, feeling cross with herself that she couldn't think of anything better to say. She was a poet. She should not be at a loss for words.

A nun in a black habit and white headveil sat down abruptly on an adjacent bench, glancing around herself surreptitiously. 'Philippa,' she hissed in a low, conspiratorial tone, leaning forward with her elbows on her knees and her fingers interlaced.

Philippa swabbed at her tears and stared at the nun. It took her a long moment to recognise the woman who was gazing intently at her. 'Mafalda, is that you?'

'I'm not known by that name here, and I can't be seen talking to you.' She unlaced her fingers and sat upright. Beatriz noted her large blue eyes, small nose, full red mouth. She had the white, translucent skin of a red-head and Beatriz imagined her hair would be red beneath her wimple. Few nuns managed to look exquisite in their drab garb, but this one did. 'Send your *trobairitz* to meet me in an hour at the top of the cheese tower.' She rose as swiftly as she had arrived and was already gone, head bowed, hands folded into the sleeves of her habit. She vanished beyond the doorway before Philippa or Beatriz could respond.

Beatriz gaped after her. 'Who was that?' She was pleased the nun had described her as a *trobairitz*, a poet, rather than a *jograresa*, a mere performer.

'Mafalda of Hautville, princess of Sicily,' Philippa told her. 'The second wife of uncle Raimon, until he discarded her for not producing babies.'

'That's an extreme change in fortune,' Beatriz said.

Philippa made sure she was facing Anna. 'Yes, she was a great lady, and now she spends her days in silence, in prayer, owning nothing.' Philippa mouthed the words distinctly, her expression more theatrical than if she had been addressing somebody else.

'It's good for her soul, I suppose,' Beatriz said, without a shred of conviction in her voice.

'Beatriz!' Philippa reprimanded her.

'Well, she is very mysterious. What did she want?'

Philippa shook her head. 'I don't know. Perhaps she has something to say to me about the inheritance of Tolosa. She used to be very well connected and embroiled in political intrigues before she took the veil. You will go and meet her as she suggested and find out.' Now that her brother was dead, Philippa was the heiress to the county.

'I daresay there are more than bodies buried here,' said Beatriz. 'Abbot Frotard has his fingers in a multitude of controversies and scandals. The secrets of many noble families are suppressed and bought off in his confession box.'

'Don't be rude about him, Beatriz,' Philippa retorted angrily. 'He is a good and pious man. Abbot Frotard is the papal legate, in service to Pope Urban and charged with great business.'

Beatriz raised her eyebrows. In her view, a cleric and a good man was a contradiction in terms, but she knew better than to rile Philippa on anything to do with religion.

Raimon, Bertrand and the abbot entered the hall from the graveyard and came towards them. Raimon had once been a very handsome man, like his son, but time, battle, and his many responsibilities had gouged deep lines and craters into his flesh.

Abbot Frotard took Philippa's hand. 'My deepest

35

condolences, Lady Philippa. Pons was a sweet and pious boy. He is resting with God now.' He bowed his head over her hand. His thick hair was white and brushed back from a broad forehead. When he lifted his head again to look into Philippa's face, his brilliant blue eyes were kindly.

Philippa bit her lip and thanked the abbot. The men moved off to sit at another table and talk together. Beatriz noticed one or other of them glanced in Philippa's direction several times, indicating that they were discussing her.

'Don't bite your lip, lady,' Anna said to Philippa. 'It will bleed.'

'I had to, to avoid sobbing in front of them.' Philippa looked down at her hands in her lap and then up again at the two girls, her eyes wet with tears. 'Oh, in truth, I fear there is at least a modicum of self-pity in my mourning.'

Anna frowned a question to Philippa and Beatriz voiced it. 'Self-pity?'

Philippa could not reply, as the men returned to stand over her. Raimon took her hand. 'My dear child. This is a very sad day for your father and mother, for you, for me.' Raimon let Philippa's fingers drop.

Beatriz saw the slight compression of Philippa's lips. She was well aware of the ambition of her uncle and his hopes of taking over Tolosa.

'What news do you have of your father?' Abbot Frotard asked Philippa.

'He is making his way to Jerusalem in hopes of a cure for his ailment,' she said. 'The news from Father, and from my mother too, is sparse. It will be some time before they hear of my brother's death.'

There was a moment's silence as they contemplated how the news that their only son had not reached maturity would land with the count and countess of Tolosa.

'Does your mother travel in the Holy Land with Count Guilhem?' the abbot asked.

'No. She is at the court of Aragon, in Jaca.'

The abbot's kindly eyes and his smiling mouth, set in a nest of cheerful wrinkles, did not fool Beatriz. The abbot came from the family of the lords of Saint-Antonin-de-Noble-Val. Beneath that pleasant façade, the abbot was a zealot in enacting his missions from the pope.

Abbot Frotard took his leave of the bereaved family to tend to correspondence, and Raimon and Bertrand decided to fly their hawks in the nearby woods. 'Do you want to come with us, Philippa?' Bertrand asked. His pale blue eyes contrasted shockingly and pleasingly with his black tufted hair. He wore a carefully barbered moustache and a beard cut close to the contours of his face. Beatriz enjoyed looking at him and had once been inveigled to climb into his bed after a little too much wine, but she wouldn't trust him as far as she could throw him.

Philippa shook her head. 'Thank you, but no.'

When the men had cleared the room, Philippa whispered to Beatriz, 'You should go to the cheese tower now. It's time.'

Beatriz screwed up her mouth and reluctantly left the refectory, pulling her grey cloak and hood back around herself. She stepped into the courtyard. The wind had died down a little at least. Several towers punctuated the abbey walls. How was she to know which was the cheese tower?

4

THE CHEESE TOWER

Mid-February 1093, Saint-Pons-de-Thomières Abbey

*B*eatriz did not want to wander around in the cold any longer than she had to. Ahead of her, the abbey latrines were in the far-right corner, to one side of the main gate, and the hospice was on the other side. Then there was a long row of stables. A tower rose at the end of the stables, but was it the right one? A young monk was feeding chickens in the courtyard. She stepped briskly to him. 'Is that the cheese tower?' she asked, pointing. He nodded. The monks were a silent order and used a curious sign language at meals.

Beatriz pushed through the door at the foot of the tower and found herself in a pungent space lined with wooden racks, holding hundreds of cheese wheels of different sizes and colourings, ranging from white to yellow and orange. The smell of cheese and beer was overwhelming. As a young girl, she had been responsible for cheesemaking for her family, back in Farrera, and she knew the cheeses had to be regularly washed with beer to help the development of their rinds.

A wooden ladder rested on the back wall, disappearing up into a hole in the ceiling. Beatriz set her foot on the lowest rung and climbed up to the first floor. Her blue, laced boots were too thin for the cold. She had regretted them at the graveside, but their flexibility was good for climbing. She poked her head up out of the hatch on the next floor. Two women were intent on their work and took no notice of her. One woman was pouring whey into a cheesecloth-lined wicker strainer. Another was using a cheese press and had bowls of vinegar and salt ranged alongside her.

Beatriz pulled herself up off the top of the ladder and made her way to a second ladder. She emerged on the top storey, where another smell greeted her nose. Brown onions were laid out on the floor on one side of the space and green apples on the other. A narrow aisle had been left between the low fields of brown and green, and the nun Mafalda was waiting there, with her back to Beatriz, at the far end of the aisle. Beatriz was glad to see she didn't have to go up the final ladder, out onto the frigid, windswept roof.

The nun turned at the sound of Beatriz's puffing as she emerged through the hole. 'Close the hatch,' she commanded. When the hatch had dropped, the nun pushed the veil from her shorn head, allowing it to bunch around her neck. She was a tall woman in her early thirties. Beatriz's guess about her hair colour had been correct. The reddish stubble on Mafalda's head framed a long, handsome face. Her beauty was as effective at transcending a shorn head as it was at defeating a nun's wimple. Beatriz picked her way carefully between the onions and apples, moving towards the nun.

A daughter of the powerful Norman rulers of Sicily, Mafalda had sailed across the Mediterranean to marry Count Raimon. She would have had riches and a lavish, eventful life. And now, here she was in her black robe, living in silence, with no status at all. After eight years of marriage, Raimon had set her aside because she was barren. Beatriz thought of the statue of the mother and baby in the graveyard. It was a fraught business, being a noble wife.

'Philippa didn't know me at first!' the nun said in a distressed voice. 'It's not just my hair and my habit. Illness, the cold, the damp, the privations here have wrought change in me.'

'I am sorry, Lady Mafalda.'

'Don't call me that. I had to give up my name when Raimon of Saint-Gilles sent me away. This abbey is the midden for those who are no longer wanted in Tolosa.' She paused and surveyed the onions and apples, regaining control after the fury of her words. 'Tell Philippa I am glad to see her looking well, grown to a woman.' She smiled at her memories, and Beatriz presumed they were memories of Philippa as a child. Beatriz couldn't imagine memories of Raimon and his harsh manner would make any woman smile. The nun's brief cheer dropped. 'I fear for Philippa and wanted to warn her.'

'Warn her?'

'She cannot trust …' She halted at a loud sound in the room below. They both held their breath, listening. Perhaps one of the cheesemakers had simply dropped an implement. When there was no further sound, she continued. 'She cannot trust Raimon and Bertrand. They stole my sister's dowry and they will steal Philippa's inheritance if they can.'

Beatriz frowned.

'My sister, Emma,' the nun said. 'You must have heard of it? She was supposed to marry the king of France, and my father entrusted her and her dowry to my then husband Raimon. But the king was already ensconced with his paramour, Bertrada, so Raimon married Emma off to another lord and her dowry mysteriously disappeared. Disappeared into Raimon's coffers. Raimon and Bertrand have no scruples. They and the abbot are garnering all the money they can for the reconquest of the Iberian lands.'

'Do you suspect foul play in Pons' death?' Beatriz asked.

The nun considered for a moment. 'It's possible, I suppose. It is certainly a convenient death for Raimon, removing another obstacle for the lordship of Tolosa. But I assisted the apothecary in the care of Pons and the boy had consumption of the lungs – the captain of death, as the illness is known.' She paused, and they exchanged a doom-laden glance at the well-known disease that afflicted so many young people. 'He was so slender, so frail, his skin almost transparent, a febrile red blooming on his cheeks, but he was funny. He was the only thing here that could make me smile. The bloodlettings and herbal concoctions the apothecary devised did him little good.'

Beatriz was conscious they might be interrupted again and was feeling the cold painfully in her feet. 'Speak plain, Sister, I beg you, and swiftly.'

The nun frowned at Beatriz's tone. She had been a great noblewoman, and Beatriz was a mere musician. The nun clamped her lips together as if she would say no more.

'Speak more, Sister Mafalda, if you know it,' Beatriz begged her as politely as she could.

'Now only Philippa stands between her uncle and her cousin and the inheritance of Tolosa.'

'Count Guilhem hopes to find a cure for his ailment in Jerusalem,' Beatriz said carefully, but she knew Philippa's letters from her mother were not optimistic about the state of the count's health.

The nun pursed her mouth, considering Beatriz. 'A *trobairitz*.' Her tone was sceptical. 'I have never known your like to be trustworthy. All spies, adulterers, and liars in my experience.'

Beatriz slapped her hand to her hips and opened her mouth to contend with the nun.

Mafalda's voice was sharp, and she held up her hand. 'Stop! We do not have time to argue with one another. Tell Philippa that I believe Raimon is conspiring with Abbot Frotard to take Tolosa from her. I advise her to write to Duke Guillaume of Aquitaine, telling him of her situation, and hinting that a marriage between them would profit them both. He is her best hope. I will also write to him and pave the way for her approach. She has the right of law on her side for the inheritance of Tolosa.'

Beatriz regarded Mafalda with a new respect. It was an astute suggestion. Beatriz had met Duke Guillaume when she performed with Imbert at the Poitiers court. He would fit Philippa's desire for a young husband. And he had the wealth and arrogance to oppose Raimon, which few other lords would dare. 'There is a rumour that Duke Guillaume is betrothed to Ermengarde of Anjou?'

'He will set Ermengarde aside for Philippa if she is swift in writing to him. Tolosa would be a greater prize for him. I have to go.' Mafalda raised her veil to cover her bald head. Her dark, rough robe, tied with a hemp rope at the waist, made an ugly, scraping sound against itself, against her thighs as she walked to the hatch, revealed the ladder, and descended quickly into the gloom.

Beatriz waited a while, strolling up and down between the onions and apples, thinking. Perhaps Mafalda was simply a woman wronged, seeking vengeance against Raimon, but her warning was credible and her proposal had merit. She followed the nun down the ladder and found Philippa and Anna still in the refectory. 'We will return to the women's guesthouse,' Philippa instructed, 'to prepare for the meal.' The white hound, Adimante, rose with her and glued itself to her calf. She lifted her skirts to avoid getting tangled with the dog as they walked.

At the door to the guesthouse, the guest master greeted them and asked Philippa if she had everything she needed for her comfort. She thanked him graciously, telling him yes. When they were sure nobody else was around, Beatriz reported on her conversation with

Mafalda. 'She did not seem to really suspect your brother's death, but warned that your uncle and cousin covet Tolosa and may be plotting with Abbot Frotard. Nobody recovers from the illness your brother had, lady.'

Philippa said, 'Yet murder is not a rarity in my family.'

Beatriz and Anna raised their eyebrows.

'My grandmother, Countess Almodis of Barcelona,' Philippa told them, 'was murdered by her stepson, and my uncle, Count Ramon Berenguer of Barcelona, was murdered by his twin brother.'

'Mafalda's proposal of Duke Guillaume of Aquitaine as husband for you is a wise idea,' Beatriz said. 'I met him when Imbert and I performed at his court in Poitiers last year. He rules a vast territory. He is young, good-looking, of good humour, and he is an excellent poet. You would like him, I believe.'

Philippa smiled keenly at Beatriz's description. 'My marriage should have been arranged long before now,' she said. 'My parents refused offers and delayed, hoping my brother would survive and that would influence who I should marry. I believe my uncle has turned away and concealed marriage offers that might threaten any attempt he makes to take Tolosa.'

'Any husband challenging Raimon and Bertrand,' said Beatriz, 'would have to be very strong and wanting war. Your Uncle Raimon will not give up Tolosa meekly now he has had his feet under the table for the time of your father's absence.'

Philippa nodded. 'My mother finally replied to my letter. My parents are set on this ridiculous match with King Sancho Ramírez of Aragon. He is a good friend of my father, and my father sees it as the safe option for me. This will be Frotard's doing too,' she said, shifting swiftly to anger. 'Not content to have near-killed my father by urging him to crusade against the Moors in Spain where he took this injury that festers still, now the abbot must sacrifice me there too. He is intent on the glory of reconquest in Spain and accruing wealth from that for Rome.'

'Or himself,' Beatriz interjected.

Philippa ignored Beatriz's criticism of the abbot. 'Can you tell me more about Duke Guillaume, Beatriz?'

'He would make you a fine husband, lady. He is a well-schooled warrior, but also an excellent wit. His court is full of gaiety and learning. He is strong-minded. I believe he would be inclined to hold Tolosa for you. And, of course, he rules a vast territory and does not lack for wealth.'

'What good is an old king in Aragon to me?' Philippa asked. 'He will not come here and keep Tolosa for me. And I am not you,' Philippa added, looking at Beatriz. 'I do not have your liberties.'

Beatriz opened her mouth to object. Philippa was referring to Beatriz having run away from an unwanted marriage arranged by her father in Farrera.

'Let's leave this,' Anna interrupted diplomatically. 'We have to get ready for the meal. Your clothes stink, Beatriz.' She pinched her nose.

'The apples, at least, smelled good,' Beatriz said.

Anna stood, fetched her brushes and attempted to remove the earth of the graveyard (and in Beatriz's case, the smell of cheese) from their clothes, only to replace it with the stone dust that hung everywhere in the air from the building work going on to expand the abbey. Crowds of pilgrims were making their way from Narbonne towards Tolosa and then on, across the Pyrenees, to the tomb of Saint James at Compostela on the Iberian peninsula. Like all the abbeys and cathedrals on the routes to Compostela, Saint-Pons-de-Thomières was preparing to milk the penitents. Developing the Camino de Santiago from here was another of the abbot's projects on behalf of Pope Urban.

Philippa stood still while Anna fixed an elaborate triple-pin brooch to her dress front. The brooch had been left to her by her grandmother, Countess Almodis. The distinctive brooch consisted of three intricately worked gold discs hinged together with short chains, each with a long, sharp pin to weave into clothing. It was beautiful and complex, and Beatriz often wished she could wear and own such a thing. 'I think you should change out of that smelly robe,' Anna told Beatriz, glancing back over her shoulder, her fingers busy with the brooch.

Beatriz came around to where Anna could see her and shook her head. This was her best dark blue gown, edged with fine yellow and blue embroidery on white linen, depicting birds and boughs. Philippa had given her the robe, and Anna had cut it down for Beatriz's shorter stature and stitched the embroidered hem back on. Beatriz had put it on for the burial and wanted to make a good impression for the performance at the meal. She did not have another fine dress to change into. 'I'm playing music,' she said. 'I'm not planning to be in a clinch with anyone who might get close enough to object to this particular perfume.'

'Beatriz, come!' Imbert's dishevelled grey head peered around the door jamb. 'You should have been in the refectory before now to rehearse. Excuse me, Lady Philippa. My condolences to you. I must steal Beatriz from you for a while to prepare the music for the meal.'

5

THE PAPAL LEGATE

Mid-February 1093, Saint-Pons-de-Thomières Abbey

*B*eatriz picked up her *vielle* and followed Imbert back across the courtyard, wafting her robe as much as possible in the fresh air, hoping the cheese odour would dissipate a little. She was amazed, as usual, by the girth of Imbert as he waddled his way across the yard ahead of her. He placed his feet carefully – they always seemed too small to carry his bulk and height – avoiding the piles of horse dung. Halfway across the courtyard, Imbert encountered Petrus Regimundus, the *vicar* of Tolosa and brother to Viscount Ademar. Petrus collected taxes and managed the financial matters of the city on behalf of Philippa's father, and lately on behalf of Raimon. He was a large man in all directions – over six feet tall and broad in the shoulder. But his muscle was turning to fat;

his bright green tunic strained over a large belly that made him look like he might birth twins at any moment. Imbert and Petrus appeared to exchange a few cross words, but Beatriz was not near enough to overhear what was said. Did Imbert owe yet another gambling debt?

Beatriz and Imbert would usually rehearse in the cloister, but it was too cold for their instruments out there today. 'This will do,' Imbert said, leaning his *oud* against the wall of the storeroom adjacent to the refectory. He was flustered by his encounter with Petrus and took a moment to settle before being able to play music. They were surrounded by sacks of flour and salt, racks of warm bread, and more cheese wheels. Smoked and salted meat and fish hung from the ceiling beams and more meat was curing in deep dishes of salt set out on the table.

'What did Petrus want?' Beatriz asked.

'Nothing. None of your concern.' Imbert closed down her curiosity. 'We are only permitted to play hymns in the monks' refectory,' Imbert told her. 'No lyrics, no cavorting.'

'I never cavort,' Beatriz said with hauteur.

Imbert refused Beatriz's request to perform some of her own music. 'It is not seemly, in this holy place, for a woman to be the lead strummer.'

Beatriz scowled.

'Oh, don't scowl so, my pretty Catalan strumpet, sorry, I mean strummer, of course,' he joked. He gripped her about the waist. She pushed Imbert's large hands from her, wriggling and rolling away to free herself.

'I am no strumpet,' she declared vociferously, although

she felt less than certain of that when Lluis came in, picked up two loaves, and winked at her. She turned back to Imbert and saw he was following Lluis' departure with a look of speculation on his face.

She returned her attention to her instrument. Imbert and Beatriz played the opening melody of their first song several times until they had it fluidly together. Beatriz listened with pleasure to the sound of Imbert's skilful playing. Four years ago, Imbert heard Beatriz piping on a recorder and singing for her supper in the street in the Catalan mountain town of Sort. She was a dirty thirteen-year-old beggar, and he was impressed by her voice. Imbert was a very talented musician and poet, but his own singing voice was poor. He sang like a frog in a pond. He needed a singer to be a success as a *trobador* at court, and Beatriz had been his salvation.

'Let's try the opening of the second tune,' Imbert told her and tapped his foot three times before they began, on cue, together. 'Good,' Imbert pronounced. Her ability to play the *vielle*, to project her voice, to follow the complex composition rules of the poetry and melodies had come with Imbert's patient tuition. It didn't hurt their performance value that Beatriz, with her youth, her thick black hair, her black eyes, and her rather sulky, haughty habitual expression, was a good deal better to look at than Imbert. 'You must learn courtesy and charm, how to conduct yourself among noble people,' he had told her, and that was sometimes the hardest part, if she had to be obsequious to someone who did not deserve her respect.

Beatriz liked Imbert. He was funny and intelligent. She

repaid him for saving her from beggary by enhancing his performances and, often, by rescuing him from his proclivity for dice. His skill at dice was as poor as his singing and had frequently proved catastrophic to their joint fortunes. Yet exchanging herself, her bed, was too high a price to pay for Imbert's kindnesses. He was forty years older than Beatriz and a prodigious size because he loved to eat and drink. He often suffered from piles, especially after a long, wet ride, and then Beatriz had to tend to his suffering. She would draw a hot bath for him and suppress her gagging as she applied a herbal concoction to the affected area.

'They are going in,' Imbert declared, still a little flustered.

'And we are in the way here,' Beatriz told him, as a gaggle of servants flooded in to collect bread and other supplies. She pulled Imbert by his sleeve towards the door.

The monks and nuns and their grieving noble guests were filing into the refectory for the meal. Six knights had accompanied Raimon's family, including Philippa's bodyguard, Roger. Lluis was one of ten servants and companions in the entourages of Raimon and Bertrand. Beatriz and Imbert began to tune their instruments. It was a fish day, and Imbert and Beatriz would not be served until later. They must strum lugubriously in the corner while the others ate. Beatriz's empty stomach growled over on itself again.

'Get on with it man! Will you be tuning all day?' Raimon exclaimed loudly to Imbert. Servants paused mid-step, knives and spoons frozen in place. Shocked faces looked up at Raimon and then to the abbot. This was a silent order, and there should be no speech in the refectory. Raimon, realising his error, signalled an apology to the abbot, who evinced an expression of forgiveness and gestured to all to continue eating and serving. The sound of movements resumed. Imbert and Beatriz played the quiet, stately melody of several hymns. Imbert had the music from the school at the cathedral in Limoges.

The hands of two monks flew to Beatriz's left – they were silently chattering with each other in their sign language. One moved his hand like the tail of a fish in water and, sure enough, his companion passed a dish of fish to him. One raised a little finger to his lip and Beatriz watched, bemused, as a servant poured milk into his beaker. Another placed a bent finger on his lip and was served with wine. Another gestured for the large silver salt cellar decorated with waves and ships. Anna, a still point among the company, was watching, taking it all in. Her thick golden hair was tightly plaited and subdued under a modest, opaque headveil.

Mafalda had come to the meal, along with a handful of nuns. Mafalda's eyes were fixed on Raimon, who took no notice of her whatsoever, as if she were invisible and had not shared his bed and his life for so many years. The hatred on her face was scorching. To be confined to a nunnery, reduced to nothing, was not Mafalda's intention when she set out on her voyage from Sicily. Roger sat with his bulging, tattooed forearms crossed in front of

him on the table. Silence was Roger's prevailing charac-
teristic, so he was at home here, Beatriz thought. She tried
to decipher his expression as he looked at Mafalda. Was
he distressed to see her so reduced and discarded? It was
always impossible to tell with Roger.

Beatriz fluffed a note and looked guiltily to Imbert.
'Concentrate on the music,' Imbert muttered under his
breath. Beatriz bent her head to the *vielle*, intent on
making up for her error. The notes of the instruments
soared and Beatriz smiled a private smile to herself at the
beauty of the sound.

At the end of the meal, the abbot gestured graciously
to Raimon, Bertrand and Philippa that they should follow
him, and Philippa glanced to Beatriz to indicate she
should accompany her. In the abbot's chambers, the
mason responsible for the abbey extensions spread a
sketch on the table for their perusal. The abbot was
looking for more donations from his noble guests to pay
for his building work. The sketch showed a grand new
gate – death's gate, he called it, cheerily. The great arched
doorway was flanked at the top by a woman with a moon
on the right side and a woman with a bird on the left.

'The extensions are vital for the pilgrims passing
through,' the abbot told them. Beatriz thought she heard
avarice in his voice.

'The building work in Tolosa on the great basilica of
Saint-Sernin is progressing well,' Bertrand remarked
provocatively.

'Indeed,' said the abbot tersely. When it was
completed, Saint-Sernin would far outshine Saint-Pons-

de-Thomières. Saint-Sernin would accrue many more donations from the awed pilgrims. 'The pilgrims will have so many heartwarming stories of the saints to contemplate,' said Abbot Frotard, 'as they make their way along the pilgrim road from here to Tolosa, up into the high Pyrenees, and on to the tomb of the blessed Saint James in Compostela.'

'Let's get to the business, Abbot,' Raimon said impatiently.

The abbot inclined his head graciously. 'Lady Philippa, we needed to speak with you now that your brother has died. Perhaps you would rather conduct this conversation in private?' He looked towards Beatriz. The mason was already rolling up his sketches and making to leave.

'Beatriz will stay.' Philippa's tone was decisive.

'Very well.' The door closed behind the mason. 'We wished to make you aware of an agreement drawn up between your father, Count Guilhem, and your uncle, Count Raimon.' The abbot gestured politely towards Raimon.

'I see,' Philippa said.

The abbot passed a rolled parchment to Philippa. Beatriz could see the inked sentences, the flourishing signatures at the bottom and two seals attached.

Philippa read swiftly and then threw the parchment onto the table with force. 'My father did not inform me of this agreement. I don't believe it!'

The abbot was perplexed at her outburst and looked to Raimon for steerage on how to deal with it. Beatriz glanced at Bertrand and saw a smug smile on his face.

'My brother and I made the agreement before he left

for the Holy Land. It was witnessed by the abbot here,'
Raimon said calmly. 'He knew his son was ailing and
unlikely to survive. He knew that Tolosa would need a
man at its helm,' he held his palm up to Philippa and
spoke louder to override her attempts to interrupt, 'to
guard it from its rivals and enemies.'

'My father would have informed me if he had made
this agreement!'

'My dear!' the abbot's face expressed theatrical shock.
'Are you suggesting the document is a forgery? That we
are lying to you? I assure you we are not.'

Raimon put his hands on Philippa's upper arms to still
her angry gestures and words. 'Desist! Let us speak.' He let
go of her. 'When my father died, he divided his territory
between your father and I, knowing it was the best way to
safeguard it for the family. You will go to Aragon and be
queen there. This is the best way to safeguard our county
for all the family.'

Philippa, who was red in the face and on the verge of
tears, looked at Beatriz and pointed at the rolled parchment. Beatriz picked it up. Philippa looked from Raimon
to the abbot and to Bertrand, who straightened out his
features to a solemn expression, as her glare alighted on
him. 'This will not stand.' She gripped Beatriz's hand and
removed them both from the room.

In the guesthouse, Anna studied the parchment. 'It
looks real,' she said.

Philippa paced up and down, her fists balled at her
sides. 'It can't be. My father would have informed me if
this was his intention.'

Beatriz, who had experience of her own of a father's betrayal, said nothing.

Philippa accidentally trod on Adimante's paw, causing her to make a high-pitched yelp. 'Oh, I'm sorry.' She patted the dog's head. 'You are always underfoot, Adimante.' She looked at Anna and Beatriz with decision in her face. 'I will write to both my mother and father to ask about this so-called agreement. I am the heiress of Tolosa. Bertrand is not the heir.'

AT THE MASS before their departure, Abbot Frotard exhorted them from the lectern. 'Men are nothing. It is their virtues, it is holiness above all, that attracts. At the smell of this perfume from the sky, generations come running, full of generosity and love, edified, already remade by the spectacle of a soul engaged in the ways of perfection.' Beatriz regarded the abbot with distaste. She could almost see the hypocrisy wafting from him, like incense.

Soon after the mass, the party assembled in the abbey courtyard. Beatriz was curious to see Bertrand and Imbert emerge from the stables together, both looking out of sorts. Had they argued? Bertrand's huge black hound, Bragge, was at his heels and Imbert was glancing nervously at the dog.

Roger and three other knights took the head of the entourage. Philippa rode a fine brown mare and sat alongside her uncle Raimon. Bertrand's horse was as black as his hair and as wild-mannered. Imbert was riding alongside Bertrand and already squirming, uncomfortable in his saddle. Lluis assisted Beatriz onto her black mule. 'You are looking very fine this morning, proud Beatriza,' Lluis murmured in Catalan, his mouth brushing her hair. She suppressed a smile at the touch of his firm hands on her waist and hip. He handed Anna up to mount behind Beatriz. The other servants and knights who had accompanied the party from Tolosa assembled behind Beatriz and Anna. The abbot and several monks stood on the steps of the church watching the departure, and Beatriz glimpsed Mafalda at the back of the crowd. The nun looked on glumly, and Beatriz noticed Roger exchanging a nod with her.

Raimon signalled to Roger, and they kicked their horses on, out through the arched gateway. From Saint-Pons-de-Thomières, the party followed the course of the River Jaur. The rushing water course wound through the sinuous Olargues valley and flowed into the Orb river at the foot of Mont Caroux, near Tarassac. They took the road west towards Tolosa. In Venerque, they rested the horses and broke fast, and then moved on into the wood near Orzvals. Riding a slow mule in freezing weather behind the dust kicked up by the nobles' horses was not a pleasure. Beatriz wrapped her cloak more closely about her mouth and cheeks and looked forward to the comforts of Chateau Narbonnais.

At last, they were crossing the vast plain towards the city. The hard fields would soon be ploughed and planted with corn and millet. It was a clear, cold day, and the snow-capped Pyrenees were visible on the horizon. When they passed the old Roman cemetery, Beatriz knew they were close. She craned her neck to see around the horses ahead of her. The pinkish Roman city walls rose up before them. Chateau Narbonnais, with its two imposing towers and defensive ditch before the monumental Narbonne Gate, was one of the ten city portals. If Beatriz's father could see her now, in the midst of all this grandeur, what would he think?

Suddenly, the broad River Garonne came into view. Several boats of various sizes with coloured sails moved fast under a good breeze towards the port, reefing and furling their sails to prepare to pass under the bridge. Beatriz could see the millers hard at work on the floating mills. Donkeys carried sacks of grain across the narrow jetties, and men hefted the sacks up ladders to the millers, who poured the grain into the funnel above the mill stone. She saw the constant turning of the water wheels, the pale puffs of grain as the sacks were emptied. She could just discern, above the racket of the river itself, the chug chug of the mill wheels and the deep-throated rattle of the millstone in its housing.

The gate opened as the garrison recognised Count Raimon's party and they rode under the central arch in the gigantic entryway. In the courtyard, Beatriz's mule was transferred to a stableboy, and Beatriz and Anna hurried across the cold cobbles into the warmth of the Great Hall. Raimon, Bertrand, Petrus Regimundus and Philippa were already being greeted by Viscount Ademar, who had held command of Tolosa during Raimon's absence. Imbert came in and hastily made himself comfortable close to the fire and close to the group of men around Raimon, always alert to pick up information and gossip. The viscount began his report to Raimon on matters that had occurred in the week of their absence. 'I had a tally made of the salt supplies and income again and there is definitely a shortfall,' the viscount said.

'Would you like me to investigate …' Petrus began.

'No,' Raimon said. 'I will get to the bottom of this myself. I will travel to Narbonne in a few weeks. I am leaking coin as if I had stabbed a great hole in every one of my salt sacks.'

'*My* salt sacks,' Philippa whispered to Beatriz. 'They are more mine than his.'

'I have business in Narbonne,' Imbert called over. 'Might I accompany you again, lord?'

'Do what you like,' Raimon said. He was not at all pleased to hear about the shortfall.

Anna tapped Beatriz's hand and surreptitiously pointed at Petrus. Beatriz was surprised to see Petrus directing a look of fury in Imbert's direction. She shook her head imperceptibly to Anna to indicate that the tensions were a mystery to her.

Raimon waved a hand dismissively at Philippa. 'See to your household duties.'

Philippa frowned but signalled to Beatriz and Anna to follow her from the hall. 'I should be party to this report by the viscount and vicar on the business of Tolosa,' she muttered, as they turned towards the courtyard and the exterior stone staircase that led to Philippa's chambers.

'Lord Raimon,' Beatriz heard Imbert's voice behind her. 'I would ask a favour of you concerning my girl.' She turned to stare at Imbert, and Philippa and Anna turned with her. Imbert gestured with his head towards Beatriz, and Raimon glared at her. 'I've a mind to marry her if you would give me leave.' Beatriz's heart plummeted into her boots, and she heard Philippa's indrawn breath. They had not expected this problem to erupt so soon.

'My lord,' Beatriz began, intent on at least voicing her objection.

6

VALENTINES

14 February 1093, Chateau Narbonnais

*B*eatriz and Philippa leant from the window overlooking the courtyard, watching Imbert and Raimon ready their horses to begin the journey to Narbonne. The two men and their escort mounted. Raimon gave the command, and the group rode out beneath the gateway. Beatriz heaved a sigh of relief as she watched Imbert's broad rump, almost as wide as his horse's, disappear from view. Several days ago, Raimon had angrily put off Imbert's request for permission to wed Beatriz, telling him it was no time to be talking of marriage, when the count had just buried his nephew. Imbert had patted her arm and told her, 'Don't worry. I just have to catch him at the right moment.'

'We both have a reprieve,' Philippa said in response to Beatriz's sigh. 'A temporary stay of execution. I have written letters – one to my father in the Holy Land and one to my mother in Jaca protesting against my intended marriage and against this usurpation by my uncle and cousin. I asked about the agreement Abbot Frotard revealed. But I know my letters and their replies will take months on the road!'

'And Imbert will use his journey as an opportunity to work persuasion on Lord Raimon to allow him to marry me.'

'Clap! Clap!' Beatriz and Philippa turned their heads to look over their shoulders at the sound of Anna's wax tablets being slapped together.

'What is it, Anna?' Philippa asked. The two small tablets in Anna's hands were hinged. She carried them everywhere in case reading mouths didn't suffice and she needed to resort to written communication. She slapped the tablets shut, repeating the sound one more time, and slid them back into the dark green woollen pouch on her hip. Two yellow plaits of wool suspended the pouch from her belt. The pouch was decorated with a yellow bird and was another example of Anna's handiwork.

'Let me give you your Valentine hearts and then come and see what we have done in the hall!' Anna was sporting a pink silk heart pinned to the shoulder of her robe and was grinning broadly with excitement.

Philippa smiled at Beatriz, took her by the hand and grabbed Anna with her other hand, dragging them both in her wake, past Roger at the doorway, back into her own chamber.

'Stand still!' Anna commanded as she pinned a bright

blue heart to Philippa's dress and then a green one to Beatriz's.

Suitably adorned, Philippa stepped to the window. Her room looked out across the city. 'Are you watching the birds seeking their mates?' Anna asked, joining her. 'If you see a kingfisher on Valentine's Day, you will marry a happy man. If you see a golden oriole, you will marry a rich man. If you see a sparrow,' she turned in Beatriz's direction, 'you will marry a poor man.'

Beatriz smirked at her gullible companions and joined them to look at the view. She put her fingers on the cold stone of the windowsill and smiled at the morning sunshine and the birdsong, which had been absent for so many long, cold months.

'I sent it this morning,' Anna confided to Beatriz. Beatriz glanced at Philippa's hopeful expression. Anna was referring to Philippa's letter to Duke Guillaume of Aquitaine. Philippa had wasted no time in taking Mafalda's advice and writing to the duke, noting she was unwed and should be the heiress of Tolosa. Folded inside the letter was a small painting of Philippa's face that Lluis had made, although he had not known he was making the likeness to send to Duke Guillaume. They couldn't trust him not to spill the information to his friend Bertrand. If only Beatriz's marriage dilemma could be resolved with a letter to a duke.

'What you are doubtful of will come into your hands,' Philippa recited, reminding them of the prophecy of the Holy Lots. 'I am staying hopeful for the outcome of my letter to Guillaume.'

'Come and see the hall!' Anna begged.

. . .

THE HALL WAS SWAGGED with yellow and white mimosa flowers, which gave off a strong, honeyed scent. Anna held out her arms, waving her hands towards her face and breathing in deeply. Beatriz was forced to laugh at her delight. The maids had hollowed out vegetables for candle lanterns and carved a smile into each lantern. An excited crowd of people were arriving for the midday feast. With Raimon away, Bertrand was presiding. Philippa joined him on the high table, along with Petrus Regimundus. Behind Bertrand, Gauzlin perched on a stool. The discoloured lump off-centre on his tonsure was exposed as he bent his head over his tablet and stylus. When the company were assembled and had taken their seats, Bertrand instructed the unmarried men and women to write their names on strips of parchment or get a friend to scribe for them if they could not. Since the majority could not write, this took some time. Anna and Gauzlin (much to his evident distaste at such a frivolous undertaking) moved up and down the trestles writing names for others. Anna had to keep instructing people to look her in the face as they said their name.

'Lluis!' Bertrand commanded, tapping the two pots on the table in front of him, one black and one white.

Lluis grinned, put one pot under each arm and strolled along the trestles. 'Men in the black pot! Women in the white!' he instructed, holding out the yawning mouth of the appropriate pot and catching, with panache, the strips of folded parchment that were pitched and slipped towards him. 'Is that everyone?' Lluis finally asked, and there was a shout of Yea! Lluis placed the two pots back in front of Bertrand, who began to take out pairs – one man from the black pot and one woman from the white.

'Acibella!' Bertrand shouted, pointing at a giggling maid, 'and … Sauvaric!' Sauvaric was one of Bertrand's soldiers and looked well pleased to take his seat next to the smiling and pretty Acibella. 'Philippa … and Roger!' Bertrand called out, laughing openly at the incongruity.

Reluctantly, Roger took a seat next to his lady on the high table, and Philippa smiled graciously to him. 'Sorry,' he said, taking care not to tread on her dog as he wedged his oversized thighs onto the bench and under the table.

'Ermessenda and Raimbaut!' There was much clapping on the back as the men received their partners. 'Anna… and Bertrand!' Bertrand beamed amusement at Anna, who blushed furiously and took her seat next to him on the high table but at several removes from the reassurance and care of Philippa.

Beatriz frowned, studying Bertrand's hands as he selected the names. She wondered if he had rigged the selection of Anna. Bertrand was a notorious seducer, and Anna was among the few servants who had not yet succumbed. With his rumpled good looks, his superior position, his easy charm, seductions came easily to him. Beatriz's musings were interrupted by the sound of her own name.

'Beatriz and Lluis!'

She looked suspiciously again at Bertrand and was furious with herself at the sensation that swept over her when Lluis asked, 'May I?' as he sat down beside her. The reorganising of the seating had led to overcrowding on the benches. Lluis' thigh was pushed up against her own. She felt both nervous and delighted at his proximity. But above all, she felt angry with herself for these emotions and angry at this ridiculous festival.

Once the couples were seated together, the food was served, including heart-shaped pies and cakes. When the plates were cleared away, two male servants processed up the hall with an arch of brambles to banish unwelcome spirits, and Bertrand set about coordinating the flirtatious love games. Beatriz observed Gauzlin's discomfort. The clerk had been trained at Cluny. He mentioned his association with the great monastery at every opportunity. He glanced around at the company, disapproval writ plain on his long-nosed face. In Bertrand's service, he must be often discomfited.

'Beatriza!' She looked up at Bertrand. What foolishness now? 'We must have love songs!'

Beatriz inclined her head. Lluis placed a stool in front of the high table for her. She lifted one blue-booted foot onto the stool and rested her *vielle* on her raised knee, tuning it. When she was ready, she stood straight again, her *vielle* nestled along her arm. She sang a few of Imbert's best love songs. She was saving her own songs for the Easter feast.

> *The winter that comes to me*
> *Is white red yellow flowers;*
> *My good luck grows*
> *With the wind and the rain,*
> *And so my song mounts up, rises*
> *And my worth increases.*

I have such love in my heart,
Such joy, such sweetness,
The ice I see is a flower,
The snow, green things that grow.

I could walk around undressed,
Naked in my shirt,
For perfect love protects me
From the cold north wind.

Beatriz stopped and sat on the stool to rest a moment and take a beaker of wine. Two other musicians took up the task of musical entertainment and strummed a tune. Beatriz watched Anna responding slowly, uncertainly to the jokes and conversation around her, where she sat on the high table next to Bertrand. Bertrand did not take the trouble to face her when he spoke, so she was isolated, marooned by his neglect. Anna smiled and smiled, the smile becoming more and more fixed as the festivities wore on.

Beatriz rose from her stool. Bertrand didn't notice that she had stopped singing. He was immersed in Julia, his current mistress, who he had seated on his other side. His back was turned to Anna now. Beatriz tapped Lluis on the shoulder. 'I'm tired and will retire.'

'I will escort you.' She took one last look at Anna staring into space and caught Philippa's eye. Philippa nodded and Beatriz hoped the lady had understood the message she was trying to convey. In the arched doorway to the courtyard, Lluis gently pressed Beatriz to the wall and kissed her. She allowed and revelled in the kiss for a while and then pushed him away. 'Saint Valentine's could be a night of love, Beatriz,' he said, his eyes limpid, his pupils huge, his pale hair glinting in the torchlight.

'It is very tempting, but ...,' she murmured, dodging past him to the safety of Philippa's side, as the lady emerged from the hall. Philippa had rescued Anna from Bertrand, and Roger stood silent and huge beside the two young women, waiting to escort them up the stone steps to the second floor.

As Philippa prepared for bed, Anna placed a yarrow sprig on Philippa's pillow and sprinkled it with rosewater. She decorated the pillow with five bay leaves, to encourage Philippa to dream of her husband-to-be.

'Did you find Lluis a delightful Valentine partner?' Philippa asked Beatriz as they watched Anna's preparations.

'Yes,' Beatriz said slowly, flushing at the memory of the kiss.

'Can you trust him?' Philippa asked. 'He is tight with Bertrand.'

'I don't trust any man.'

'What about you, Anna?' Philippa asked when Anna looked in their direction. 'How was Bertrand as your Valentine?'

'He finds my deafness exotic. He thinks I am mute as well as well as deaf.'

Beatriz raised her eyebrows. 'Yes, probably you are right. The notion of a mute bed partner would delight him. Be careful with him, Anna. He is only interested in conquest.'

'I know,' Anna said, the anger plain in her voice. 'He thinks I am stupid.'

There was a moment of silence. 'Bertrand's *actual* Valentine, his betrothed wife, Helie of Burgundy, will soon arrive,' Philippa remarked.

'Poor girl!' exclaimed Beatriz.

'This is a prestigious marriage for Bertrand. The house of Burgundy is a rich and powerful court, with ties to Cluny. The marriage is another way for my uncle to silence whispers of Bertrand's illegitimacy. Another emphasis on his suitability to inherit Tolosa.' Philippa's last phrase was pronounced in a tone of great irritation. Raimon had been forced to put aside Bertrand's mother by Abbot Frotard when consanguinity was ruled in that marriage, but Raimon had no intention of putting aside his only son.

Beatriz grimaced. 'Perhaps this Helie will take one look at Bertrand and run for the hills.'

'But Bertrand is very good-looking,' Anna blurted.

'Good-looking in a profoundly louche way,' Beatriz responded. 'I think he has slept with just about every loose woman in this castle.'

'Including you,' Philippa said tartly.

Beatriz stood, swirling her cape dramatically, insouciant to Philippa's declaration. 'Well, goodnight, and sweet dreams.' She poked her head from the door to check no one – Lluis or Bertrand – was lurking there, emboldened with Valentine's ardour, and she slipped along the passageway to the Galliarde Tower to climb the ladders to her eyrie.

.   .   .

69

IN THE MORNING, Beatriz only had time for a brief practice with her *vielle*. Yawning, she strolled into Philippa's chambers, hoping the lady had received the romantic answers she wanted from her superstitious practices. Otherwise a lengthy and tiresome discussion would ensue. A wilted sprig meant no love, but a healthy one meant eternal love. As she entered, Philippa held up a healthy-looking sprig for Beatriz to see. It was silly, but Beatriz could not begrudge Philippa her hope. She smiled at Philippa. Like enough, the lady would be married off to the wrinkly old king of Aragon before long. 'And what did you dream of?' Beatriz asked.

'Duke Guillaume, of course!' Philippa beamed. 'He was riding a white horse and was very handsome.'

'Did he have a big lance?' Beatriz asked and was gratified to watch Anna giggle and to hear Roger shuffle his feet.

Philippa closed her eyes and pursed her small mouth. When she opened her green eyes, Beatriz was relieved to see there was laughter in them. 'You are incorrigible, Beatriz. I don't know why I keep you about me.'

'Because, lady, you have to save me from Imbert,' Beatriz flashed back.

'I will do my best,' Philippa promised.

7

THE RED DRESS

Late March 1093, Tolosa

*B*eatriz stepped out from the shadow of the gateway into the city, encountering bright sunshine. She was intent on making her way to the basilica of Saint-Sernin. Imbert had instructed her to go there while he was away and collect new music sheets from the canon in charge of the church, Dean Gayrard.

It was a relief to be out of Philippa's chambers, out of the chateau with its crowd of people, and in the open air, alone. She had spent a year living on the street as a runaway with no comforts or certainties and then four years travelling with Imbert. They had spent more time on the road than performing at a great variety of courts. It was wonderful to have the security of Chateau Narbonnais, but sometimes she felt cooped up, too cheek-by-jowl with nosy others. Sometimes she longed for a little uncertainty.

She had tied her hair up under a boy's cap and wore breeches and her long cloak, hoping to avoid too much attention as a woman walking alone in the city. The proprieties made her smile when she thought of the year she had spent as a beggar in Sort and what she had had to fend off there. She took her time, observing the details around her. There was no reason to hurry. To her right was the Mint, a solid building with high, small windows and two guards on the door. To her left was the Salin, the salt spring next to the chateau. In the summer, the water evaporated in the heat, leaving behind salt for the kitchen staff to collect. Beatriz sniffed at the air, enjoying the slight salty tang on her lips. This pond could only supply a tiny fraction of the vast amount of salt used in the chateau kitchens to preserve meat and fish and make cheese. Salt was ubiquitous.

She strolled on through the Jewish quarter at Carmes, walking up the street called Changes, which took her to the Saracen Wall. The wall separated the city – the seat of the counts – from the bourg – the newer part of the city, where the bishop took taxes and tolls. She passed through the wall at the Capitol and made her way past La Taur towards the worksite where the great basilica was rising up from the ground in a haze of stone dust and a racket of hammers. She heard and smelt the site before she saw it. Wood-smoke and the scents of cooking, leather, stone, heated metal and sweating men were on the air.

The narrow roads leading to the worksite were lined with hastily constructed workshops, small timber-framed houses, lodges and material stores. A temporary encampment of food stalls, hostels and alehouses catered for the construction workers. Wagons loaded with stone and timber shook the ground as they rolled past Beatriz.

As the basilica close came into view, she stopped for a moment to marvel at the thrumming chaos of so many workers rushing to and fro. Craftsmen checked their measurements; apprentices passed tools to their masters; muscled labourers balanced on high wooden scaffolds or swarmed up ladders; men carefully buttered mortar onto dressed stones. A blacksmith swung a rebounding hammer, tending to the workers' tools. More stones were slung in leather cradles being raised into position with a small crane. A team of oxen circled a large wheel, driving a windlass to raise a heavier load. Beatriz moved closer and craned her neck, peering up at the activity on the underside of the roof. The scaffolding looked impossibly fragile, with labourers teetering on planks held up by rough poles lashed together vertically and diagonally. The seeming chaos was closely managed by overseers in each section who ensured there was, in fact, an underlying order, else the basilica would not rise well, and valuable, skilled workers could be injured.

The old shrine of Saint-Sernin and the crypt were already enclosed with a vast circumference wall and more spaces to be built were marked out on the ground with ropes and wooden pegs. When it was finished, Saint-Sernin would be a huge rectangular structure with a massive central nave, four aisles – two on either side of the nave, an ambulatory and several minor chapels. Pilgrims milled around with the edges of their cloaks held up over their mouths and noses in a vain effort to protect themselves from the dust.

The building work had proceeded in stop-start fashion for the last few years – held up by rivalry between the Saint-Sernin Augustinian canons and the Cluniacs from Moissac, or by disruptions in the supply of marble and stone, or by a lack of skilled workmen. Beatriz turned in a circle, her eyes wide. The scale of Saint-Sernin certainly reflected the majesty of heaven and would awe the visitors. The enormous new church was being conjured in stone and imagination all around her.

She realised the *portarius* was looking at her with a bemused expression on his face. 'I would like to see Dean Gayrard,' Beatriz told him.

'What is your business, girl?' he asked, looking askance at her unusual attire.

'I will tell my business to him.'

The *portarius* was far from impressed by her stubborn rudeness, but after some blustering, which she ignored, he went to see if the dean would let her in. Gayrard was known as a man of principle. He had fought his ground with the Cluniacs and had appealed to the pope. He had been successful in evicting the Cluniacs from the basilica. The whole controversy held up work at Saint-Sernin for two years and the pope was not pleased. Work on the cathedrals and churches on the pilgrim route to Compostela was for the glory to God, and, of course, there was the small matter of the profits that would flow from the hordes of visitors. Gayrard was greatly loved in the bourg of Tolosa. There were many hospices and hospitals in and near the city, each with their own particular job – the leper hospital outside the city walls, hospitals for the old, for orphaned children, for the sick and poor, for wounded soldiers who could not work. Many of these were the initiatives of the Augustinians, and of Gayrard, in particular. He had recently opened a new hospital for beggars in the close of Saint-Sernin.

'Mistress Beatriz, isn't it?' he asked as she came in and took the seat he indicated to her on the other side of a desk covered in parchment rolls and ink pots and a vase of spring flowers. She took off her cap and let her black hair free. The dean made no remark on her unusual clothing.

'Yes, Dean, Beatriz of Farrera. Thank you for seeing me. You promised new music from Limoges to myself and Imbert.'

'Indeed.' He sifted through the many parchments on his desk and at last handed one over to her. It was rolled up and tied with a black ribbon. 'This is the one I promised to Imbert.' Gayrard was a busy man, overseeing the construction, managing the cathedral staff, meeting with benefactors, leading the canons' chapter meetings, dealing with the church hierarchy. A model of the basilica in miniature constructed in wood and plaster sat amidst the sea of parchments and ledgers on his desk.

'Thank you, Dean. It is very kind of you to think of Imbert and me and make time to share this with us. I look forward to trying the melodies.' He didn't need to know Beatriz couldn't read the parchment and would rely on Anna to decipher it for her.

'Is all well with the Lady Philippa?' he asked.

'Yes. Lady Philippa is well. Count Raimon and Imbert

are away in Narbonne, but will return soon for the Easter Assembly.'

'And will you be singing at the assembly, Beatriz?' Gayrard was an accomplished composer and singer, although he, of course, sang of the love of God rather than the love of man or woman.

'Yes. I have composed five of my own songs.'

'Love songs?' he asked.

'Four are love songs and one is a *tenso*, a debate song that I will perform with Imbert.'

'I suppose you think I know nothing of your love lyrics?' Gayrard asked with a smile.

Beatriz smiled back, but said nothing.

'I was married for a long time, before I became a canon, but my wife died.' Beatriz could see the warm memory of his wife in his eyes and in the lines of a smile grooving his cheek. She was about to respond when they were interrupted by a loud screeching.

'Get off me! Let go! Get off!' The *portarius* burst in with two dark-haired boys pinched painfully by the ear, one to each hand.

'*Portarius*! Please! Let them go. What is this?' Gayrard asking standing.

The *portarius* let the boys go abruptly, and they both fell, one skinning his knee and starting to snivel instead of screech.

'These heathens were snooping around the worksite, looking what to steal,' the *portarius* asserted.

'We're not heathens!' exclaimed the bigger boy who had got up and aimed a kick at the *portarius*' shin, causing him to dodge quickly out of the way.

Beatriz bent and helped the injured child up and sat him in the seat she had vacated. Gayrard wetted a cloth from his water jug and passed it to her to clean the boy's bloodied knee.

'No indeed,' Gayrard said to the boys. 'You are not heathens. I know your father. The boys are the sons of Zachary the Jew,' he said to the *portarius*. 'I can vouch they are not thieves, but simply curious, eh? About the work?' He asked the older boy, who nodded.

'Aye,' asserted the *portarius*. 'Heathens, as I said.'

'Not at all.' Gayrard frowned at the man. 'I'll thank you not to be so rough with children. You may leave.'

The *portarius* scowled, gave the older boy a last furious glare and departed.

'However, boys,' Gayrard turned back to them. 'You should not be about the worksite. It is a dangerous place. I would not wish to have to tell your father that you were seriously injured. I will see they are escorted home safely,' he told Beatriz.

She thanked him again for the music, ruffled the younger boy's hair, crammed her own hair back into her cap and stepped out into the hubbub of the worksite. Amid the general cacophony, she heard the chink chink of stone hammers to her left and decided to look in at the sculptors' workshop. The last, low rays of late afternoon sun streamed in through the large windows and thick dust motes from the work hung in the streams of light like constellations. Beatriz had expected dust and noise but was surprised to find how delicate the tools and movements of the sculptors were. They were using small hammers to tap at stone and marble, carving wonderful pictures for the capitals for Saint-Sernin. Each man drew on detailed knowledge of the qualities of stone to create their images.

She spotted Lluis on the far side of the workshop. He was wearing a thick hessian apron and a pair of stout gloves were looped over his belt. The stone dust muted everything to a uniform cream hue, but Lluis' fair hair glinted through, the light sparking off his head. His hair fell in unruly curls to the side of his face. He was intent on his work and had not seen her. She moved closer to see what he was doing.

An image of a cleric was emerging on a capital and was near finished. The carved man stood with a bible in his left hand and his right hand was raised, palm out, in blessing. His two large bare feet were squarely planted beneath the folds and drapes of his habit. It was an astonishingly lifelike image to be creating from such hard, inanimate material. Beatriz smiled to herself, thinking how Lluis had complained to her that he could never hope to compete with his father, who was a famed fresco artist. His father's name and exquisite work were known throughout Occitania and Catalonia. Rather like Bertrand, Lluis struggled for his own light in the shadow of his father. But looking at him now, Beatriz felt sure his own light would succeed in shining through.

Lluis' drawings were pinned to the wall around him. The sketches, made in charcoal, showed birds in foliage, an angel with straining neck muscles, squat figures with flat torsos and protruding stomachs draped with the folds of their tunics. Beatriz's glance halted, astonished, at a vivid drawing of her own face. She glanced quickly at

Lluis, but he was working with his nose close to his work, his lips gently blowing and his broad fingers carefully dusting away excess material as he made each tiny chip. Beatriz backed away quietly.

The sky was beginning to darken, and the fortified tower houses of the Tolosa nobility were stark, crenellated silhouettes all around the basilica close as Beatriz emerged from the workshop. Moving towards the path, she noticed a woman standing framed in the tall ground-floor window of one of the tower houses, wearing a brilliant red dress. The woman had her back to the window, exposing the intricate lacing of her dress, running from low in the small of her back up to the nape of her neck. Her head was wrapped in a veil. Candlelight blazed from the window and projected out onto the ground at Beatriz's feet. Dusk was gathering the last light like the slow sweep of a raven's wing. A man in dark garb came up behind the woman and Beatriz could only see his back. Delicately and slowly, he unlaced the woman's red dress, and Beatriz watched the looping movements of his hands, mesmerised, thinking of Lluis' hands. He finished and moved to the side so that Beatriz could see that the back of the red dress had fallen open and slipped a little on the woman's shoulders. The skin of her naked back had a golden hue. The tops of her round buttocks and the crease between them were visible as the dress slid down a little further. It was near full dark now and Beatriz reluctantly turned away to hurry back towards the chateau. The city gates would be closing soon, and the curfew bell would ring in an hour or so.

8

FOOL'S DAY

1 April 1093, Chateau Narbonnais

*T*he hall was busy with men doing business. Beatriz sauntered through, bun in hand, hoping to overhear something useful, as Imbert had taught her. Information is coin, he always said. The flamboyantly dressed young stranger seated to Bertrand's right at the high table must be Henry of Burgundy, who had arrived late last night with his niece. Abbot Frotard and Mafalda were seated to Bertrand's left. The group were looking over two family trees spread out on the table before them. Beatriz eyed Henry with pleasure. He was an island of vivid colour surrounded by the black habits of the abbot and Mafalda. Even Bertrand was wearing black today, but in his case, it only served to heighten his good looks, to contrast with the blue of his eyes.

Henry was the brother of the duke of Burgundy and the uncle of Bertrand's wife-to-be, the duke's daughter Helie. Henry's clothes told the tale of his status. His tunic was a pale yellow, elaborately embroidered in blue and gold at the hem, cuffs and neck. His mantle was a deep, rich blue with a thin edging of black and white fur and held in place on one shoulder with a finely wrought gold and blue-gemmed brooch.

Gauzlin was seated, as usual, on a small stool behind Bertrand, writing on a wax tablet. The abbot was tracing the lines of descent on the family trees with a broad forefinger. Beatriz guessed he was checking that a marriage between Bertrand and Helie of Burgundy did not transgress the rules of consanguinity, of seven degrees of relationship. And if it did – Beatriz's voice inside her head was sour – the abbot would no doubt be amenable to a donation to make such a problem evaporate. With Bertrand's marriage approaching, Philippa's unwelcome fate came closer.

Beatriz sat down at a trestle and turned her eyes away from the high table, looking around the hall at the other occupants. Petrus Regimundus sat at the long trestle opposite. He was in conversation with a couple of merchants and *vectuari*. They too had papers strewn before them, but these looked more like account books, charts and maps of sea and road routes. The vicar was discussing the price of salt with the merchants. Bernard Gelduinus, the master architect at Saint-Sernin, entered and made his way over to Petrus. The draw on the count's coffers for the building of the basilica was enormous, and

Petrus and Gelduinus would soon be haggling long and hard.

Beatriz's breakfast and observation were interrupted by the appearance of the hulking form of Roger at the doorway to the courtyard. The man was huge. He had to dip his head under the arched door frame. As he walked through the hall towards her, he was a clear head and shoulders taller than any other man there. Beatriz looked towards Mafalda and saw the nun had noticed Roger. A look passed between the two, Roger's eyes grazing Mafalda's cheek. Roger turned his attention back to his quarry. He stopped in front of Beatriz, and she studied the broad strips of tattoos across his forearms, patterned in blue ink like chain mail. 'What is it, Roger?' He jerked his head over his shoulder back in the direction he had come from. His unkempt, long hair and beard hung about his head and neck like a wolf pelt. 'Lady Philippa wants to see me?' she guessed. He nodded and turned. She compressed her lips but rose to follow him. It wasn't as if he couldn't talk. He just couldn't be bothered!

Philippa was hosting Helie of Burgundy in her chambers. Helie was slight, with sandy-coloured hair and extraordinary turquoise eyes. She was a childish thirteen. She had arrived with a retinue of six ladies, and all these ladies had their own maids. This marriage to the daughter of the duke of Burgundy was a grand coup for Bertrand and Raimon. Entering Philippa's chambers, Beatriz felt she had stumbled into a rainbow. Helie's ladies were clustered about her, each in a different brightly coloured gown. Helie picked up a pinch of fragrant cardamon and liquorice from the bowl on the table and chewed it. A gentle buzz of conversation emanated from the young women. Beatriz nodded a greeting to Anna. Philippa patted the padded bench beside her, and Beatriz joined her, leaning towards Philippa's whisper. 'It's frustrating to have to engage in these social duties.'

Helie, perhaps jealous of their whispering, offered, 'Your cousin Bertrand is very handsome.'

Philippa politely smiled her agreement.

Helie looked around at Philippa's chambers. 'I suppose,' she ventured hesitantly, 'since you are leaving for Jaca soon, that I might be installed here, in these chambers.'

Philippa blinked her green eyes. 'My departure is not settled yet,' she replied tightly. Beatriz looked with sympathy at Philippa. She had inhabited these rooms for seventeen years and now she was to be displaced and exiled. Beatriz looked coldly at Helie. The only consolation was that the girl would have to marry Bertrand.

'What is Bertrand interested in? What makes him happy?' Helie asked.

Beatriz raised one eyebrow. She picked up her *vielle* and looked down at it, strumming and tuning.

'Oh,' Philippa stumbled, no doubt needing to cover the same thoughts Beatriz was having in response to Helie's question: wine, sluts, dice. 'He loves to go riding and fly his hawk,' Philippa responded diplomatically.

Helie beamed. 'Those are my favourite pastimes, too.' Her ladies twittered and smiled, many of them barely out of the nursery. Beatriz conjured an image of them all scrubbing out the latrines in the guards' tower in their fine dresses. She struck a chord dramatically and smiled with her best hypocrisy at Helie.

> *A knight once lay beside and with*
> *the one he most desired,*
> *and in between their kisses said,*
> *what shall I do, my sweet?*
> *Day comes and the knight goes*
> *Ai!*
> *And I hear the watcher cry:*
> *'Up! On your way!*
> *I see day*
> *Coming on, sprouting behind the dawn!*

'That's beautiful,' declared Helie, her fingertips to her mouth, 'and rather rude!'

'It is an *alba*, lady,' Beatriz told her, 'a lover's dawn song.'

'Will you sing more?' Helie asked eagerly. 'Do the lovers wed?'

'True lovers are never *wed*!' Beatriz said, her voice acerbic. Philippa frowned and poked Beatriz's calf with the tip of her shoe to warn her to be polite. But as Imbert often said, politeness was frequently beyond Beatriz.

Bertrand and Henry of Burgundy entered, accompanied by Lluis and Gauzlin. Bertrand's large hound, Bragge, was at his heels and both Philippa's dog Adimante and her cat Tibers rose, readying for antagonism. 'We wondered if we might trouble you ladies for more entertaining conversation than we can find downstairs with priests and nuns,' Bertrand stated. Beatriz watched Gauzlin's mouth purse at Bertrand's words.

'We have concluded our business in the hall,' Henry added, looking meaningfully at Helie.

Beatriz noticed Bertrand appraising Helie's ladies and maids and how Helie *did not* notice it. Abbot Frotard had complained to Raimon on several occasions about Bertrand's licentious behaviour.

Bragge commenced a low growling in the direction of Adimante. 'Silence!' Bertrand commanded with a hand gesture, and the dog subsided at his side. Adimante similarly resumed her place, resting her chin on Philippa's shoe. Tibers, not so easily persuaded, stalked off to a back corner and concealed herself in the folds of a long curtain pooled on the floor.

Philippa smiled a welcome to the men and saw her guests seated and provided with beakers of wine. Beatriz half-heartedly resumed her singing.

> *Time comes, and turns, and goes,*
> *in days, in months, in years,*
> *and I, weary, know not what to say of it.*

She sighed and set her *vielle* down. She leant to pet Adimante, who snuggled closer to her ankles.

'Oh, do sing more, *jograresa*,' Helie begged.

'I have lost the will, I fear, my lady.'

Helie's eager expression transformed to crestfallen. She glanced shyly at Bertrand, who continued not to take notice of her. He had fixed on the most buxom of the six ladies who was dressed in yellow, and they were exchanging glances.

'Does everyone know the game of the king who does not lie?,' Henry asked. His niece clapped her hands happily. 'Yes! I love that game!'

Philippa shook her head. 'I don't know it, I'm afraid.'

Henry sat down in the chair opposite Philippa and Beatriz, swagging his heavy blue cloak to one side. His hair and beard were dark brown. He had soft brown eyes, a well-shaped nose and mouth. He leant forward, talking to Philippa with a pleasant smile. 'The rules of the game are we begin with one "king" by drawing straws and that king must tell us a love secret and then nominate the next "king".'

'I see.' Philippa's tone was hesitant.

'We must fashion a crown,' Henry said. 'Do you have anything suitable, Lady Philippa?'

Philippa stood and lifted the lid of a chest at the side of the room. Anna and Beatriz exchanged a look as they saw Henry regarding Philippa intently. She was wearing another of her new-fashion dresses. This one was a rich green. Anna had plaited her lady's hair and wound it around her head in an elaborate circlet that morning. Philippa drew a heavily jewelled diadem that belonged to her mother from the chest. 'Will this do?' The reds and greens of the jewels glinted as she turned it in her hands, holding it out towards Henry.

'Perfect!' He took it from Philippa and set it on the table in front of them.

One of Helie's ladies made the straws ready for drawing. Many hands reached to the bunched straws held out to them. Beatriz found she was the first reluctant 'king' and must be 'crowned' by Henry. She worked not to look in Lluis' direction. 'Well,' she stammered, 'umm...'

'Come along now, *Trobairitz*,' Henry encouraged her, 'no doubt a beauty such as yourself has many love secrets.' He laughed with Helie, who was very excited and practically bouncing in her seat.

'Well, *if* I marry,' Beatriz stated firmly, 'I would expect to have at least a morsel of love's bread in that marriage, and I don't mean to suffer the cuts of love's knife.'

Henry's eyes flashed. 'Well said!' he declared, impressed. 'Although not really a secret,' he jokingly reprimanded her. 'More an aspiration. Who do you nominate?'

'Lady Helie,' she said, desperate to get the girl's keenness out of the way. Henry lifted the heavy diadem from Beatriz's hair and set it on his niece's head, where it looked comically over-large.

Helie closed her pale turquoise eyes for a moment. Her long sandy lashes fluttered on the white skin of her cheek. She opened her eyes. 'I am secretly in love,' she declared.

Beatriz swallowed. This was a very annoying game.

'And ....?' Henry queried.

'I am in love with a man with dark hair,' she said, looking at Bertrand.

Henry rolled his eyes. 'Alright. Good enough. Who do you nominate?'

'Lady Philippa.'

Philippa sighed, clearly also finding the game tiresome. 'I love music,' she said.

'Wait, the crown!' Henry called out, placing it carefully

on Philippa's head and brushing a stray lock of pale yellow hair to a more becoming location.

'Oh no!' Bertrand said loudly. 'You don't get away with just that. We are talking the love between men and women here, cousin, as well you know.'

Philippa pressed her lips together. 'Alright. I would wish to marry a *young* man.' She flushed and did not look at them. Beatriz heard a snort of amusement from Bertrand.

'And who do you nominate, lady?' Henry asked gently. No doubt Henry was as aware as Bertrand of the negotiations over Philippa's marriage to old King Sancho. Henry's aunt was the queen of Castile, and he had spent time fighting against the Saracens on the Iberian peninsula. He would be well versed in the business going forward there.

'Cousin Bertrand,' Philippa said.

Bertrand, appearing both foolish and rakishly delicious in the woman's diadem, looked around the room dramatically, jousting with the eye of each lady in turn. Even Gauzlin appeared to be amused at the sight of him. When Bertrand's glance rested on Beatriz, she scowled at him, which made his grin wider. 'I am in love with a girl with *fair* hair and fetching freckles scattered across her nose,' he declared, looking at Beatriz, who did not, of course, match this description. Helie did, but then so did his mistress Julia. 'And I nominate you, Henry.' Bertrand stood briefly to lodge the glinting crown in Henry's brown curls.

'I am in love with a lady in this room,' Henry said quietly, looking down at the tips of his polished black boots. The crown slipped from his head, and he caught it in both hands. There was a quiet moment as everyone took in his statement. He looked up at no one in particular. 'She shines as brightly as the moon compared with which the stars are but tiny candles. And I nominate Lluis,' he added swiftly, depositing the crown on Lluis' head.

'I am also in love with a lady in this room,' Lluis said, smiling to himself, 'and I nominate Gauzlin.'

There was general laughter in response to this nomination. The monk looked up crossly from a prayer book. 'It is hardly fitting for me to play such a game. My love is reserved for Christ.'

'And you love Cluny, your motherhouse,' Bertrand said.

'Of course.' Gauzlin exchanged a tight smile with Henry of Burgundy. The Burgundy family were strong supporters of Cluny. Gauzlin waved off their attention and the crown and returned his gaze to the small book in his hands. Beatriz noticed he was not reading the book itself, but rather a letter he had lodged between its pages. Beatriz took the crown and waved it at Anna, who shook her head and warded it off with a hand.

'You know, the Romans exposed a newborn with an impairment,' said Bertrand. 'And if one such should survive, they were barred from marriage.'

Beatriz looked swiftly to Anna and saw she had thankfully been looking in another direction during Bertrand's mean speech. She had not read his cruel words on his mouth.

'Anna was not impaired at birth.' Beatriz and the rest

of the company were startled by Philippa's anger. 'As well you know, Bertrand.' Anna was following Philippa's words now and her face flushed to find herself the subject of discussion. 'Her deafness is the result of a childhood illness,' Philippa continued.

'Such abnormalities are generally caused by sin,' Helie pronounced primly. 'Your maid should consider a pilgrimage to beg …'

Philippa stood abruptly, knocking over a beaker of wine with her skirts. 'I beg you will excuse me. I grow tired. Roger!'

Bertrand smirked. He was delighted to have let loose dissension. Henry frowned his niece to silence and rose. 'I beg forgiveness, ladies,' he nodded to Philippa and then to Anna, 'that offence has been given.'

Philippa stared angrily at Bertrand, barely containing her impatience that they should quit her rooms. Henry reached a hand towards her, but Bertrand plucked him by the sleeve and gestured with his head towards the door. Roger stepped in front of Philippa and loomed like a great Cerberus at the unwelcome guests. Helie, her face an unbecoming red, rose with her ladies and the group rustled to the door. 'To horses, to hawks, my lord,' Bertrand murmured to Henry as they left. Henry turned in the doorway to throw one more wistful glance towards Philippa. 'I look forward to conversing with you, Lady Philippa, at the feast later today,' he said.

PHILIPPA WORRIED at the absence of response from Duke Guillaume. She paced up and down, bewildering Anna and Beatriz with a torrent of excuses and reasons for his neglect. 'There was the rumour that he was betrothed to Ermengarde of Anjou… I have humiliated myself… He is afraid to confront my uncle. Beatriz, find Mafalda and invite her to come and speak with me. Perhaps she knows something.' There was no reply yet from Philippa's parents either.

Beatriz hoped Fool's Day might lighten Philippa's mood. On this first day of April, the jester ruled the hall and everything was widdershins. The jester sat in Bertrand's place on the high table and Bertrand had been demoted to the trestle and made sure to sit between Beatriz and Anna. Petrus had also been demoted from the high table and sat opposite Beatriz. During the meal, everyone was trying to outdo each other with ridiculous tales. It was permissible to play practical jokes until noon. Earlier that morning, Roger had been unamused to find himself and his dignity covered in flour when he opened the door of Philippa's chamber. Philippa and Anna had balanced a bag of flour atop the door, and he had been the unfortunate recipient. There was a little flour still lodged in his hair and beard.

'I just heard something that will amuse you, Beatriz, seeing as you are a woman of the world,' Bertrand said.

Beatriz cast a distrustful glance at him. The things Bertrand thought would amuse her rarely did.

'I was given a manuscript from Burgundy that talks of the salting of virgins,' said Bertrand in his overloud voice. Petrus focused on Bertrand, an interested expression on his face. The taxes for the count's salt were his responsibility, and anything salt interested him.

'Whatever do you mean?' Beatriz suspected she would regret asking.

'It's a kind of comedy,' Bertrand said, a little hesitant now everyone around them was listening, but he ploughed on. 'If young women have failed to find a husband before Lent, the poem recommends they are "salted down" to preserve them for future consumption.'

Petrus slapped his thigh and laughed loudly. The bench shook with the man's huge movements.

'Like stock fish?' asked Beatriz, anger burning in her chest. Gauzlin shifted unhappily in his seat on the other side of Anna. It must be a kind of torture for him to be in Bertrand's service, and Beatriz wondered why he had chosen to stay in Tolosa instead of returning to the serenity of Moissac Abbey.

'It's a comedy,' Bertrand said defensively.

'It's not very funny,' asserted Beatriz.

'Don't look like you are sucking salt, Beatriz,' Bertrand chivvied her, and Petrus rocked the bench again, laughing at the quip. 'Can't you see the humour in it? It is *very* funny. It recommends packing young women in salt to neutralise their cock-hunger.'

'What!'

'It's a joke,' Bertrand reiterated, 'a conceit.'

'Conceit indeed,' said Beatriz angrily.

'Salt will preserve *anything*,' Petrus told her smugly. 'And it is an aphrodisiac.'

She looked with distaste at the flecks of food lodged in his blond beard.

'The priest rinses the salt off the virgins after Easter,' Bertrand went on talking across the table to Petrus, ignoring Beatriz, 'and the young women are made delectable again.' He started laughing behind a hand, as he was halfway through eating a slice of pie. 'The salt prevents the girls from getting mouldy down in their cracks!' He guffawed loudly. Anna was regarding them, confused, unable to follow Bertrand's words.

'Do you get it, Anna?' Bertrand asked. 'The poem presents young virgins as toothsome but perishable commodities.'

Anna smiled pleasantly, not understanding, humouring him.

'Make sure you don't have any salted virgins in my shipment, Petrus!' Bertrand yelled and thumped his fist on the table.

'I will, my lord,' Petrus struggled to say, his shoulders shaking with laughter and tears squeezing at the corners of his eyes.

Beatriz stood and signalled to Anna to accompany her. She reached across the table for the fish-tail handle of the silver salt cellar, topped by the figure of Neptune. She thumped it down in front of Petrus. 'Here, Petrus and Bertrand! Take your medicine! Salt will cure your impotence and give you Neptune's foam.' She allowed herself a moment to take in Gauzlin's face turning brick-red, Petrus' mouth hanging open, and Bertrand's expression of shocked delight. She turned on her heel.

'What did you say to them?' Anna asked, hurrying to keep up with Beatriz. 'What were they talking about?'

'Beatriz! You are my salt-born goddess!' Bertrand yelled down the hall after her.

9

BLACK SATURDAY

Easter Saturday, 16 April 1093, Tolosa

*A*nna walked slowly along the passage to Philippa's chambers, carefully avoiding the rush of other servants and the occasional soldier passing her. She read the expressions on their faces – anxiety, fury, happiness, sexual satiation. They glanced at her, but most quickly looked away again, unsure how to deal with someone who could not hear, embarrassed at her difference.

Spring had arrived at last, and she stopped at a casement window where the sun streamed in. The broad Garonne river and banks offered a sparkling, shifting mix of greens and golds. A slight breeze tickled her cheeks. She breathed in the smell of spring. Somebody stumbled hard against her, and she gripped at the shutter edge to stop herself from falling. She turned to see that the woman, Julia, one of Bertrand's maids, was shouting at her, but she was too shocked by the sudden collision and the woman was too furious for her to read the words on her lips. But she could guess at them. 'I'm sorry,' Anna said.

Julia threw one more furious word at her. 'Deafie!'

Anna saw that one. She cast a look of hatred at the woman's retreating back, which she would never have shown to her face.

The passageway was empty again. Sunlight dappled and slipped on the wall opposite the window. She reached her fingertips out to the liquid light, feeling the warmth the sun had already managed to infuse into the stone. Nobody else knew how silence reveals itself in a thousand inexpressible forms: in the quiet of dawn, in the noiseless aspiration of trees towards the sky, in the stealthy descent of night, in the silent changing of the seasons, in the falling moonlight, trickling down into the night like a rain of silence. Anna smiled to herself and continued up the passageway.

Just inside the door of Philippa's chamber, Roger stood at his usual post. He was the first person to greet her this morning, as he always did. He bowed his head to her and placed his palm flat against his heart. Anna returned the gesture, smiling. Philippa and Beatriz were in their usual seats. They sat together on one side of the table so Anna could sit on the other side and watch their mouths.

'Flying bells!' she caught on Beatriz's lips.

'What are flying bells?' she asked.

'The city bells are silent today and yesterday to signify

the absence of Christ, taken down from the cross and laid in his tomb.' Beatriz leapt to her feet to demonstrate her point. 'The priests tell us the bells have flown to Rome to be blessed by the pope. Flying bells!' Beatriz mimed the flying bells and then threw up her hands in disbelief.

Anna delighted in Beatriz's theatricality and in her scepticism. She responded to the curving of Beatriz's mouth, which was more often sullen. Even when Beatriz was not in performance, her stance and the positioning of her feet retained their drama – placed at right angles to each other, stomping with one heel to emphasise a laugh or a point in her conversation. Her face was long and soft, but suggested a wisdom beyond her years. She had, after all, spent a year aged only thirteen, living rough and begging on the streets and then travelling to many marvellous courts far and wide with Imbert. Beatriz's eyes were dark brown. Her nose had character. Her mouth was wide. Her eyebrows were high on her forehead, straight and often rising up and down, as she widened her eyes dramatically, comically. Beatriz had an expressive face and body – always mobile, and often, when the drama of her face and her gesticulating hands did not satisfy her, she would jump to her feet and enact and perform her words. It was an exaggerated body language particularly well suited for communicating with Anna, and well employed in Beatriz's art of interacting with a large audience as a *jograresa*.

'Your cynicism is too much, Beatriz!' Philippa told her. 'Sit down. It's a lovely idea that the bells go on pilgrimage.'

Anna had attended the service in the cathedral yesterday with Philippa and Beatriz when the chalice containing the host was moved from the main altar to a side altar covered in flowers to represent the garden of Gethsemane, and now the host had been removed from the church altogether. The three young women stayed together in the church for an hour, keeping company with Christ through his days of suffering. Anna had closed her eyes to breathe in the strong scents of lilies and hyacinths on the side altar, and she had opened them again to delight in the composition of pale pink chrysanthemums, deep pink primroses with yellow hearts, and purple hyacinths and irises.

'What are you two doing today?' asked Beatriz.

'Making the menu and seating plan for the Easter Assembly feast,' Anna said, setting out a scraping knife and an old parchment. When she had scraped an adequate surface, she took a quill and sketched the plan of the Great Hall with its high table across the width at one end and two long trestles set down the lengths on either side. The Easter Assembly was the big event of the year. Raimon and Imbert would return in time for it. Taxes were paid, justice was meted out, important visitors arrived. Marriages were contracted at the Easter Assembly.

'What's on the menu?' Beatriz asked avidly. Forty days of Lenten fare were drawing to an end. Beatriz carelessly deposited her satchel on the table, knocking Anna's sewing to the floor.

Anna picked up the sewing and rearranged the objects on the table, setting Beatriz's satchel to one side, on top of the princess chest. 'Don't put your things there, Beatriz.

We have order here and you bring chaos. You have to wait patiently to see what is on the menu.'

Beatriz pouted. 'Well, tell me who's on the seating plan. Who is coming? I need to know *that*, for my performance's sake.'

'The papal legate – Abbot Frotard, Abbot Hunaud from Moissac,' said Philippa, 'Bishop Izarn and Gayrard, the dean of Saint-Sernin.'

Anna wrote down the names after she had seen them on Philippa's mouth. Beatriz leant over and touch her on the arm. 'Musty old clerics! No young knights to swoon over?'

Anna smiled and watched the exchange between Philippa and Beatriz as if it were a play. They were both careful to ensure she could see their mouths. 'The clerics are the tricky part,' Philippa said, 'because Bishop Izarn and Dean Gayrard have been in dispute and must not be seated anywhere near each other.'

'The bishop has more pearls on his cope than the dean?' Beatriz asked, straight-faced.

'No doubt he does,' Philippa laughed, 'but that is not the reason for their conflict, as you know. The bishop is a Cluniac and a Benedictine and tried to eject the dean and his Augustinian brethren from Saint-Sernin. Pope Urban upheld Gayrard's complaint and reprimanded the bishop! The grudge between them persists. The bishop still thinks the Cluniac monks from Moissac should be in control of Saint-Sernin ...'

'And its donations from pilgrims,' interrupted Beatriz.

'Put them at opposite ends of the high table, Anna.'

'Yes,' said Beatriz. 'Then they will be able to glare at

each other down the length of the table. In Christian fashion, of course.'

'As long as they don't poison each other,' said Philippa, 'I don't care what they do with their eyes. I need to finish this. There are so many more people to seat.'

'Henry of Burgundy is a young knight to swoon over,' Beatriz stated, and Anna glanced at Philippa, who did not take the bait.

'I will have to seat Viscount Ademar and Vicar Petrus Regimundus on the high table too, and then that is full. And what should I do with Mafalda? I can't seat her on the high table with my uncle and yet if I don't, surely she will take offence? Everyone else will have to go on the two long trestles. Do you think I should put artists and masons on one side and merchants and scribes on the other? Or mix them up?'

'Mix them up,' Anna asserted.

'Imbert and I need to be near the front,' Beatriz said, 'so we can easily take our positions for the performance.' Anna made a few more annotations to her drawing.

'Did you speak with Mafalda yet, Beatriz?'

'I haven't found the opportunity. She keeps to her quarters.'

'My uncle will intend to make marriage arrangements at this assembly. You know, Beatriz, Imbert would be considered a good catch as a husband by some girls,' Philippa said. 'He is a renowned *trobador*, welcome at all the great courts of Occitania, Catalonia, and Aragon. His patrons bestow gifts upon him. He is kind to you?' Philippa raised her eyebrows in enquiry at her last words. Anna looked to Beatriz's mouth for her reply.

Beatriz shrugged. 'Yes, Lady Philippa, all true and I am grateful, and I like Imbert – like my grandfather, not as a husband in my bed.' She grimaced and Anna mirrored her grimace. 'He is ancient. Wrinkled blubber from head to toe,' Beatriz said with disgusted gusto.

Philippa smiled sadly and shook her head. 'My husband, it seems, will be the same.'

'Not if it is Guillaume of Aquitaine. He is your age,' Beatriz told her.

'Don't keep harping on, Beatriz. It won't be Guillaume. He hasn't replied. Sancho Ramírez is even older than Imbert.'

They lapsed into silence. Beatriz took up her *vielle* and continued working on her composition. Anna watched her movements, imagining the sound. She loved to watch Beatriz play and to see the concentration and joy on her face. Anna slipped off her shoes beneath the table and felt the cold stone on the soles of her feet. She closed her eyes and felt the vibrations of sound. She played the rhythm out on her thigh with a silent forefinger. Bertrand had looked askance at Anna going barefoot, seeing it as a lack of propriety, but Anna persisted, despite his and others' disapproval. She had to use every means available to her to experience her world.

ANNA LEANT against the huge open gate of Chateau Narbonnais, waiting for Philippa and Beatriz to join her, watching the spectacular sunset. Bertrand's party were assembling in the courtyard and included Helie and Henry of Burgundy. Philippa arrived, accompanied by

Beatriz and Roger. The group walked together towards Saint Etienne Cathedral at dusk for the start of the Easter vigil.

The streets were crowded with city folk making their way in the same direction, but Bertrand's guards were ahead, calling out, clearing a path for them to walk unimpeded. At the cathedral square, the bishop, deacons, priests and choristers were lined up outside the east door, which faced Jerusalem. They were vivid in their vestments – the bishop and deacons in white and gold, and the others in Lenten purple. The sky was darkening, and stars began to appear and look down on the fire kindling in the brazier outside the cathedral door. Anna watched the flames dance red and yellow, higher and higher, swinging a little this way and that with the night breeze. She watched anxiously as the deacons and choristers stood close to the flames, their silky vestments fluttering with the wind.

Beatriz tugged at Anna's sleeve, and she followed Beatriz into the cathedral. They each took a small candle from a nun standing at the door. They entered the vast, dark space, moving as close to the altar as they could. In the deep gloom, Anna could just discern the gleam of Philippa's blonde head, where she stood in front with Bertrand, and alongside them were Henry and Helie of Burgundy. She was jostled and was grateful Beatriz kept a firm grip on her arm.

The absence of Christ was palpable in the blackened church. Anna could not see it, but she knew the tabernacle where the host was usually kept on the altar was wide open and empty. The tabernacle lantern was put out.

Some people were rocking themselves gently on the balls of their feet, their mouths moving in prayers of contrition. Without the host, without the bells, without confession for two days, many must be feeling the weight of their misdemeanours or worse. Beatriz liked to say, 'You could scrape the sin off the walls in here!' Anna looked around, noting the comical contrast of small, thin Gauzlin standing beside the bulk of Petrus Regimundus. People directly behind Petrus shuffled and craned their necks trying to see past him in the darkness.

Anna glanced back over her shoulder and gently elbowed Beatriz as the light of a candle appeared at the doorway. The congregation moved to either side of the cathedral nave to leave a path for the deacon to advance with the candle. He was preceded by the altar assistants swinging thuribles on chains. Anna inhaled the sweet, piney scent of frankincense. A delicate wave of light began to move slowly up the nave and gather strength. The deacon was processing up the space cleared in the middle of the nave, carrying the Paschal Candle lit from the brazier and allowing those to either side of him to light their own candles and then those of their neighbours. Anna knew from her missal that the priest called out 'Lumen Christi!' as he advanced and the congregation responded heartily, 'Thanks be to God!' Beatriz tapped the back of Anna's hand to tell her when to make the response, and they smiled, shouting it together.

Eventually, the deacon was at Anna's shoulder. She lit her candle and cupped the flame to pass it to Beatriz. Ahead of them, Philippa was lighting her own candle from Bertrand's. Despite all the small candles, the vast space of the church was still dark, with hands and faces illuminated in a flickery, white glow. The deacon processed on with the Paschal Candle towards the sanctuary. Two enormous candles on either side of the altar, each the height of a man, were lit. They represented the angel at Christ's head in the sepulchre and the angel at his feet. The bishop took his place before the altar and began the readings of the Scripture in semi-gloom.

Beatriz nudged Anna, pointing at the nun Mafalda, who was standing nearby. Keeping her hands low, at the level of her hips, Beatriz opened her palm to reveal the small, white square of a folded note. 'Give it to Mafalda, secretly,' Beatriz mouthed. She pressed it into Anna's palm and closed her fingers over it. Anna took a step, bringing her closer to the tall nun. Gently, she tugged at the sleeve of her habit. Mafalda turned to her, an angry look on her face. Anna held up a placatory palm and briefly uncovered the note in her other hand. Mafalda took the note and concealed it in her sleeve with a surprising rapidity. Anna took a step back closer to Beatriz, who nodded her head without turning her face towards her.

Anna looked at the statue of the Virgin Mary and asked that she not be offended at this subterfuge. It was necessary for the sake of her friend, Philippa. Anna begged the Virgin to bring Duke Guillaume to Philippa soon. Please let him attend the assembly feast, Anna asked in her head. She did not relish the idea of having to go to Aragon and learn a new place, new people, any more than Philippa wished to be married to old King Sancho. If Philippa married Guillaume, they might stay in Tolosa.

The vigil service went on all night with lessons, canticles, blessings, baptisms, which she could not hear, but her eyes, adjusted to the gloom, focused on the candlelight sliding over the lavish vestments of the priests, caressing the contours of people's faces, lingering with the tranquil features of the Virgin, and probing the deep folds of her cloak. Beatriz squeezed her hand now and then.

It was cold in the cathedral. Anna, like everyone else, had been fasting since the afternoon and there had been weeks before that of sparse Lenten fare. She felt lightheaded. Sometimes they stood, sometimes they knelt on the frigid stone of the ground. Anna swept her fingertips across the stone, trying to clear a space where her knees would not be painfully pressed against sharp pebbles. The cold was making Beatriz sleepy and, as they knelt, Anna saw her eyelids fluttering and her head jerking on her droopy neck, as she caught herself on the threshold of sleep. Anna elbowed her awake.

At cock crow, as the faintest glimmerings of dawn began to lighten the long cathedral windows, the vigil rose to its joyful climax. Anna just had enough light to follow the service in her missal. The congregation stood for the Gospel of Saint John: 'In the beginning was the word....' Then came the *Alleluia* and *Gloria in excelsis Deo.* Next to Anna, Beatriz drew herself up straight and lifted her face and voice upward, throwing herself into the song. She took Anna's hand and placed it flat on her chest so Anna could try to keep time with Beatriz's breath and with all the other singers in the jubilant church. Beatriz signalled to Anna with her hand when the volume of singing rose, when it fell to a low murmur, or when it stopped altogether. Then Beatriz cupped her hand upside down and swung it from side to side. 'Bells?' whispered Anna. She had been able to hear for the first eight years of her life so she could imagine, now, the jangle of the pealing bells, and she hoped this new season would bring all three of them happiness.

'Yes,' she saw that Beatriz was yelling, 'the flying bells just got back!'

REHEARSAL

Easter Monday 1093, Chateau Narbonnais

*B*eatriz fled from the hubbub in Lady Philippa's chambers. A messenger had ridden in on an exhausted, sweating horse with the news that Raimon was on the road from Narbonne to Tolosa. Anna had set out Philippa's clothes for the feast to welcome her uncle home and for the start of the Easter Assembly, but discovered that one of Philippa's jewels was missing. Servants were emptying caskets, shaking out pouches, lifting bedclothes and riffling through gowns in an increasingly frantic search for the triple-disc brooch. Beatriz needed somewhere quiet where she could work on her song, but it had to be somewhere with more space than her attic room, so she could practice her gestures and dance movements. Solitude was hard to come by in the Chateau Narbonnais, crowded as it was with the households of Lady Philippa,

Lady Helie, Lord Bertrand, Lord Henry and, soon, the returning entourage of Count Raimon and the guests for the assembly. Beatriz took a final glance back from the doorway and winced sympathetically at Anna's frustrated gestures. The search was proving fruitless.

Beatriz turned from the scene of chaos and stepped out into the gloom of the cool, stone passage, sifting in her mind through potential quiet but large places. She held her bow and instrument lightly in one hand behind her back, keeping them safe from collision with the servants and soldiers rushing up and down, brushing and sometimes more brusquely bumping against her shoulder. In addition to the disruption in Lady Philippa's chambers, the castle was in anxious preparation. The feast must be cooked, and the Great Hall readied. The cooks would be flushed and sweating in the kitchen. Their assistants would be constantly coming and going to the buttery and the pantry, collecting ingredients. The soldiers would be cleaning their armour and weapons in the courtyard and the gatehouse, shouting to one another. They would be lining up on the battlements, watching for the approach of Raimon.

Beatriz sometimes tried out the final versions of new melodies in the Great Hall itself, but that was no good today. It would be full of servants slamming up extra trestles, thumping down pewter dishes and jugs, screeching in self-importance at their alarmed assistants. Beatriz frowned. Was there nowhere quiet? If it hadn't been raining, she might have ventured into the fields in front of the chateau and the city walls, but her *vielle* was a sensitive soundbox. It was hard enough to keep it in tune to complete one song. It certainly couldn't be exposed to damp. She must give her very best performance tonight. The wine vaults beneath the buttery and pantry might work. She moved in that direction. The ceiling of the vaults was low, so the acoustic was nothing like the Great Hall, but she could at least finish composing the song and test out its timing.

Lady Philippa would ask Raimon to allow her to take Beatriz as her *trobairitz*. If the song was well received, if the request was accepted, it would free Beatriz. Raimon had only ever seen Beatriz as Imbert's *jograresa* – singing Imbert's songs, accompanied by his skill on the *oud*, or playing the second to Imbert's lead in a melody for two instruments. Beatriz must impress Raimon, or there was no hope he would take Philippa's request seriously.

Imbert always spoke cheerfully of their eventual marriage as if it were a foregone conclusion. Being *jograresa* to Imbert was a good situation. She could do a great deal worse if she entrusted herself to the road once more. And she really liked the work. Imbert had taken pains to teach her his art of composing in words and music. She could play six instruments and understood the complex wordgames and rhyming of the various types of songs. He was kind-hearted, fair, humorous. But Beatriz would run away again, if she must, to avoid the marriage. The self-damaging act of throwing herself once more on the mercy of fortune, to leave this comfortable berth at the court of Tolosa was not what she wanted. She hoped having to run could be avoided.

She moved to the arched opening that led to the exterior staircase down to the courtyard, which was also chaotic with rushing servants, arriving guests, stableboys taking care of many horses. Quickly, she turned into the doorway to the Great Hall and made her way towards the partition at the back of the hall. Behind her, Bertrand was standing on the dais, shouting out commands to the servants as they made ready for his father's return.

'Beatriz?' Her name was spoken in a low hiss. She turned to find Mafalda close behind her. 'Keep walking.' Mafalda pushed her gently in the small of her back. They both passed through the curtain across the partition doorway. The steps down to the buttery and pantry were here. 'I read Philippa's note. Tell her, I did write to the duke, and he replied saying he was receptive to the suggestion.'

'Philippa has not received a reply from him,' Beatriz stated, keeping her voice low to match Mafalda's.

The nun frowned. 'I'm surprised she has not heard from him yet, but she must be patient. He is intending to reply positively. I'm sure of it.'

'I will tell her.' The nun moved back through the curtain. Beatriz frowned. Why would the duke of Aquitaine bother to correspond with a nun? How could Mafalda be continuing to exert political power when she no longer had any? Beatriz turned down the steps into the buttery and, glancing to her left, saw the expected melee of servants shouldering past each other, laden with bowls of fruit, bladders of wine, cuts of uncooked meat.

'Hello, luscious Beatriz,' puffed the kitchen boy, Simo, leering at her. He looked very red in the face, and she was glad to see his hands were well occupied with a loaded dish of uncooked capon. He was a big, precocious boy.

'Hello to you, Simo, and mind your manners, boy.' She did not pause, but hurried on down the next set of stone steps that led into the undercroft.

The vaults ran the entire length of this side of the chateau and were filled with iron-strapped barrels arranged in clusters in the niches of the crypt-like space. Only a dim light filtered in through small, half-moon windows set at regular intervals high up near the ceiling. There was plenty of space down here. Two boys were tapping a barrel at one end of the vaults, filling jugs with wine. Another two were using a long-handled silver spoon to carefully fill an array of glinting salt cellars lined up on a table. The spoons dipped in and out of a salt sack. It was likely that any business for tonight's feast would stay down that end of the undercroft. She moved to the opposite far end and ensconced herself in a U-shaped area created by barrels piled high on top of one another. She was concealed from view here. It was a kind of solitude. If anyone heard her playing or singing, they would know she was rehearsing and, she hoped, they would leave her in peace.

She pulled a stool into the space and took a seat. She rested the *vielle*'s rounded bottom just above her left breast, nestled the instrument comfortably along her left arm, and drew the bow experimentally across the four strings. As she expected, the tone was terrible, completely off again. After considerable droning and sawing with her bow and minute adjustments back and forth with the pegs on the leaf-shaped head of the *vielle*, she was satisfied with the sound.

I must sing of those bitter matters between us.

Hopeless. No good at all.

Of things I'd rather keep in silence I must sing.
So bitter do I feel toward you

Yes, better rhythm.

Whom I love more than anything.

The thought of Lluis rose unbidden. Hmphh. Also, no good. She could have no distractions. He had large, soft tawny eyes and a rather luscious mouth. His hair was that particular shade of dark blond she especially liked. She smiled at herself and shook her head. No distractions. Her fingers should caress her strings, not Lluis' imagined curls. She plucked a few notes on the strings. Pretty young men were as bad for a girl's ambitions as fat old ones.

I send you there on your estate

Like her, Lluis was from the Pyrenees, and they had a wealth of common stories to discuss together. They could relax into the familiarity of their own tongue instead of struggling to be correct with the differences of the Occitan spoken here. Lluis was tall and slim. He was always smiling, winking and open-faced, holding the palm of his hand up to slap with you at some fine joke. He had a modest demeanour and was a paradox of shyly gregarious. He was a tactile man, unconsciously caressing Beatriz's arm, or clasping her shoulder when he passed the back of her chair.

This song as messenger and delegate.

One barrel tap to her right was dripping very, very occasionally. Faint sounds filtered down through the ironwork of the air vents on the stairwell. A metal knife tinkling on a glass. A laugh. Outside, a golden oriole called to its mate. That was a good omen for her song.

Beatriz had all the words of the song and the general melody more or less right when she heard the unmistakable racket of many horses arriving in the courtyard. She pulled the stool beneath one of the tiny windows that punctuated the top of the wall and stepped up to try to get a view, but mostly saw legs – horses' and men's. She heard Raimon's voice issuing orders. Those armoured feet with wickedly sharp spurs, a long, red cloak skimming them – that must be Raimon. She thought she saw Imbert's feet alongside, but she couldn't be sure from this angle. It looked like his shoes and thick ankles.

She stepped down, moved the stool back and ran through the song one more time. She would ask Anna to transcribe it before the feast if there was time. Showing the written melodies and words would be an important part of Lady Philippa's bid to her uncle Raimon, proving the songs were Beatriz's own and not Imbert's, or copied from another singer.

Boots were coming down the steps – two men, perhaps. They did not go to the end where the serving boys were preparing wine jugs but instead moved towards her hidey hole. She frowned, picked up her *vielle* and bow, keeping a silencing finger on the strings and stood with her back to the wall of barrels, moving even further out of sight. She did not want her concentration broken by being forced into inane conversation with whoever it was. And she certainly did not want to talk with Imbert at this moment.

'You say a letter has come?' She recognised Raimon's voice. Why was he holding a conversation down here?

'Yes, Father.' Bertrand's voice sounded young and anxious. In his father's forceful presence, he always seemed reduced.

'And is his reply positive?'

'It is.'

'Give it here.' Beatriz heard a rustle of parchment exchanged between father and son and a pause as Raimon, she guessed, read the letter.

'You will need to escort her to Jaca with haste,' Raimon said. 'This letter will be better for a bit of cooking.' The count's voice was gleeful and was moving away, back towards the stairwell. She moved forwards to keep them in earshot, peering around the edge of a barrel. She smelled burning – the letter? Raimon and Bertrand's voice came through the ironwork of the air vent. 'Is all ready for tonight's feast?' The sounds trailed off as the two men mounted the stairs.

She was about to step out and rescue the burning letter, when a shadow, almost opposite, moved, and she drew back rapidly. She glimpsed the back of a man who was also moving towards the stairs. It was Imbert. His broad girth was unmistakable. If he had been down here with Raimon and Bertrand, he had not spoken. Unusual for him! He always had a lot to say. She had the distinct impression his presence had been furtive, that he had concealed himself to listen to Raimon and Bertrand's conversation about the burnt letter. She saw him snake out a hand to lift the smouldering parchment from the bowl, where Bertrand had left it on top of one of the barrels. He gently shook the parchment and tiny, brilliant sparks of fire fell from it in the gloomy undercroft. She waited.

When she was sure he had gone, Beatriz made her way back to Philippa's rooms. The song still needed a little polish and transcribing. She had to search out her best tunic, and she hoped Lady Philippa's chambers were returned to a calm oasis. It would be good if there was time to allow herself the luxury of imbibing a little liquid courage before her performance.

As Beatriz entered Philippa's room, her satchel of songs clutched under one arm and her instrument and bow held carefully in the other hand, Philippa turned worried green eyes in her direction. 'My uncle Raimon has returned,' she said in a flat tone.

'Yes, my lady.'

Beatriz looked sympathetically at Philippa's bleak expression. Beatriz reported what Mafalda had said about Duke Guillaume. She held back the information about the burnt letter for now. She needed to puzzle it out in her own mind, see if she could quiz Imbert about it.

'Well, where is the duke then? He will not come in

time,' Philippa stated. 'And there is no reply from my mother or my father.'

'Anna,' Beatriz said. Philippa tapped the maid's arm again and pointed at Beatriz. 'Did you find the brooch?' She mouthed the words distinctly.

Anna was holding Philippa's open jewel casket on her knees. She shook her head miserably. 'No.' Anna stirred her finger through the jewels. Beatriz's ear tuned to the jingling of the rings and necklaces in the carved wooden box. Philippa's small cache of treasure and gifts included earrings, rings, a silver bracelet, a golden cross on a pearl necklet. The distinctive triple-disc brooch was large and not easily overlooked.

'It was a gift from my grandmother,' Philippa said, 'and my favourite. Its loss is an omen I will be made to marry an old man I can't care for.'

'Take heart,' Beatriz said. 'You don't know that. Anna and I will stick with you and help you through whatever is to come.'

Anna placed a comforting arm around her mistress's shoulders. Briefly, Philippa rested her forehead against Anna's.

Philippa looked to Beatriz again. 'And Imbert has returned?'

'He has indeed.'

'We may both be offered in marriage tonight, then. We may not be able to stick together.'

'Surely not tonight,' Beatriz denied. 'There will be some breathing space, some arriving time.'

'My uncle will not delay. He will be swift about it. You know how he is.'

'Will you write out my latest song for me, Anna?' Beatriz asked. She contemplated Philippa's words at the same time as asking her question. If Philippa had to go to Aragon, and Imbert tried to marry her, perhaps she could run away and make her way to Aragon. It was a plan forming in her head.

Anna laid out parchment, quill and ink to transcribe the song. First, she watched Beatriz's mouth and transcribed the words, set out neatly in lines for the pausing of breaths. Then Beatriz played the melody, one line at a time and several times over, and Anna transcribed the melody. Beatriz found the combination of the silence she imagined in Anna's head and her friend's ability to see and feel sound instead of hear it quite fascinating. Could Beatriz make a song about that?

'If you are ready, Beatriz, let's go down. I'm just worrying myself sitting here,' Philippa said.

'I have to choose a dress, my lady,' Beatriz responded, moving towards the gowns Anna had laid on the bed. 'I will be quick, I promise. Go down. I will follow you and Anna.' She glanced at the wine jug on Philippa's table, hoping there would be time for a beaker before she must appear in the Great Hall below. The letter in the undercroft was from Guillaume of Aquitaine, surely? That would explain Raimon and Bertrand's words and actions. But why was Imbert lurking there, and why did he pick up the burnt parchment?

EASTER ASSEMBLY

Monday 18 April 1093, Chateau Narbonnais

*B*eatriz looked up at the colourful woven banners lining the high walls on either side of the Great Hall. They were wafting with the air stirred by the movements of many people preparing for the feast and with the hot air rising from the blazing hearth. The banner with a blue field of yellow *fleur de lys* with a red-and-white-striped slash was the family crest of Emma of Mortain, Philippa's mother, who was from a Norman family and related to the king of England. The banner with the yellow Occitan cross on a red background was the banner of Philippa's father, Count Guilhem IV of Tolosa and of his brother, Raimon of Saint-Gilles. The arms of the counties of Rouergue, Nimes, and Narbonne hung beside the arms of Tolosa.

These counties were all claimed by the count of

Tolosa, who was effectively the king in this southeast area, which, under Charlemagne, had been called the kingdom of Septimania. At the death of Guilhem and Raimon's father, the holdings of Tolosa had been divided between the two brothers, as was the old way of inheritance. Philippa's father had not, in Beatriz's view, made a particularly astute division of the lands. Raimon had taken the lordship of Saint-Gilles, Narbonne and Montpellier, giving him control of all the lucrative trade flowing through those cities near the coast, and he had very effectively built on that wealth through a mixture of aggression and negotiation.

Looking down from the banners, Beatriz was assaulted by the sight of all the people animating the hall. Two long tables ran almost the whole length of the space. The table for Philippa's family and important guests was set on a raised dais. The final touches were being made by the servants. They were setting vases of gay flowers on the tables, building up the fire, lighting torches along the walls and on either side of the enormous double doorway from the courtyard. Trenchers were laid out, wine jugs and salt cellars were in place, and the servants were setting out the best glass beakers and silver knives on the high table.

Beatriz's eye alighted on Anna, who gestured to show Beatriz where they were seated, at the far end of one of the trestles, close to the dais. Beatriz rested her *vielle* against the wall behind her and greeted Imbert, who was seated on the other side of the trestle. Imbert acknowledged her greeting but appeared preoccupied with his own thoughts. Beatriz saw that Lluis was among the many servants waiting on table.

'Imbert,' Beatriz spoke in a low voice and touched his arm. He glanced up at her, raising his eyebrows. 'Do you know anything about a letter for Lady Philippa from Duke Guillaume?'

His expression changed rapidly, from surprise to displeasure. 'No!' he said shortly, and Beatriz was sure he was lying. 'Quiet, now,' he said.

Beatriz watched Count Raimon's party progress through the huge door, up the aisle between the trestles, and onto the raised dais, taking their seats at the high table. The clerics were splendidly dressed, rivalling the vases of flowers in their colourful silks. Lady Philippa sat at her uncle's right hand. Abbot Frotard sat next to Philippa and then Ademar, viscount of Tolosa and his wife, and then Petrus Regimundus and his wife, who was as small and thin as Petrus was tall and fat. Beneath her left eye was the half-circle of a green, fading bruise.

'Why all the clerics?' Beatriz asked, knowing Imbert would like to show off his knowledge.

'Here to discuss the development of the pilgrim route to Santiago de Compostela with Count Raimon. It passes through Tolosa, and Saint-Sernin is an important point along the route.' Imbert rubbed his right thumb and forefinger together, raising a speculative eyebrow. Beatriz looked up again at the clerics and Raimon on the dais. Yes, plenty of cash in pilgrims! Abbot Frotard appeared to be dominating the discussion, no doubt urging the noblemen to dedicate themselves to reconquest in Spain.

Gauzlin and Poncius Vitalis, Raimon's scribe, were seated to Beatriz's left. A *vectuari* named Jacques was seated to her right and regaled her and the scribes for most of the meal with information and stories about his trade. Jacques freighted goods, and especially salt, from the marshes of the River Rhone delta in the Camargue. Mafalda was seated beyond Jacques, looking discomfited to be in the company of such low folk. She maintained a haughty silence.

'Your Lord Raimon there,' Jacques gestured with his knife in the direction of the high table, 'is sitting on a white gold mine with all the saltpans he controls. The caravan of pack ponies I am running at present is destined for the markets in Champagne, in the north. Over there,' he gestured across the aisle to the opposite table at two well-dressed, dark-haired men who were deep in conversation, 'those are Armand Amalfitanus, a merchant out of Amalfi and his ship's captain, Emmanuel Piloti, who hales from Crete. They are negotiating with Count Raimon for the contract to ship the salt up the Rhone. Myself, I would far rather brave the road than the sea. I don't fancy drowning. But occasionally, I ship the salt instead, with the aid of the Genoese.'

Beatriz nodded, only half-listening, her eyes roving over the strangers, preoccupied with her nervousness at the coming performance and Philippa's promised request to her uncle. Everyone was wearing their best clothes – bright greens, oranges, pale pinks, reds, yellows, deep blues and meandering embroidery presented a feast for the eyes to match the dishes being loaded onto the tables. Candlelight and firelight glinted on daggers and brooches. Dogs wound in and out of human and table legs. Beatriz listened to the cacophony of voices, the clatter and clink of vessels, knives and spoons, and the glug, glug, glug of wine poured into jugs and beakers. Raimon's three minstrels strummed gently. Beatriz noted Roger's eyes on Mafalda when he served wine to the group on her table.

Beatriz's glance alighted next on Bernardus Gelduinus, the master sculptor leading the work on the new church of Saint-Sernin. He was elderly but still had power in his body from sculpting stone, a power, Beatriz realised with a guilty pang, that reminded her of her blacksmith father. She wondered how her father was now, alone in the mountains without his daughter. She had a sudden vivid memory of the dull jangle of myriad goat-bells in the mountain pastures, two black donkeys grazing, the vivid greens of the patchwork fields and crops cladding the valley, the dark dense green of the forests, and the great birds of prey circling the peaks.

She looked again at the high table. Raimon's head was tilted towards Abbot Hunaud and Abbot Frotard. She strained to hear their conversation. 'The pilgrims will have so many heartwarming stories of the saints to contemplate,' said Abbot Frotard, 'as they make their way along the pilgrim route from here to Tolosa, up into the high Pyrenees, and on to the great cathedral of Compostela, when it is finished. And the Christian rulers in Spain are making great strides in reclaiming all Iberia from the infidels for the glory of Rome.'

There was a short silence in response to this remark, and Beatriz admired Raimon and Bertrand's constraint in not pointing out that 'the great strides' had been minimal and often lost again as soon as gained. The latest assaults on the Saracen kingdoms by King Alfonso of Spain and King Sancho Ramírez of Aragon had been unsuccessful. Most of Iberia had been under Saracen control for close on four centuries.

'The pope aims high with his talk of Roman sovereignty of Iberian territories,' Henry of Burgundy declared, a deliberate contention in his tone. The Burgundian families favoured Cluny, and donations of gold from the Iberian kings were of great importance to that monastic foundation. Henry intended to travel later in the year to the court of his aunt Constance, the queen of Castile.

'One can no more accuse the pontiff of ambition than one can accuse the sea of soliciting the rivers to take refuge in its bosom,' Abbot Frotard retorted. 'The actions of the pope are for our good, my son, and for the good of all Christendom. A multitude of abominable customs have been brought into disuse by an infinity of persuasion,' the abbot declared in that mild-mannered way he had of making a statement that was actually a kind of punch in the face. He beamed at Bertrand, who clenched his jaw. 'Let us give praise to God that the pope's civilising influence has introduced order, rule, respect, security in the midst of a furnace of unrestrained lusts that reaches even to the king of France.'

Raimon mumbled an assent. Bertrand retained a stony silence. The church was intent on forcing the nobility to amend their marriage customs. The king of France had been threatened with excommunication for his recent marriage to Bertrade of Montfort, whom the king had abducted from her husband, the count of Anjou. Raimon had reluctantly complied with the new marriage rules and repudiated Bertrand's mother, who had been his first cousin, but Bertrand was distressed at the taint of illegitimacy these new rules gave to him.

Beatriz's attention was suddenly claimed by Raimon's loud exclamation: 'Missing?' He was addressing Philippa. 'The one handed down to you from my mother?' Philippa nodded, and Beatriz realised conversation had turned to the lost brooch. 'It shall be found ... and so shall the thief,' said Raimon, leaving little room for doubt about the thief's regret in those circumstances. 'You will have jewels aplenty, before long, Philippa,' Raimon cupped her chin and slanted her face up to his. 'I see something of my mother in you. You have the same colouring.' Beatriz watched Philippa hold her uncle's eyes. 'We will search out this jewel thief.' Raimon suddenly fixed Beatriz with a basilisk stare and Beatriz felt like patting herself down for the missing jewel.

As her gaze passed along the high table from Raimon, she noticed that Henry was staring at someone close to her. It was Mafalda, but the nun's face was turned away and Beatriz could not tell what her expression might be. Henry and Mafalda probably knew each from the time before her marriage to Raimon. One of her cousins had married into the Burgundian family. Or, perhaps, Henry was simply as engaged by the nun's beauty as Beatriz had been on first encountering her. An attraction between them could serve neither one of them, surely? Henry was a youngest son of a great and powerful family, but without land or wealth of his own. The only way he could win what he needed would be through a marriage.

Mafalda could no longer offer what he needed and worse, was proven to be barren. Beatriz felt pity for the nun. She was barely thirty and her life was as good as over.

The stream of dishes finally ceased. Servants refilled beakers and cleared away the debris from the tables. Acrobats tumbled artfully over each other into the hall. One set about juggling knives, while three others clambered and contorted around each other. Another three set up willow hoops and took it in turns to hold and leap through them. Another danced precariously with a glass goblet balanced on his finger, head, shoulder, foot, knee, and bottom. Some feast guests applauded politely, but most continued their eating, drinking and conversations.

When the acrobats had tumbled out of the hall, Imbert stood and placed two stools in the space in front of the dais, one for himself and a second for Beatriz. He fussed around, arranging and tuning his instruments. Beatriz followed suit, quelling her unusual nervousness. 'All these beans in the meal do not agree with me,' Imbert complained under his breath, and Beatriz silently congratulated herself on removing her straw mattress from his room and the miasma of his flatulence. 'We are here to accompany their sloppy eating and inane conversation with fiddling and trilling,' he grumbled. 'At every third word of your exquisite song, they will be whispering and telling each other their tawdry news and gossip.'

We'll see about that, Beatriz told herself. As she and Imbert had agreed in advance, Beatriz made her way inconspicuously to the back of the hall. Imbert struck a note, and the hall fell momentarily silent. Imbert quavered to the conclusion of his *razo* introducing the next song, and as usual, claimed the song as his own, although it was hers.

Beatriz advanced into the hall, singing the *stampida* – a dance song she had composed. The sound of her song and the vibrancy of her presence gradually captivated her audience and silenced their chatter. She brought an imperious hauteur to her performance, stamping her feet, slapping her thigh, moving one leg suddenly far to the side and sweeping her foot around in a half-circle, moving her arms in elegant shapes, turning from side to side or looking straight ahead at the dais, staring her audience members in the eye. She had seen these dance techniques used by the Romany of Andalusia. Beatriz was not tall, but her arms and legs were long. She was full-breasted, with a narrow waist emphasised by an embroidered girdle. When she sensed she had the full attention of her audience, she abruptly stopped singing, turned her back on the dais, and began to move slowly back towards the hall door.

There was uproar behind her. 'Where are you going, *jograresa*! Come back!' It was Bertrand's voice. 'More! More!'

She stopped walking and left them her back for a moment, her feet and arms posed elegantly, allowing their doubts and silence to gather. She turned around. Smiling slightly, she moved steadily forwards again and lifted her *vielle* from where it leant against the stool, raising it to her chin.

There was a racket of response as they laughed and shouted, slapped the table, jangled their knives against the glass and metal goblets on the trestle. Dramatically, she held a long, straight finger up against her lips, swivelling around to take in everyone seated in the hall, and they silenced immediately. She had them in the palm of her hand.

Imbert's face was aglow with a mix of sweat and goose fat. Beatriz blinked to remove the impression from her eyeballs and to find her way instead into her song of passion and betrayal. Her hand shook as she found the position for her fingers on the *vielle*, but she did as Imbert had trained her. She fixed her eyes just above the heads of her illustrious audience on the dais, stood up very straight and symmetrical, and let the song resound from her. She lost herself in the song.

When she reached the end, she sat down on the stool a little too fast and indecorously and breathed relief with the applause. Bertrand bellowed 'Brava!'

Lluis was at her shoulder with a beaker. 'Brava, Beatriza, songbird,' he whispered against her ear, his fingers lingering on the exchange of the beaker to her fingers. Beatriz gulped down the wine, and he poured her another.

Imbert pressed Lluis out of the way and claimed her hand. 'I knew you could do it, my little wife.'

Beatriz flinched at the word. She looked over Imbert's shoulder to Lluis' glance of commiseration. He pantomimed knocking back her wine as consolation, and she did so.

'Uncle, I have a request to make.' Philippa's voice was loud and clear. Beatriz swallowed and fixed her gaze on Philippa. Raimon was smiling indulgently at Philippa and raised his eyebrows. 'I would like to take Beatriz as my own *trobairitz*, to take her into my household and be her patroness.' The men on the dais smiled, as if a child had asked for a puppy.

'Beatriz is *jograresa* to Imbert, my dear,' Raimon responded in a patronising voice. 'No *trobairitz* for such a grand lady as yourself, I fear.'

Beatriz stole a rapid glance at Imbert. His mouth was agape, and he was staring at her in consternation. He dropped his hand from her shoulder. He would know she and Philippa were colluding in this request. She guiltily swallowed more wine and returned her gaze to the dais.

'No, Uncle, you are wrong. Beatriz is indeed a *trobairitz*. The song she just sang is her own. She penned words and melody herself and can prove it. And she has at least five songs of her own invention.' Philippa had chosen her moment carefully and well to make this claim and request in front of witnesses.

Raimon looked towards Imbert, who raised his palms and shrugged his shoulders as if in confusion. Raimon looked at Beatriz now. 'How can you prove this?'

Beatriz stood, glancing at her satchel leant against the wall. 'I have my songs written down, lord.'

'Well,' Raimon said, turning back to Philippa, 'I will review these documents tomorrow and we will speak more of it then, Niece.'

Beatriz let out a breath. It was something. It would be difficult for Raimon to refuse with the evidence of her five songs. She avoided looking at Imbert. Beatriz's attention swung back to Philippa, who was now exclaiming to her uncle in a strident voice: 'King Sancho! My mother and father ....'

Raimon's voice overrode Philippa's. 'Your parents approve the match. You will be a queen. King Sancho Ramírez has expressed himself open to the match, and who would not with such an offer of a healthy, young mother to his heirs?' Philippa dropped her glance in embarrassment.

'Two fecund young females who will be covered, eh?' stated Imbert, placing a large proprietary hand back on Beatriz's shoulder, a cross expression on his face.

Raimon laughed and clapped his hands at his *trobador*. 'Another song, Imbert, to celebrate my niece's coming betrothal!' Beatriz gestured to Lluis to refill her wine beaker. Above the rim of her beaker, she noted Henry's soft, sympathetic eyes on Philippa now.

After their final song, Beatriz moved to resume her seat at the trestle, but Imbert gripped her elbow and walked her to the side of the hall. 'So this is your gratitude to me for rescuing you from the gutter?'

'Imbert, the songs are mine. That is the truth. And I am worthy of the title of *trobairitz*. You know it. I am grateful to you for your tutelage and protection these last years.'

'So grateful that now you would slough me off!'

Beatriz had never seen Imbert this angry before. 'We could still perform together on occasion, but I wish to join Lady Philippa's household.'

'In Aragon!'

A fleck of Imbert's spittle landed on her lower lip and she swiped at it quickly. 'Wherever Lady Philippa goes. That is what I want.'

'It doesn't matter what you want. I need you to wed

me, and Raimon will see to it.' Imbert turned his back on her and moved off to talk with Henry of Burgundy.

The night wore on and the wine jugs were refilled over and over. Philippa and Anna excused themselves, and most of the clerics retired to the chambers set for them in one of the towers. Beatriz knew she should follow, but she was still excited from her performance and worried about Imbert's assertions. She was exhausted, but she could not bring herself to leave. It seemed by staying put she might stave off the threat of marriage to Imbert and the need to run away – hold off the progress of the night and the next morning.

She looked over at Imbert, who was now in an altercation with Gauzlin in the far corner of the hall. Bertrand approached them with Henry. Bertrand shook a set of dice beneath Imbert's nose. That would distract him from harassing the clerk, for sure. Bertrand swilled wine into Gauzlin's beaker. The clerk did not usually drink wine. He was shaking his head but being cajoled by Bertrand to take another beakerful.

Beatriz was growing sleepy with the alcohol, exhaustion, the heat of the fire. Jacques, the *vectuari*, struck up a drinking song with Imbert, and the Greek captain and Bertrand joined them, clashing their goblets together and roaring the song. Despite the untuneful racket, Raimon's head was drooping at the high table, and the scribe, Poncius, fussed around him, encouraging him to retire. No doubt, thought Beatriz, her own eyelids drooping, the lyrics of the song were as bawdy as Bertrand's salted virgins.

THE UNDERCROFT

Morning, Tuesday 19 April, Chateau Narbonnais

*B*eatriz's eyes startled open on the ceiling of her attic room and the sound of muffled screams coming from below, as she surfaced to consciousness and wished she had not. She rolled her thumping head to one side and found herself in close proximity to Lluis' slumbering face. His mouth. His eyelashes. Beatrix briefly closed her eyes on the agony of the hangover and opened them again, but Lluis was still there.

She lifted the bedclothes a little and groaned quietly. They were both naked. He breathed gently, oblivious to the increasing commotion outside the chamber. Beatriz sat up gingerly. Her left temple throbbed. She fished her discarded tunic towards her with a foot and slipped it over her head. Familiar remorse rolled over her. She picked up one shoe and found the other beneath the bed.

She stole towards the opening and ladder. Would she never learn? Strong wine and pretty boys. Again! Had Imbert seen? Philippa? Who else knew? She couldn't remember a thing. She might be pregnant. What an idiot she was. She set foot on the top of the ladder.

'Goodbye, fair songbird,' Lluis said from her straw pallet.

She glanced at him, smiled, and moved swiftly down the ladders. She could hear running feet. Sobs. A guard ran down the passage towards her and she stayed him for a moment. He swung around the axis of her hand at his elbow, interrupting his momentum. 'What's going on?'

'Someone's dead in the undercroft.' He pulled his arm away and set off running again.

'Someone…' she echoed. She slipped on her shoes, tried to smooth her mussed hair, and crossed the walkway to the Tour de Sire Claude, then made her way down via the courtyard, back into the Great Hall, to the stone steps leading down to the undercroft. Bertrand was standing at the bottom of the steps, looking up at her, white-faced.

'What the devil?' Raimon pushed past Beatriz.

'You'd better come down, Father.'

'What is it?'

'There's been a death.' Bertrand's voice was cracked and shocked. 'Over here. You'd better come.' Bertrand turned away. Raimon, and then Beatriz, clattered down the steps.

Bertrand led his father to the end of the vault, where Beatriz had practised the previous afternoon. The opening between the barrels was crowded with servants and half-dressed soldiers jostling each other to look over the shoulders of the people in front. Some of the women were weeping, gasping, fanning themselves with their aprons. Raimon's approach parted them cleanly and swiftly. He advanced into the gloomy space between the barrels, and Beatriz stayed close on his heels. Her gaze slid over stacked flour sacks, and – propped awkwardly up against the far wall of barrels – the shape of a man seated with his legs extended in front of him on the floor. There was a dark stain on his right collar and shoulder, continuing down the front of his tunic.

'I came in search of a beakerful to cure my headache and found him like this,' Bertrand said.

'Who is it? Bring lights,' Raimon commanded. There was more pushing and shoving in the opening and more clattering on the stone steps. Anna appeared at Beatriz's shoulder. Beatriz pulled her out of the way of two of Raimon's men, who came back in carrying torches they had snatched from holders in the Great Hall. The crowded space, the frightened faces were suddenly illuminated as the men held the torches high.

'Hold that flame away from the flour, you idiot,' Raimon chastised one of the men. Beatriz and Anna looked with trepidation at the flour sacks. Flour was highly flammable, and it was foolhardy to hold an open flame close to it. Raimon knelt next to the body. 'Bring the torch over here so that I can see.'

'Should we call a surgeon?' Bertrand asked.

'A surgeon would be pointless,' Raimon announced. 'He's dead.'

Beatriz and Anna craned to see over Raimon's shoulder and gasped together, recognising the dead man, despite the horribly googling eyes, the protruding tongue and the discolouration of the face. 'Imbert!' Beatriz exclaimed. 'It's Imbert!'

'Yes,' Raimon said tersely, glancing up at her. He stood and turned to the crowding onlookers. 'I am sorry to say the *trobador* Imbert has been foully murdered, and in great sacrilege on the Easter feast.' There were cries and gasps from the crowding people. Craning to see around Raimon's bulk and his red cloak, Beatriz saw something was wrapped around Imbert's throat and the fingers of one of his hands were cut and clawed where he had scrabbled to loosen the cord that had strangled the life – and the song – out of him.

'Everyone out of the way. Bertrand, fetch the priest and the viscount. You two,' Raimon pointed at Roger and at Lluis, who had just arrived straightening clothes he had donned in a hurry, 'carry him upstairs to the hall and don't disturb the corpse any more than you have to. I will look into this foul murder in the light of day.' Raimon strode out, and those concerned jumped to obey his orders. Before they turned to leave, Beatriz noticed that Imbert's tunic was rumpled up and his hose were awry, as if he had come down here in search of the privy, or perhaps a private moment with a woman.

Beatriz and Anna trooped upstairs with the others, relieved to regain the fresher air and natural light of the Great Hall. The two men struggling with Imbert's not inconsiderable bulk, dumped him unceremoniously on the first trestle they could stagger to. The priest bustled in, tutting aghast at the body, and began to lay out holy oil and a prayer book. Raimon and Viscount Ademar circled the trestle, studying Imbert's corpse.

Imbert had been a tall and wide man, full of loud jest and laughter, always strumming an instrument, taking a stance, singing in a deep, if croaking voice. Now he looked shrunken, grey, and it was hard to see the life fled out of him, his body turned to a mere paltry thing.

Raimon carefully found an edge of the thing embedded in Imbert's neck and began to unwind it from the flesh, having to hold up Imbert's gruesome head now and then as he did so. Beatriz screwed her face up in disgust at the unpleasant task, but did not look away. There were three bloody holes in Imbert's neck on the right side. Philippa came to stand next to Bertrand, holding a hand to her mouth, her eyes appalled. Gauzlin was staring, horrified, at Imbert's corpse. Raimon's men-at-arms formed an outer circle, protecting the corpse and Raimon's investigation from curiosity. The servants went about their business beyond the circle, but they craned and glanced in the direction of the body at every opportunity. Raimon held the thing he had unwound aloft. It was a length of sheep-gut, a bloodied instrument string. In its absence, Imbert wore an ugly, red welt necklace beneath the horrid grimace of his face. 'Note his hose,' Raimon said loudly. Imbert's penis had slipped out of his gaping hose and was pathetically on show to all and sundry.

'Perhaps he offered violence to some young woman,' Ademar said, 'and she defended herself.'

'I can't believe a woman could do this,' Philippa said.

'And note this curious stab wound in his neck – three small holes,' Raimon said.

Beatriz frowned. Imbert had pestered her to marry him, but he was motivated more by the success of his business than by licentiousness. It dawned on her that she might come under suspicion, since many people knew of her resistance to his marriage offer.

Raimon raised the grisly lute string again. 'Everyone will stay here. You two,' he addressed Lluis and Roger again, 'go and examine all the instruments in the castle and find one with a missing string, and look for any weapon that might have made these three holes.'

Beatriz gulped down rising panic. Yesterday, she had been in the very spot where Imbert had been found. She had no idea where her *vielle* was since she couldn't remember the last few hours of the previous night.

The priest finished his prayers and Raimon took a woollen cloak, placing it over Imbert, mercifully covering the contortion of his face. 'When we have finished our investigations, Father,' he told the priest, 'I will have him carried to the church for the vigil.'

There was nothing to do but wait. They all sat as far away from the covered body as possible, and the servants put bread and beer in front of them. The mood was subdued, and nobody had anything to say.

Lluis and Roger returned, carrying a lute. Beatriz felt Anna shift beside her. She saw, with relief, it was not her *vielle*. 'We found it,' Lluis said, showing Raimon the gap in the strings. Raimon compared the bloody string that had killed Imbert and found it to be a match.

'Whose instrument is it?'

'It was in Lady Philippa's chamber,' Lluis said reluctantly.

There was a long silence. Raimon looked at Philippa and she turned to Beatriz and Anna. 'Well, whose?' Raimon demanded.

'I think it's Imbert's. Anna was restringing it for him,' Philippa said, 'but Anna couldn't have done this.' She frowned. 'Nor Beatriz,' she added swiftly.

'Who else had easy access to your chamber?' Raimon demanded. 'What do you say?' Raimon turned to Anna. 'Well?'

'Anna is deaf, sire,' Beatriz said. 'She can't hear you.'

'I know what is happening, what is said,' Anna protested, ignoring Beatriz's restraining grip. Anna's pronunciation was smudged. 'It is Imbert's lute, which I carried to my lady's chamber, lord, but I know nothing of Imbert's death.'

Raimon stared at her, unblinking. 'Did he offer you rudeness, violence?'

'No!'

'Were you down there in the cellar with him last night?'

'No!'

'Anna did not commit this crime,' Beatriz interrupted. 'I'm sure it can't have been Anna!' She tried to quell the shaking of her hand, which she knew Anna would be feeling.

'A search of the girl's possessions will be made for the weapon used to stab Imbert in the neck. Bring her,' Raimon told Lluis, who gently took Anna's arm, pulling her up and with him, to follow the count, shrugging apologetically as he did so to Beatriz. Beatriz and Philippa hurried to follow the group of men. Beatriz looked at

Roger and noticed something like panic in his usually impassive expression.

In the tiny closet off Philippa's main chamber where Anna slept, her few possessions were neatly placed on a stone shelf protruding from the wall. Lluis and Roger sifted through the bits and pieces on the shelf, lifted up the bedclothes to look under the mattress, lifted the lid of the small chest where Anna kept her clothes. The search was fruitless.

'Lady,' Beatriz tugged at Philippa's sleeve and spoke very quietly. 'Have a search made of Imbert's room. I think you will find a part-burnt letter there from Guillaume of Aquitaine. The viscount will help …'

She stopped mid-sentence as Raimon suddenly announced, 'The *jograresa* sleeps in the Galliarde Tower. We will search there.' The maid Julia, who was often unkind to Anna, was standing next to Raimon and had probably whispered this information in his ear.

Beatriz struggled to stay on her feet and keep a reassuring grasp of Anna's arm as they were manhandled along the walkway to the opposite tower. The whole party moved up the ladders to the third and fourth floor, but they could not possibly all cram into Beatriz's attic space.

'Petrus, go up and search,' Raimon instructed.

Beatriz glanced at Lluis, who did not meet her eye. She hoped he had left no evidence of their night together up there. She wished she could remember it, but there was just a blank in her mind, after the late-night carousing of the men. The group stood at the bottom of the ladder, looking up and listening to Petrus riffling through Beatriz's possessions. She heard something fall to the floor. 'Be careful with my …' she began to call out, but her words froze in her throat. Petrus' face loomed in the opening at the top of the ladder. He was holding out Philippa's gold triple-pin. The tips of the three sharp prongs were smirched with a dark, rusty red. Petrus lumbered awkwardly down the ladder and handed the brooch to Raimon.

'Your missing brooch?' Raimon asked Philippa. 'Stolen by one of these strolling players and used to stab Imbert in the neck.'

Philippa's eyes were wide with shock, but she rallied to argue with her uncle. 'They are not strolling players! Anna has been with me since I was born. Beatriz has been in Imbert's service for the last four years and has served me too for the last year, as you well know, Uncle. Beatriz is a *trobairitz* of great talent, as Imbert himself would have told you.'

'Well, here is your stolen pin smeared with Imbert's blood in her possession. It matches the stab wounds in Imbert's neck. And the deaf girl's lute string was the second murder weapon,' said Raimon.

'I did not put that pin in there,' Beatriz declared. 'I did not kill Imbert.' Had Lluis planted the pin in her room, slept with her for that reason? Had he drugged her? Was he the murderer? She stared wild-eyed at him.

'No doubt,' Raimon addressed Philippa, 'she planned to sell the pin and use the money to get away and Imbert caught her at it.' He turned suddenly on Beatriz. 'I understand Imbert wished to marry you and you had objections. You had motive to kill him. The two of you did it together.'

Beatriz stammered. 'No! My lord, this is not the truth of it!'

'Take her and the deaf-mute,' Raimon commanded. 'They will be tried for Imbert's murder at the Michaelmas Assembly. The evidence is solid against them.'

Roger grasped Anna's arm gently. 'I'm sorry,' he said. Petrus took hold of Beatriz.

Philippa stepped in front of Roger and Petrus to prevent them from leaving with Anna and Beatriz. She addressed her uncle again. 'Neither Anna nor Beatriz can have murdered Imbert. They do not have the strength for such an act. And what reason could Anna have, Uncle?'

'They could have given him drugged wine before strangling him,' Raimon said. 'It seems he was about bad business down in the undercroft, trying to take the virtue of the simpleton or the dancing girl, but it is a foul murder, nonetheless. Or one of them seduced him to soften him up, while the other murdered him.' He nodded again to Roger and Petrus.

'Lady, please,' Roger said quietly to Philippa. Philippa stepped out of his way, breathing heavily and frowning furiously at her uncle. Anna's face was white with panic, and she held an arm out desperately to Philippa as Roger pulled her towards the ladder, one burly but gentle arm around her waist. 'I didn't do it, Philippa!'

Petrus gripped Beatriz's wrist painfully and pulled her towards the ladder. She cast a glance of supplication towards Lluis, but he would not meet her eyes.

PART II

April–June 1093

13

ACCUSED

Evening, Tuesday 19 April 1093, The Dungeon, Chateau
Narbonnais

'They will hang us, Beatriz.' Anna clung
piteously to Beatriz, shaking violently with
fear and cold.

Beatriz pushed Anna back to arm's length so that Anna
could see her mouth. 'No, they will not!' She swallowed
and immediately hated the thought of both her own
hanging and Imbert's garrotting that the act of swal-
lowing conjured. 'We will prove our innocence.' She
injected as much bravado as she could into her voice, for
her own sake.

'How? From here?' Anna looked around, gesturing at
the three damp walls and low ceiling of the cell. The
fourth wall was an ironwork gate securely fastened with a
heavy chain and padlock. Moss grew lavishly in one

corner of the cell. The stones of the walls were unfinished. At least they weren't shackled, thanks to Roger. He
had persuaded the guard that shackles were not
necessary.

The dungeons were in the space beneath the west
tower, as the undercroft was the space beneath the east
tower and the Great Hall. The damp and cold seeped
relentlessly into Beatriz's bones. The cell smelled bad – of
old, stagnant water and other things it was best not to
dwell on. The passage they had come down to get here
had been long, narrow and dark. The guard had taken pity
on the two frightened girls and left them a torch, but its
light would not last forever.

'Philippa will be working for our release,' Beatriz said.

'It suits Count Raimon to blame us. You saw that. He
termed me a simpleton and you a dancing girl.'

'Yes. It helps him to separate Philippa from her
friends.'

Anna pressed her lips together in agreement. 'Poor
Imbert! Why would anyone kill him?'

'It was not a gentle death. I wonder what he had done
to provoke it.'

'You think it was a woman he assaulted? Julia?'

'No. Imbert was not lecherous. He wanted to marry
me for his business. It's likely the murderer untied his
hose and left him like that to mislead everyone. Just as
they deliberately used the lute string and the brooch to
incriminate us.' Beatriz frowned furiously at the thought
of someone in her room, someone acting with such
malice towards them, and of course, towards Imbert.
Lluis had been in her room.

At least they were together. The thought of being in here alone, with images of the gallows vivid in her imagination, was horrifying. She must focus on something else, think back through her conversations with Imbert, her observations of his actions and look for a motive for the murder. And she must conjure up for herself the awful sight of Imbert's dead body in the undercroft and then on the table in the Great Hall, searching for clues about the real murderer. The more she thought about it, the more she convinced herself that Lluis could have been involved, could have deliberately got her drunk and duped her. Why else did he remain silent when she was accused, since he knew they had been in bed together?

Anna clutched at Beatriz's shoulder, terrified by her own thoughts.

Beatriz must keep talking to her. 'I would dearly like to know what Imbert was up to,' she said, mouthing the words clearly, as it was difficult for Anna to see in the gloom.

'Why would someone kill Imbert?' Anna repeated.

'Oh, there could be reasons.'

'What reasons?'

'Imbert had his nose in everyone's business. Someone took umbrage. He must have gone too far with the wrong person.'

Anna threw her a look of incomprehension.

'His gambling was an expensive habit,' Beatriz said. 'He had to feed it with coin somehow.'

'He was spying?'

'Oh, yes. For sure. He did more of that than composing.'

'Spying for who? On who?'

'I'm less sure of that. He didn't tell me. But I know he was sometimes flush with silver that was unlikely to have come from our performances. He met with many great men in the course of our travels from court to court. I always assumed he was spying.'

They lapsed into silence, and Beatriz listened to the slap of the dark water. She glanced at the torch. It would only last a short while. She nudged Anna to look at her again. 'I think he was spying on Raimon and Bertrand. I overheard them talking, and then they burnt a letter yesterday in the undercroft. And I saw Imbert after they had gone. He had concealed himself. I think the letter was from Guillaume of Aquitaine to Philippa.' Beatriz hung her head, pondering the things that she knew.

'What is it?' Anna placed a palm under Beatriz's chin to bring her face up to her view again. 'What are you thinking?'

'I was in bed with Lluis last night,' Beatriz said and hurried on before Anna could respond, 'but I don't remember anything. One minute I was in the hall drinking, the next I woke up, in the morning, naked with Lluis, with screaming below in the passageway.'

Anna digested this information. 'Lluis …. You remember nothing?'

'Nothing. It's a blank.' An awful thought suddenly occurred to Beatriz. What if she *had* done it? Perhaps she had murdered Imbert!

Anna shook Beatriz's arm to regain her attention. 'You stayed up late, Beatriz. You were still there when Philippa and I went to bed. Did you see who Imbert was with?'

Beatriz pictured the scene in the Great Hall and the last things she remembered. She was drinking with Lluis at the trestle, and idiotically drinking in his love talk, still thrilled at her own performance and its effect on the audience. Bertrand, Petrus, Imbert, Jacques – the salt merchant, some of the other merchants, were standing by the fire, singing and clashing their goblets together. 'I confess, my memory of the end of the night is hazy. Imbert had an argument with Gauzlin, but that was a bit earlier. What did you see, Anna? Sometimes, you see a great deal more than I do. I am intent on listening and talking and can miss something right under my nose.'

Anna shook her head. 'I don't remember seeing anything that would be reason for murder. Lluis will speak on your behalf to Count Raimon, surely. He knows you were with him. In bed.' Beatriz could not see for sure in the gloom of the dungeon, but she guessed from her voice that Anna was blushing.

'Well, he did not speak up, did he? Perhaps he was part of it. That's what I'm thinking.'

'Lluis?' Anna's voice was loaded with disbelief.

'He is Bertrand's friend, his tool.' Beatriz felt furious with Lluis. 'Perhaps he committed the actual murder. I doubt Bertrand would get his hands besmirched with blood.'

'But Lluis likes you, Beatriz. He likes you a lot. And I can't believe he would do this.'

'My lack of memory suits them all very well. Perhaps it wasn't just the wine. Perhaps they drugged me. Lluis is a sculptor and has the strength in his hands and arms to have so cruelly killed Imbert. And he has a need to prove

147

himself, because of the great fame of his father. Bertrand could have played on that.'

She could hear scurrying at the edges of the darkening cell. Mice or rats. Speaking was better than listening to the furtive claws on the stone and thinking of trying to sleep in such circumstances.

'So you believe Imbert was a spy for Guillaume of Aquitaine?' asked Anna.

'That's possible,' Beatriz said. 'The letter was likely destroyed, but he could still carry the tale to Lady Philippa. It would not suit Raimon and Bertrand at all to have Philippa wed to the duke. He would claim Tolosa on her behalf and he has an army to back him.'

Anna nodded. The torchlight distorted the little that could be seen, casting strange red and black shadows looming over them, which Beatriz knew were only their own heads moving, but still the shadows were alarming.

'We should try to sleep,' Beatriz said, feeling certain she could never sleep in here. She strained to see what scrabbled at the edges of their prison. There was nothing to sit on, nothing to lie on. She could already feel the frigid dankness of the place, and perhaps it was not night-fall yet. There was no way to know how long they had been here, if the sun had set, if there was a moon. Some-where nearby, she could hear a regular dripping of water. There was nothing for it. They would have to sit on the filthy floor. They could not stand shaking together forever. 'We'll have to sit,' she told Anna, who looked with alarm at the grime of the stone flags. 'We won't be in here long.' Beatriz heard the doubt in her voice and was glad Anna could not hear it, but perhaps she read it in her face.

Gingerly, they sat, doing their best to keep their tunics from the worst of the dirt. Neither of them had a cloak. Philippa would surely come to see them if she couldn't get them out quickly, and Beatriz could ask her to bring their cloaks, straw mattresses, a jug of wine to give them courage? She hoped for that.

Anna's eyes were huge. 'If Raimon or Bertrand is the culprit, we will be judged by the murderer and have no hope of justice.'

'It's likely Raimon will delegate the matter to Viscount Ademar. There is hope there for us. He would not allow an injustice to stand. As Philippa noticed, such an act required more strength than one or even two girls could muster. Imbert was a big man.'

'But Raimon suggested we drugged him. I suppose then it would be possible?'

'Hardly. A woman might have stabbed Imbert in the neck with the pin, I suppose. But garrotting? That is the brutish act of a strong man. Ademar will see the truth of that.'

Anna put her face into her hands and breathed in and out in distress. 'The smell here is awful,' she said, looking up, cupping her hand to her nose. Yes, like something rotting, like we are rotting, thought Beatriz, and pushed the thought away.

The torch began to fizz, and the light stuttered. They focused on the torch, willing it to last, until it made a final, feeble splutter and they were plunged into an impenetrable darkness. Eyes shut or open, it made no difference. How dark darkness was. All Beatriz could see were spots swimming in her own eyes. Now Anna could no longer read her lips. They could only communicate through touch.

'It is darker than Black Saturday,' Anna said, her words coming in halting gasps. 'But we emerged from that, and we will emerge from this, Beatriz. I am praying to the Virgin.' Beatriz squeezed Anna's hand and kissed her forehead.

Beatriz imagined the layers of stone and life going on above their heads – the cook's boy dropping a hot pan in the sweltering kitchen, a maid laying a fire, a soldier pulling on a damp boot in the gatehouse, a horse shifting its weight to another hoof in the pungent warmth of the stable. And the murderer somewhere, congratulating himself that Imbert was silenced, and he had got away with it. Was there malice in the implication of them, or were they merely an easy target? As Anna had implied, her disability made her an object of suspicion for some people, and Beatriz had no man or family here to speak for her. Their hope rested now with Philippa, and Beatriz took some comfort from that. Anna was, in effect, Philippa's sister. She admitted to herself that, although Philippa's spoilt girlishness sometimes irritated her, the lady was also brave, opinionated, a staunch friend. She would get them out.

Anna shivered against her. It was like being buried, in the grave. Now that Anna could not see, they could no longer talk to one another. Beatriz felt for Anna's shoulder and the girls drew closer together in the blackness.

14

POWERFUL SERPENTS HIDE

Wednesday, 20 April 1093, Chateau Narbonnais

*B*eatriz had doubted sleep would ever come to her in this hard stone place. Anna had eventually slept, her breathing soft against Beatriz's neck. Beatriz continued to listen to the drip of water and to imagine how far down they were, immured with rats and crawling things, but she must have lost consciousness eventually, because they were both wakened by a sudden flood of light. Roger and Lluis stood at the opened grate, torches in hand. 'You're safe now,' Lluis said, reaching to pull Beatriz to her feet, while Roger bent his great frame and picked Anna up, hugging her to his chest. She blinked at him.

'What's going on?' Beatriz asked groggily.

'Let's get out of here. Count Raimon requires you both in the hall,' Lluis told her.

Her legs and feet felt numb. She staggered against Lluis as they followed Roger, who carried Anna up the long passage and steep steps and into the Great Hall. 'I'm so sorry you had to go through this, Beatriz,' Lluis said, his arms carefully placed about her to keep her upright.

In the Great Hall, Philippa was pacing up and down with her hands on her hips. Bertrand leant against the trestle table. Raimon and Ademar were seated opposite each other, close to the fire. 'Look at the state of them!' Philippa exclaimed, her face full of anxiety, as she rapidly took in the details of Anna and Beatriz's appearance.

'Bring wine, bread and the *aquamanile*,' Ademar told a maid, concern in his voice. 'Sit here.' He directed Roger to place Anna on the fur-covered bench where he had been sitting and indicated that Beatriz should sit next to her.

'Well, Ademar, you said there was a good reason for this,' Raimon demanded. Beatriz studied his face, trying to read his intentions. Ademar nodded to Lluis, who stepped forward and placed his hand on a prayer book that Ademar held out to him.

'Beatriz was with me, lord, when Imbert was murdered. I swear it.'

Raimon took a deep breath through his nose. '*When* was she with you?' he demanded.

Lluis glanced at Beatriz and looked back to Raimon, a flush on his cheeks. 'We were together from the end of the feast, lord. All night.' He stared at his boots for a moment, and Beatriz felt the blaze of her own face and saw Raimon's lip curl. She watched a smirk form on Bertrand's face at Lluis' revelation. Lluis looked up again. 'Imbert was in the hall when we left, I'm sure. I had to help Beatriz out. She was … she had taken too much wine. Imbert was laughing near the fire with the *vicar* and *vectuari*. She was with me all night.' His voice had gathered a certainty as his narrative progressed, and Beatriz wished he had not been quite so loud with his final statement. She glanced at Philippa and saw surprise and disapproval in her expression.

Raimon considered Lluis and then Beatriz. 'Well, you, Beatriz de Farrera, are exonerated then by this testimony.' He turned to Philippa. 'And this is who you want as *trobairitz*, is it niece?' Philippa did not answer the question. She was busy washing Anna's face and hands and coaxing her to take a beaker of wine. 'The deaf girl has no such excuse, I presume,' Raimon stated.

'But we have seen fit to place her in my custody until trial,' Ademar added quickly, speaking to Beatriz. 'Lady Philippa argued that to leave her alone in the dungeon was a great cruelty given her affliction.'

Beatriz looked at Anna and saw she had not understood any of this. She was simply immersed in the emotion of her reunion with Philippa, in the touch of their hands and the speech of their eyes. They would have to explain the situation to her later.

'The maid will be tried at Michaelmas,' Raimon stated. 'I leave the matter to you, Ademar. I have other business to deal with. This murder has been an appalling stain on my assembly and Bertrand's betrothal. The murderer,' he looked at Anna, whose mouth trembled at his stare, 'will swing for Imbert's murder. He was a fine poet, and I'll not find another like him nor let his murder go unpunished.' He rose and left them.

Bertrand stepped to Lluis and clapped him on the shoulder, grinning. Lluis looked uncomfortable at the gesture. He found Beatriz's eyes, an apology in his own. Beatriz compressed her lips. They were all the same, all alike in their machismo and vanity.

'Lady,' Ademar addressed Philippa. 'I will leave Anna in your care during the daytime – under the eye of Roger, but she must spend the nights at my house. Roger will escort her to me before nightfall each day.'

'Thank you,' Philippa said. Roger nodded his comprehension of the orders.

'You know she didn't do this, Viscount,' Beatriz asserted.

'I know I need proof that someone else did, Beatriz. Something that contradicts the proof of the lute string used to garrotte Imbert, which had been in Anna's possession.'

'And you see,' Beatriz persisted, 'that somebody deliberately tried to implicate me by placing the bloodied brooch in my possessions? They did the same with the instrument string that had been in Anna's possession. It's clear!'

'It must be proved,' the viscount said, reluctance in his voice. 'This someone must be identified and proved.'

Beatriz opened her mouth to continue her objections, but Philippa interrupted. 'Let's go upstairs,' Philippa said. 'Anna needs to recover.'

'Thank you,' Beatriz murmured to Lluis as she went to move past him. He touched the back of her hand and tried to look in her face, but she kept her eyes down and moved on.

. . .

PHILIPPA ORDERED two tubs to be set before the fire, and they watched the maids fill them. 'If Anna is to sleep at Ademar's house, will you sleep in here with me, Beatriz? Keep me company?'

She nodded. After all, there was a murderer in the castle.

'I did what you said, Beatriz,' Philippa told her.

Beatriz looked confused. 'What did I say?'

'You told me to search Imbert's room. I found the burnt letter you mentioned. I've got it here, and I collected up all the papers in the room.' She gestured to two leather satchels on the table. Beatriz recognised them as Imbert's.

'Wonderful! Can Anna look through these documents – see if there is anything other than songs and music?'

'After the bath,' Philippa gestured at the steaming tubs. Roger shifted his position to outside the door, and Beatriz stripped off her filthy clothes and eased into the warm water. In a role she was not accustomed to, Philippa moved around the chamber, looking in chests and eventually found two sets of clean clothes, which she put on the bed. She sat on a low stool at the side of Anna's tub and explained the situation to her. Anna put her face in her hands and wept loudly. 'It will be alright,' Philippa told her repeatedly, stroking her hair and arm. 'I won't let harm come to you.'

But Anna's mood shifted suddenly. She looked up again with red fury in her face. She thrashed at the surface of the water, soaking Philippa. 'This is no justice!

This is prejudice! This is just hatred for someone different!'

Philippa grabbed for her arms and stilled her. 'You are right! You are right, of course. And we will not allow it to stand. I solemnly promise you that.'

When Anna had calmed down and sunk back low into the water, Philippa turned to Beatriz: 'I have a sentence of sorts, too.' Beatriz raised her eyebrows. 'My uncle has declared I will travel to Aragon after the Michaelmas Assembly. I'm to be betrothed to Sancho Ramírez by proxy at the assembly and then travel to my marriage. Now that Imbert is gone, you will accompany me as my *trobairitz*, Beatriz.'

Beatriz nodded sombrely and looked at Anna, who was staring into space and not interested in looking at what they were saying. 'We will *both* come with you.'

After they had stepped from the tubs, dried themselves and all three had donned fresh clothes, Philippa lifted the edge of a cloth on the table to show Beatriz the charred pieces of the letter from the undercroft. She covered it again. She began to spill the papers from the satchels onto the table in front of her and sift through them.

Beatriz felt impatient that she was unable to read and help in the task. 'Tell me about the letter.'

Anna sat next to Philippa but did not join her in sorting the papers. The hound Adimante sensed her distress and wound herself around Anna's ankles. Anna looked awful. Her face was blanched, and there were dark stains beneath her eyes. Absent-mindedly, she petted Adimante's head as she nuzzled her knee. Anna stared blankly at nothing in particular.

Roger reentered the room. 'I require you to stand guard *outside* my room from now on, Roger. Not inside,' Philippa stated. An expression of mild surprise crossed Roger's face. He glanced with concern at Anna and then returned to the other side of the door.

'You don't trust Roger?' Anna asked, snapping out of her reverie.

'I don't trust anyone except us and Lluis.'

'Lluis?' Beatriz repeated.

'He is your evidence of being elsewhere when the murder took place, and you are his.' Philippa did not look Beatriz in the eye as she spoke.

'I can't remember anything. He could have slipped out. Perhaps he drugged me.'

Philippa's look of distaste intensified. 'Or perhaps you just drank an enormous quantity of wine.'

Beatriz suppressed her irritation. 'Why don't you trust Roger?'

'Killing Imbert like that was the act of a strong man.'

'But what reason could Roger have? There are other strong men at court. Petrus, for example. And Lluis, as a sculptor, has very strong hands.' They pondered in silence for a moment. Anna excused herself to curl up on Philippa's bed and quickly fell asleep.

'Was it awful in the dungeon?' Philippa whispered to Beatriz.

'Yes.' She could not bring herself to make any further description. They glanced at Anna. 'She is exhausted with worry.'

'Our time is best spent proving her innocence.' Philippa gingerly uncovered the burnt letter again.

'In the undercroft, I overheard Bertrand tell Raimon that the reply in the letter was positive,' Beatriz said.

'Could it be a reply to me from Duke Guillaume?'

'Yes, that is credible.' There was a tap on the door, and Philippa held a finger to her lips. Swiftly, she draped the cloth back over the burnt letter. A maid came in, leaving the door ajar. She carried a basket of firewood and a jug of wine. She set the wine on the table and knelt to add logs to the fire.

Beatriz reached over to pour more wine into their beakers. Lifting the beaker keenly to her mouth, she hesitated. 'Should Roger test your wine?'

'Already tested!' Roger called from the other side of the slightly open door.

Beatriz swallowed a large mouthful. The maid rose, and Philippa thanked her. When the doorlatch dropped again, Beatriz resumed. 'We know Raimon and Bertrand are ambitious to rule Tolosa. Getting you out of the way, married off to King Sancho Ramírez, is their intention.'

'Yes. Tolosa is already as good as my uncle's. He would be acclaimed by the knights and the city because of his military prowess. He will be a popular choice of count to succeed my father,' Philippa said morosely. 'The townspeople would never accept me, a mere girl, unless they knew I was backed by a warrior husband – such as Duke Guillaume.'

'What does the letter say? What remains of it, at least.'

Philippa carefully moved it a little closer. There were large brown holes burnt in it and many parts were precariously dangling and hanging on. It was more hole than parchment. 'It's almost indecipherable. I can't tell who it's from or what it says. There are just a few marks of ink left.'

'Can you tell anything from these marks?' Beatriz asked.

Philippa pored over the parchment and pointed here and there at brown ink squiggles as she spoke. 'There are no whole words. I see at the bottom here what is probably 'aume'. Nothing else is legible.'

'It seems likely to be Duke Guillaume's signature?'

Philippa nodded. 'We have only four months before Michaelmas to stave off my marriage to Sancho Ramírez and prove Anna's innocence. I could send you to Guillaume, to Poitiers, to confirm if the letter was from him and what it said. I can give you another letter to carry to him.'

'Yes,' Beatriz said slowly, 'but let's ensure we have pursued all clues here, before I go. The journey will take some weeks, months even. What else did you find in Imbert's papers?'

'Partly written poems. Receipts for gambling debts. Do you know where Imbert went the few days before the feast? I asked my uncle, and he said that Imbert pursued his own business and did not stay with him in Narbonne.'

Beatriz shook her head. 'Imbert just told me he had business and would be away for a few weeks. I was relieved to have the time to myself. I wasn't curious about where he went. I see now, there are many things I did not know about Imbert.'

'You must be careful, Beatriz,' Philippa said. 'If Imbert was killed because he witnessed that conversation between my uncle and Bertrand in the undercroft, about the letter, then the murderer would be willing to act again. If we can find out *when* Imbert was murdered, we can think about *who* could have committed the act at that time. Perhaps someone saw him going into the undercroft with another person.'

Beatriz frowned. If only she could remember more of the night. She could not have done it. That thought had just been the desperation of the dungeon working on her. 'When did you last see Imbert yesterday, Philippa?'

'He was still in the hall drinking and talking when I left, when Anna and I left. You were still there too, drinking and slurring.'

'Yes, alright!' Beatriz gave Philippa an exasperated stare. 'I can barely remember you and Anna leaving. I can't remember when I left the hall with Lluis and whether Imbert was still there or not. I could ask Lluis, except …'

'Except you are ashamed to be so drunk you don't remember.'

'No, actually, that's not it.' Beatriz looked crossly at Philippa again. 'Do you want to exonerate Anna or just argue with me about Lluis?'

Philippa stared at Beatriz, affronted at her tone. 'It's not the first time is it that you've got yourself into that situation?' Philippa demanded. She was referring to Beatriz's brief liaison with Bertrand. Philippa waved her hand at Beatriz's petulant expression. 'Do you think Lluis would murder Imbert in a fight over you?' Philippa asked.

'No, I don't. It's not that.' Philippa's glance asked Beatriz to elaborate, but she said nothing more and instead stared at her boots for some time, noting miserably that they had not fared well in the dungeon. She had a sense of something … something about Imbert prompted by Philippa's question, but it slipped round a corner in her mind and she could not catch its coat-tails. 'Let's start again,' Beatriz said. 'I will discreetly ask around when people last saw Imbert to try to ascertain when he left the hall and who else was in the hall late.'

Philippa sighed. 'I think that might prove a waste of time. Most of the people there were in much the same state as you, including Imbert himself – inebriated!'

'Perhaps our best line of attack then is to find out who Imbert was spying for and if that was the reason for the murder. Bertrand was the one to discover the body, or so he said.'

'I can't see my uncle murdering someone,' Philippa said. 'He doesn't need to. He can just command anyone hanged from the nearest tree. He has the right and authority. He could have dealt with any threat from Imbert without resorting to murder.'

'I will go and look at Imbert's room again,' Beatriz said. 'See what I can find out from the servants, to discover if anyone saw Imbert late at night going to the undercroft with somebody else.'

Philippa nodded and reached to put a hand over Beatriz's own two, which were clasped tightly in her lap. 'I'm sorry to be … critical of your behaviour. We must stick together, work together on this, for Anna's sake.'

Beatriz left Philippa's chamber and stepped into the passageway. At the far end, there was a ladder she could climb to the third floor, where Imbert's room was. Near the ladder, two men were standing in shadow. As Beatriz approached, the shadow resolved into the shapes of Gauzlin and Lord Henry. They were an unlikely pairing. Their only common ground was Cluny, surely. Henry glanced up, saw her and rapidly stepped back into his own guest room, off the passageway. Gauzlin moved towards and past Beatriz with his hands folded into his habit and his eyes fixed on the floor.

15

SAINT CECILIA

Wednesday 20 April, Chateau Narbonnais

*I*mbert's chamber was on the third floor of the west tower, and Beatriz had to climb a short ladder to reach it. She moved off the top of the ladder and stood for a moment, looking around the empty room. A bed, a table and chair, a few clothes hanging from a hook near the slit of a window with his boots set beneath, a small hearth, his instruments carefully wrapped and placed. A candle stub in a cracked wooden holder, quills and an ink bottle on the desk. The chapel bell was tolling for Imbert's passing – tolling for each year of his abbreviated life. The bell was close, and Beatriz felt its vibrations in her teeth.

She would never sing and laugh with Imbert again. He was lying in the cathedral, as cold as the stone walls. He had been kind to her, and she had felt safe with him until lately, until he started pressuring her to marry him. She was angry at how he had died, that someone had seen fit to strangle him so horribly and silence his song, erase from the world his intelligence and humour. She swiped at an annoying tear that was cold on her cheek.

She collected up his instruments, readying to move them to Philippa's chambers. She would have to ask Roger to help her get them down the ladder later today. She could use them all now, and Imbert had painstakingly taught her how to. As far as she knew, there was no one else who could lay claim to anything that belonged to Imbert. She felt around the hems of his tunics in case there was anything stitched in there, but found nothing. If Imbert had been spying and there was any evidence of that, he would have concealed it. She searched under the mattress. Nothing. She searched inside his spare boots. It was rather an unpleasant and intimate act. She ran her fingers along the top of the small shelf above the fireplace and reached up inside the chimney. There was nothing but dust and ashes.

'What were you up to, Imbert?' she said aloud. She sat down hard on his bed. Until recently, she had slept on the floor in this chamber and she knew it well. She took a deep breath and looked again around the sparse room. Opposite where she sat, a small painting of Saint Cecilia was hanging on the wall. Cecilia was the saint of musicians and was shown holding a harp. Beatriz revelled in the lush blue of the saint's robe against the gold of the background, a brilliant patch in the gloomy room. She stood up to inspect the painting more closely. It wasn't quite straight. She reached to straighten it, but as she touched the frame, she thought she should take it instead. Keep it, for Imbert's sake. She was his legacy now. Carefully, she lifted it from its hook. 'Imbert!' she exclaimed. Behind the painting, some bricks had been removed, creating a niche. In the niche rested a small black book.

Beatriz manoeuvred back down the ladder from the third to the second floor with Imbert's book and the Saint Cecilia painting held carefully in one hand. She moved back to Philippa's door where Roger was standing stiffly. If he was offended at his exile, his curt nod and expression gave nothing away. Inside the chamber, Anna had woken and was seated opposite Philippa again.

'I found something!' Beatriz said triumphantly. She waggled the small leather-bound book in the air and handed it to Anna. It was a gather of parchments folded inside a black leather cover and tied together with a thong. Anna untied it and began to read. Beatriz set down the painting of Saint Cecilia and explained where she had found the book. Philippa watched Anna reading.

'It's a songbook,' Anna said after a few moments. 'Imbert's songs.'

Beatriz frowned. 'I've never seen that book before. Surely Imbert would have shared his songbook with me. It was concealed.'

'You can't read.'

'No, but I would have seen it. He would have had it in front of him when we discussed our performances, rehearsed.'

'I will study it,' Anna said and set it to one side on the table. Beatriz noted that Anna had pulled herself together. There was a new resoluteness about her.

'Anna has a plan.' Philippa's statement concurred with Beatriz's perception.

'We need to get better organised,' Anna said. 'We have too many suspicions, too many clues to follow.'

'What do you propose?' Beatriz asked.

Anna pointed at a small chest on the floor next to her. Its lid was leaning open, and Beatriz could see various loose scrolls and parchments and a large wooden binding of the sort that could hold parchments together. 'I will collect all our evidence in here, in an ordered fashion, so that we can present it later to the viscount.'

Beatriz cocked an eyebrow. 'We have some evidence?'

Anna fished two pieces of parchment from the chest and set them on the table. One she pushed towards Beatriz to look at and the other she began to draw on herself with a piece of charcoal.

Beatriz moved the completed drawing closer to her on the table and studied it carefully. It was a detailed sketch of Imbert's body laid out on the table in the Great Hall. Beatriz leant over and touched Anna's arm to bring her out of the concentrated world of her head she had entered to make the new drawing. 'You did this?' she asked.

Anna shook her head. 'No, Lluis came and gave me that while you were searching Imbert's chamber. He thought it might help us.'

Beatriz stood and moved to look over Anna's shoulder at the drawing she was making. It depicted the moment in the undercroft when Imbert was discovered murdered, surrounded by barrels and flour sacks. The scene was emerging like magic beneath Anna's fingers. She blurred a line here and there with the tip of her forefinger. Sometimes she rubbed a line out entirely and started again. Gradually, the image lived on the parchment. Anna looked up to encounter the rapt expressions on Philippa and Beatriz's faces. 'That's uncanny,' Beatriz said. 'You have caught it exactly.'

'Well, I hope so. I thought if I could trace the memory back out on the parchment, we might find a clue there.'

'You can see from Lluis' drawing, the two injuries,' said Beatriz, pointing. 'Three stab wounds in his neck from the brooch and the circle of the garrotte. And you can see his hose awry.'

Anna stood. 'Imagine you are Imbert in the undercroft with someone, Beatriz.' She manoeuvred Beatriz into a position she was happy with. 'Imbert was tall, but perhaps he was bending to the wine spigot.' Beatriz complied in pantomime. 'Imbert was stabbed in the right side of his neck.' Anna looked again at Lluis' drawing and then, stylus in hand, she acted out stabbing Beatriz, trying out a range of positions, in front of, beside, behind 'Imbert', and using first her right hand and then her left.

'It would have been very awkward, almost impossible, to stab him using the left hand,' Philippa observed with excitement.

Anna nodded. 'The murderer was very likely right-handed.'

'But you are right-handed. That doesn't help us much.'

'No, but we can make a note of anyone who is left-handed and exclude them from our suspicion!'

Beatriz looked back at Anna's drawing and continued to imagine her way into it. 'After he was stabbed, Imbert staggered and slumped against the barrel behind him, and then the murderer got behind him and slipped the garrotte over his head.'

'Anna had an idea about that too.' Philippa was suppressing excitement.

'The murderer must have cuts on their fingers surely from pulling on the catgut,' Anna said.

'I have mentioned this to Viscount Ademar, and he is organising an inspection of hands in the Great Hall,' Philippa announced, a note of triumph in her voice.

'Some people who were at the feast have already left. The *vectuari*, the clerics.' Beatriz did not want to dampen their optimism, but felt she had to sound a note of caution. It might not be easy to find the murderer and clear Anna.

'No man of God committed this act, Beatriz,' Philippa said firmly.

Beatriz sighed her disagreement, but did not argue.

'Of course, he might have worn gloves, falconry gauntlets, for example, to protect his fingers,' Philippa suggested.

'Then the gloves would be damaged,' Beatriz interrupted. 'This murder was carefully planned in advance. It wasn't committed in the heat of the moment. The murderer took Imbert down to the wine vault and had the cat gut, gauntlets, and the brooch with him. And, beforehand, he stole the lute string and brooch from this room, intending to cast suspicion on us.'

Philippa shuddered. 'I suppose anyone could have entered this room when we were in the Great Hall.'

'We could search people's possessions and try to find the gauntlets,' Beatriz said, 'but ...' Her excitement faded.

'He could easily throw the gloves away. That's what I would do.'

Philippa shrugged. 'If we are right about gauntlets – not everyone would have easy access to them. They are expensive items to own and discard.'

'We should search for damaged gauntlets. I will ask among the servants.'

'It's difficult for me to question people,' Anna said, 'since I am accused myself. Nobody will want to talk to me or trust my motivations. They don't trust me anyway, because of my deafness,' she added bitterly, but hurried on. 'So Philippa will make enquiries among the nobility, who will speak with her, while you will question the rest of the household, Beatriz, and I will collect what we find and keep it organised, help us decide what to do next.'

'That makes sense.' Beatriz said. 'I will talk to the servants and riff-raff of my own ilk!' Having a plan of action felt good.

'I have asked Ademar to include Raimon, Bertrand, Henry, Petrus, Mafalda, everyone in the hands inspection,' Philippa said. 'They have all agreed.'

'Henry? You suspect him?' asked Beatriz.

'As you said. It could be anyone.'

'I suspect that Henry is your running stag rather than Guillaume,' Anna said, referring to the Holy Lots prediction and smiling.

Philippa frowned. 'I don't have inclination for such nonsense now. And while I could provide Henry with a kingdom, which he craves, he could not supply me with the army to contest against my uncle.'

Anna grimaced, her expression conceding agreement.

'I cannot play anymore with a romantic eye. I must look with a politic one,' Philippa said.

'Perhaps Mafalda has something to do with the murder.' Beatriz drummed her fingers on the table. 'Mafalda is full of hate for Raimon. Perhaps Imbert somehow …' Beatriz halted, running out of ideas. 'Roger is obviously still quite taken with Mafalda. He looks at her at every opportunity.'

'Petrus too,' said Anna.

Beatriz turned to her in surprise. 'What do you mean, Petrus too?'

'Petrus was also staring often at Mafalda at the Easter feast.'

'How would they know each other?' Philippa wondered, knitting her brow.

Beatriz shook her head in bewilderment. Mafalda was beautiful. That was reason enough for any man to stare at her. 'Why is she still here if Abbot Frotard has left? She was part of his party.'

'The abbot is only away briefly,' Philippa explained. 'He will return soon and rejoin Mafalda. That is what I understood from her. Bishop Izarn was also staring at Mafalda a great deal, but …' she held up a palm to halt Beatriz's inevitable sour remark on clerics.

'I was thinking, too,' said Anna, 'Imbert was arguing with Bertrand and with Petrus around the time of the burial of your brother. Do you remember?'

Philippa shook her head. 'I didn't notice that.'

'And,' Anna added, 'Beatriz saw him arguing with Gauzlin at the Easter feast.'

'Imbert argued with people a lot,' Beatriz said. 'It was

usually over his gambling debts. And drinking made him argumentative.'

'But you said he was spying, Beatriz?' Anna said. 'That would be cause for argument, surely, if someone found out, feared exposure by him?'

Beatriz nodded slowly.

'Who do you think he was spying for and on?' Philippa asked.

'Perhaps for Duke Guillaume. Perhaps for the pope,' Beatriz ventured.

'The pope!' Philippa exclaimed. 'That's ridiculous. You are determined to blame a godly man.'

'Are you saying the pope does *not* employ spies?'

Philippa compressed her lips. 'Well, who would Imbert spy on for Pope Urban and how would that have come about?' she demanded.

'We were at Benevento in Italy when Pope Urban held council there some years ago. They could have met then. He could be spying on Abbot Frotard, on Raimon, on Henry. There is a dispute between the pope and Cluny over the development of the pilgrim routes to Compostela. Pope Urban is trying to rein in the ambitions of Cluny. Imbert mentioned that much to me.'

'Wait!' commanded Anna. 'We are getting ourselves tangled again. Let's review what we know, what we suspect so far.' She drew a few large sheets of parchment from her chest and began to set out her notes, speaking as she wrote.

'1. Imbert was murdered late on Easter Monday in the undercroft.

What was he doing there?

Who was he with?

2. He was stabbed with the brooch and garrotted with the instrument string. They were stolen from Philippa's chambers and then the brooch was planted among Beatriz's things.

When did the murderer steal the weapons and then plant the bloody brooch?

Did anyone see somebody going into Philippa's chambers and up to your attic, Beatriz, who shouldn't have been there?

It's obvious why they planted the brooch on you, Beatriz. Because of your known antipathy to marrying Imbert. I was just an accidental convenience.' Her voice turned bitter again. 'The instrument was here, and I was working on it. Implicating a deaf woman probably seemed effective. Some people think me stupid or evil, in any case …' Philippa placed a hand momentarily on Anna's arm. Anna took in a breath and carried on with her writing and reading aloud for Beatriz's benefit.

'3. The murderer was right-handed.

Who is left-handed and can be excluded from our list of suspects?'

'We have a list of suspects?' Beatriz asked.

'Yes, Anna wrote that down when you were in Imbert's room.' Philippa picked up another sheet and read out the names.

'List of Suspects: Raimon, Bertrand, Roger, Mafalda.'

'But we could add other names,' Beatriz said. 'Lluis …'

'Before we get carried away with a long list of names,' Anna said, 'let's try to think about names in conjunction with why. After all, we could put everyone on the list and, as you say, Imbert may have been murdered by someone who has already left the chateau, someone we don't know. I'll read you the list of possibilities that Philippa and I discussed so far.' She pulled another parchment from the pile and set it in front of her to read.

'Possible Scenarios:

1. Raimon and or Bertrand – to do with the burnt letter, which was probably from Guillaume to Philippa. Imbert was seen arguing with Bertrand. Beatriz overheard Raimon and Bertrand talking covertly in the undercroft and burning the letter and she saw Imbert pick it up. Philippa found the burnt letter in Imbert's room.
2. A woman Imbert was trying to assault – because of his hose being awry.'

'Julia?' offered Beatriz.

Anna's head was bowed over the parchment, and she did not hear Beatriz's interjection.

She ploughed on through her list. '3. Something to do with Imbert's spying or gambling debts. Again, spying could point to Raimon and Bertrand. He may have been spying for Guillaume.'

Beatriz nodded. 'Yes, he certainly knew and was friendly with Duke Guillaume.'

Anna dipped her pen and added two further notes: 'He may have been spying for the pope over the pilgrim route and Saint-Sernin.

'Where was Imbert in the week before the murder?

173

'What can the book Beatriz has discovered tell us?'

Roger knocked and beckoned to the girls.

'Ademar is beginning his hands inspection,' Philippa surmised. 'We must go down.'

Anna cleared the parchments and black songbook away carefully into the chest and locked it. She attached the key to her set of keys and needles and put them back in the pouch she wore on her belt. 'We should meet together every day and see what we have each found out about these questions and add to our lists, and,' her voice dropped to a whisper as they neared the door, 'look out for any lefties.'

In the Great Hall, Ademar stood close to the hearth and Gauzlin was seated beside him at a trestle, poised with parchment, inkpot and stylus, mirroring their own recent scene with Anna. Except that Anna was more handsome than Gauzlin, who was looking particularly scraggly and skinny today, Beatriz thought. The viscount had decided to call people in to show their palms in small groups. Philippa, Anna and Beatriz's hands were inspected first and found to be clear. Roger also showed his hands. Gauzlin made a note that their hands were unmarked. Next, the nobles gathered to show their hands.

Ademar first presented his own palms to view, then, in turn, Raimon, Bertrand, Henry, Petrus, and finally Mafalda showed their hands to the viscount and Gauzlin noted down that they were all unmarked. The air was ripe, however, with suspicion and resentment. Mafalda's eyes drilled into Raimon's back as if they could commit a twin stabbing. Beatriz noticed Petrus glancing at Gauzlin rather strangely, but then turning away his gaze whenever

Gauzlin looked up from his writing. Gauzlin's hand seemed to shake under the scrutiny and he dropped his stylus. Petrus bent to pick it up and hand it back to him. Beatriz exchanged a quick glance with Anna. Petrus was left-handed! Gauzlin was right-handed. Mafalda and Roger showed no sign of being aware of each other at all, which also struck Beatriz as odd, but perhaps she was seeing shadows everywhere now.

Henry passed a sympathetic eye over Anna and murmured to Philippa. 'I hope Ademar can exonerate your maid, Lady Philippa. I cannot believe her capable of this grievous act.'

Helie was tremendously excited to be playing a role in the drama, to be suspected of murder. How delicious! was the sentiment writ all over her face. She showed her palms, pulling a face at her ladies, who then, giggling, showed their own hands.

Ademar continued inspecting the hands of the household and the garrison all day. Raimon seated himself at the high table with his clerk and began working his way through his correspondence. Philippa and Anna withdrew, but Beatriz took on the task of staying with the viscount to observe the inspection. Gauzlin showed his own palms. His hands were small, like a child's and spattered with brown ink, but showed no wounded lines from the garrotte.

Lluis, Julia, and everyone trooped in and out, down to the last soldier and maid. Gauzlin insisted on inspecting Lluis' hands himself, carefully holding the tips of his fingers to his view and Beatriz also peered to see. Lluis' hands were indeed marked and notched and damaged here and there, as might be expected for a sculptor, but the straight lines of a garrotte were not evident across the bend of his fingers. Did Gauzlin suspect Lluis too? Nobody's hands showed the marks of the garrotte. 'This was fruitless then and proves nothing either way,' remarked Raimon from the high table, looking up briefly from his own pile of parchments.

16

A BAG OF SALT

Thursday 21 April, Chateau Narbonnais

*B*eatriz walked through the hall. The people talking over contracts and instructing scribes were much the same as before, with the exception of Imbert's absence. The murder and the accusation of Anna were minor matters to most of these people. Imbert was laying cold in a shroud. Usually he would have been in the thick of all this business, eavesdropping under the guise of strumming and sipping wine, looking for an angle that might benefit him or seeking out a game of dice that would not.

She walked out into the central courtyard where soldiers were inspecting carts and clerks were calculating taxes to be paid before the travellers could move on into the city. The air smelt of horse dung. She crossed the courtyard and entered the stables to find Simo, who was training with the steward and could be found underfoot all over Chateau Narbonnais, assisting in a plethora of roles as part of his training. Simo knew everything, and Beatriz had often had recourse to him. He was a precocious thirteen-year-old with a lustful interest in her. He wasn't in the stables, but she found him in the neighbouring falcons' mews, feeding bright red pieces of meat and a selection of mangled mice to the hooded birds. 'Simo!'

'Why, the beautiful and accomplished Beatriz! That was some song you gave us a few nights ago. My pants were throbbing.'

Beatriz scowled at him briefly, but worked to modulate her voice to a pleasant tone. 'Simo, do me a favour and I will write you into my next song.'

His eyebrows rose in appreciation. 'Me?'

'Yes. You will be the hero.'

His expression changed to sceptical. 'What's the favour?'

'I need you to list everyone who was at the chateau for the Easter Assembly, all the guests, all their servants, all the inhabitants.'

Now his eyes widened, and his eyebrows reached as high as they could. 'Everyone!'

'I already know quite a lot, but you, with your superior knowledge of everything that goes on here, will be able to fill the gaps.' The flattery worked, and Simo began to list everyone he could think of. Beatriz wished she had Anna with her to write down the additional names, but she did her best to commit them to memory. 'And Gelduinus and his crew,' he finished with satisfaction, referring to the masons working at Saint-Sernin. He dusted his hands together in smug self-satisfaction. 'That's about everyone.'

'Excellent,' Beatriz said. 'Now can you tell me who was in the hall late at night with Imbert at the Easter feast?'

He frowned and she could see his mental effort to picture the scene. 'Of course I can,' he said slowly.

Beatriz imagined the scene herself, the huge hearth, the fire starting to burn low. She was startled from her image by Simo's voice.

'Of course, there was you, draped drunkenly all over Lluis. You'd be better off with me, you know. I'm going to rise. I'll be steward one day. How about a kiss on credit?'

Beatriz pushed away his face as his lips advanced towards her. 'When you grow up and have a beard, maybe. And don't come near me with those bloodied fingers. Who else was there? Can't you remember?' she taunted. 'Were you so taken with staring at me?'

'Well, yes,' he admitted. 'Your tunic was almost off one of your titties there. You were quite a feast for the eyes. Lluis thought so, to be sure. He neglected his duties with his hands full of your luscious flesh and I had to do the last round of beakers. So, I know exactly who was there, actually!' He emphasised his last word sarcastically. 'Of course, if you hadn't been so drunk, you'd know yourself.'

She bit back a retort and smiled as sweetly as she could muster. 'Who?'

'Bertrand was deep in conversation with Henry of Burgundy. Bishop Izarn was talking in a corner with Gauzlin. Even Gauzlin held his wine better than you did.'

'Gauzlin was drunk?'

'A little, but not overmuch. Bertrand had been plying

him with wine for his own amusement, to observe the effect. It made Gauzlin rather ridiculously garrulous, but he is always obsequious, trying to please Bertrand. The merchants were all still there with Imbert and Vicar Regimundus.'

'Did you see Imbert leave the hall?'

He frowned. 'Ye ..es,' he said, unsure.

'Was he with somebody?'

He shook his head, again uncertain. 'I think he was alone. I think…'

She blew out a frustrated sigh. 'Can you see him leaving?'

He looked around as if looking for Imbert in the stable. 'What now?' he joked. 'He's gone, Beatriz. You are free to dally with me instead.'

Beatriz smiled sarcastically at him. 'Thank you, Simo,' she said decorously, 'but no thank you. Do you know where Imbert went last week? Did you take care of his horse when he returned from his journey?'

'I do. I did,' Simo said, rocking on his heels and raising his eyebrows smugly.

'Well?'

'Ah, not without payment of the price, Beatriz.'

'What price?' she said impatiently.

'A kiss, a feel and sight of your breasts should about do it.'

'Simo! You are appalling. That is a sin and a crime. I will bring you up before Viscount Ademar for uttering it. And I will tell him you have information on the murder and will not speak it and perhaps are implicated yourself! That will halt your rapid rise to steward, I should think.

You would more likely end on the gallows.' She stamped her foot in the hay for dramatic effect (but the muffling hay did not make for a particularly useful effect).

'Oh no! Beatriz! Please! I'm sorry.' He implored, grabbing her arm, which she wrenched from his grasp. 'Don't do that. Such an accusation might be taken seriously.'

'Well? Where did Imbert go?'

'He went to Aigues-Mortes.'

'How do you know?' Aigues-Mortes was a harbour in the salt marshes near Saint-Gilles. The count had salt warehouses there.

'He came back with a filched pack of salt in his saddle-bag. I recognised the marking on the bags. I was sent there myself once to buy a bag for the horselicks and a pretty price it was. Between the weight of the bag of salt and Imbert's, the poor horse was fair staggering. I have work to do,' Simo said sullenly, turning away from her.

The kitchen was adjacent to the mews, so Beatriz moved there next. Her gaze was captured by a vivid basket of purple beets and white carrots in the passage-way. It was infernally hot in the kitchen with the big caul-drons swinging on squeaking chains above the fires, and pots set on cooking stones at the edge of the flames. A trickle of cold sweat made its way down the back of her neck and collar. She found the head cook, and after a little small talk to soften him up, she launched into her enquiry. 'I believe Imbert was selling salt, and I wondered if you might know anything about that? I don't intend to get anyone in trouble over it. I am just trying to find out what Imbert was doing in the days before he died. To preserve his memory for myself.'

It wasn't a very good story and the cook immediately saw through it. 'To save your friend Anna, you mean. A damaged woman like that has no business at court. She should have gone for a nun.' He picked up a spoon and stirred the contents of the pot. Beatriz noted he was right-handed, like the majority of people.

'If you know something, I beg you to tell me.'

He pursed his lips, considering her, and relented. 'Imbert did sell me a bag of salt. It helped us keep within budget to have his price without the tax. It's stacked in the pantry now. It was unusual for him to be dabbling in trading food stuff. I remember being surprised. He had never come to me before with anything. He seemed more interested in asking me if anyone else had ever sold me salt on the sly – a substantial amount of it.'

'And had they?'

The cook looked at the stone flags of the kitchen. 'That's for me to know. Be off with you out of my kitchen, *jograresa*.'

Beatriz moved from the kitchen back into the courtyard and leant against the wall, watching the goings on of travellers and stableboys. Was Imbert dealing in stolen salt to cover his gambling debts, perhaps? All salt sales were supposed to go through Petrus Regimundus, who would tax each bag for the count. It was a big risk to take. If Count Raimon or Petrus had discovered the theft, Imbert would have been severely punished. A boy in the courtyard stumbled and spilt his basketful of newly baked bread rolls onto the ground. Squawking chickens and dogs rushed to take advantage of the spill, while the boy waved them off and collected up what he could. Why would someone murder Imbert because he was illegally selling a bit of salt? But if he had discovered who had been filching a large amount of salt from the count, that would be reason enough.

Beatriz knew Mafalda was housed in a guest room on the floor above the kitchen. She decided to go and ask her about her correspondence with Duke Guillaume. She returned inside and made her way to the second floor of the tower. Outside the door, she tapped, but there was no response. The bells were tolling for Terce. Mafalda must have gone to church. She tapped one more time to be sure. The door latch was faulty and her tap caused the door to creak ajar. The temptation was too much for Beatriz. She looked up and down the passage to ensure nobody was watching and quickly slipped into Mafalda's room.

There was even less in this chamber than there had been in Imbert's. No table and chair, no paintings on the wall, no clothes hanging on a hook. If Mafalda had gone to the cathedral or Saint-Sernin, she probably had her cloak and prayer book with her. Beatriz lifted the pillow on the bed. Nothing. She felt up into the chimney for any hiding place. Surely Mafalda kept writing materials somewhere, to allow her to correspond with Duke Guillaume, for instance. There were no other obvious hiding places.

She returned to the bed and lifted the mattress. 'Hello!' she said and gripped the edge of a grey sack laid out there between the two straw pallets. She set it on the bed and sat beside it. If Mafalda had just left, she would be away for at least an hour. The sack had a drawstring neck. She opened it and pulled out the contents. A couple of small books, parchments, writing materials, an exquisite ivory comb, a ring with a green gem and … 'What?' Beatriz exclaimed. A wild splash of intense red spilled and slid into Beatriz's hands.

She gathered up the material and held it up to assess its shape. That red silken dress! The same lacing up the back. The woman in the tower house window had been Mafalda! This sack must contain the few precious things Mafalda had kept from her time as a great noblewoman. So, who had been the man with her doing the unlacing? Beatriz contemplated the dress in astonishment, repicturing the scene she had witnessed. Carefully, she folded the robe and put it back into the sack.

There was also a wooden binder, like the one Anna was keeping her hypotheses about the murder in. This one had blank sheets of parchment and copies of letters. The writing materials comprised a couple of quills and a small bottle of ink. She couldn't read the letters, and none of them seemed to bear a signature akin to the 'aume' shape Philippa had shown her. At the back of the binder, beneath the parchments, Beatriz found a long plait of thick, silky red hair tied together at the shorn top with a crimson ribbon. She lifted it out and held it in her hands carefully for a moment, thinking about Mafalda. These things gave no answers, only more mystery. Carefully, she packed everything back into the sack and returned them to their hiding place.

She slipped from the room and latched the door. She made her way along the walkway above the gate to the east tower and Philippa's rooms, where she was expected for their daily meeting to update each other on what they had discovered.

'We've increased and decreased the list of suspects,' said Philippa, waving a parchment sheet at Beatriz.

'Tell me.'

'So it now reads:

List of Suspects:

Raimon – right-handed

Bertrand – right-handed

Roger – we don't know yet

Mafalda – right-handed

Petrus – no, left-handed

Lluis – right-handed

Gauzlin – right-handed

Julia – right-handed.'

'A bag of salt,' said Philippa when Beatriz reported her findings in the kitchen. 'So, he met someone in Aigues-Mortes?'

Anna was busy with her parchments, updating her lists and scenarios, adding more questions for them to investigate.

'Perhaps. Jacques the *vectuari* might know more about Imbert and the salt. There's something else.' Beatriz felt hesitant to expose Mafalda's secrets.

'I went looking for Mafalda, but she was out of her room, at prayers. Her door was ajar, so I went in.' She hesitated again.

'Yes?' Philippa pressed.

'I found a hidden bag with some letters but I couldn't read them and some other items that were clearly dear to Mafalda.'

'I should try to talk further with her,' Philippa decided. 'What were the other items?'

'A plait of her own shorn hair. I found that rather sad. And you remember, I told you about the woman I saw in the tower house in the red dress?'

'With the lacings up the back,' said Anna.

Beatriz nodded. 'Well I found that dress in the bag.'

Anna and Philippa expressed astonishment. 'You think Mafalda was the woman in the dress, with the man?' Anna asked.

'It must be,' Beatriz said.

'Then who was the man with her?' Philippa wondered.

'I thought he was a cleric from his dark clothing, but I don't know. He wasn't a small man.'

Anna made a few more notes in her dossier.

After a pause, Philippa spoke again, 'We should think more about how Imbert was murdered. Imbert was a hefty man, not young, but still strong. It would have been a tremendous struggle to strangle him.'

'If he were conscious,' Beatriz responded. 'As your uncle suggested, if he had been overpowered first with a drug in his drink, strangling him would not have been so difficult. Or perhaps he was stabbed in the neck first to make him easier to manage. No one could have moved his huge body. He was murdered in the undercroft. If anyone saw him go down there with someone else, that would give us a real clue.'

'We could try to establish where people were at the time of the murder. Eliminate all the suspects until we just have one but there were dozens of people here – a hundred even!' Philippa looked despondent.

Beatriz helped Anna pack a few clothes and books to take with her to the viscount's house. 'Don't worry, Anna. Ademar is a kind, fair man. He and his wife will take care of you.' But Beatriz knew it would be stressful for Anna to be away from her routines and everything familiar.

Roger knocked on the door. 'I have to escort Anna now, lady.'

Anna rose and Philippa squeezed her hand. Beatriz kissed her on the forehead. 'Don't worry, we are on the trail. We have the scent.' She looked at Roger. He was wearing his sword on his left hip, indicating that he was right-handed.

17

CAMINOS

Friday 22 April, Saint-Sernin

*R*oger made carrying caskets and instruments down ladders look easy. He helped Beatriz bring her chest, instruments and other belongings down to Philippa's rooms. After spending the morning practising with Philippa and Anna as her audience, Beatriz announced she was going into the city to speak with Dean Gayrard. 'I think he may know more about the possible pilgrim route motive.'

'I would like to give you another commission,' Philippa said. 'I need money for your journey to Poitiers and I need to buy a gift for Duke Guillaume at the market tomorrow. I believe Dean Gayrard is on friendly terms with the Jewish moneylenders in the city?'

'Yes,' Beatriz said. 'I think so.'

'Ask him to recommend someone to you and arrange to send that person here.'

'Yes, lady.' Beatriz picked up her cloak. At the door, she glanced back. Anna was intent on Imbert's black book, trying to decipher the code. Philippa, quill in hand, was signing documents and writing letters. 'Thank you for your help, Roger,' she said as she passed him standing outside the door. He nodded in response.

Beatriz took the external stone staircase down into the courtyard, which was quiet this morning. Many of the Easter guests had already packed up and left. A maid was filling a water bucket at the spigot. A stableboy was picking a horse's hoofs. She stepped through the pedestrian door in the gateway and out into the city.

On her left, women were working on trestles close to the river's edge, washing fleeces. Barefoot, with their sleeves rolled up to their elbows and wearing bonnets to protect them from the spring sunshine, they splashed the fleeces across the trestles and in and out of large wooden buckets bound with iron hoops that stood alongside them. Beyond the washerwomen was the pier to the floating mills. Donkeys loaded with grain sacks moved along the pier towards the mills and, urged on by the miller's boys, they returned with flour sacks. Beatriz took the direct route to Saint-Sernin, up along Changes.

Approaching the basilica, she encountered Dean Gayrard inspecting the progress of the works. 'Ah, Beatriz! How are you today?'

'I am well, I thank you, Dean. I have a commission from Lady Philippa and would speak with you.'

'Of course, follow me.' They passed close to the tower

house where she had seen the woman in the red dress – where she had seen Mafalda.

'Dean Gayrard, do you know who owns this house?'

He paused to contemplate the tall house with its long windows. 'Why, yes. It belongs to the Bruniquel family.'

'Bruniquel. You mean the viscount?'

'Yes, and his brother, the vicar. It is not their main residence. I believe they allow Bishop Izarn to sometimes house his guests there.'

'Has the bishop had recent guests?'

'There were many here for the Easter Assembly who could not find sleeping space at Chateau Narbonnais. I don't know exactly who stayed there. Possibly Abbot Frotard or Abbot Hunard from Moissac.'

The house stared back at Beatriz, empty now, but the memory of what she had seen in the window was vivid in her mind and yet the man with Mafalda remained obscure. Turning away reluctantly from the house, she followed the dean into his office. When they were comfortably seated on either side of his large, cluttered desk, Beatriz undertook her task for Philippa.

'Yes, I can recommend Elyas,' the dean responded to her question. 'He is the father of the two boys you met here on your last visit.'

Beatriz nodded. The dean dipped his quill in the inkpot and scratched out an address on a slip of paper and handed it to her. Beatriz blushed. 'I can't quite read your writing, Dean.'

He frowned and took it back briefly, reading out, 'Elyas, 7 Rue Juzaygas near Carmes Square.'

Beatriz took the slip again, thanked him and moved

onto her second objective. 'Lady Philippa and I are working to exonerate Anna of Imbert's murder. We know she did not commit the crime.'

The dean regarded her gravely. He had a long, kindly face, with two lines graven on both cheeks. 'This is a very serious matter. I will help you if I can.' The dean's expression became pained. 'Imbert's death is a terrible thing. Such an evil act. Such a loss of a fine poet.'

'I am looking for information on who Imbert was with on that night, who he had business with, what he was about.'

The dean put the fingers of his hands to his chin and pondered. 'I left quite early. Imbert was still there, drinking with some others – Lluis, Petrus, the merchants. You were also there.'

Beatriz glanced away. 'Were any of your other stonemasons there?'

'Yes, I'm sure. They work hard and like free drink and food.' He listed them for her. 'I'm afraid I don't know anything else, child. I know nothing of Imbert's business.'

'I wondered if he might have involved himself in the …' she searched for a word that would not sound too irreligious to his ears, 'the differences of opinion concerning the pilgrim route between his holiness, Pope Urban, and the abbey of Cluny.'

The dean raised his eyebrows. He nodded his head up and down, no doubt searching for his own right words. He had been a victim and then a victor of those differences of opinion. 'Not that I am aware of. What do you know about the matter, Beatriz?'

'Not much,' she said, hoping he would feel he could enlighten her.

'As you say, there is a difference of opinion, over the spiritual highroad to Compostela and over the Iberian war against the infidels. Both Cluny and the pope are working for the glory of God, of course.' He hesitated.

'Of course,' Beatriz murmured.

'Castile has been making very large donations of gold to Cluny, and Cluny urges the knights of Occitania and the Iberian kingdoms to reconquest, to battle against the Saracens.'

Beatriz wondered if he would tell her anything she didn't already know.

'The pilgrim route will bring in significant offerings for the churches along the way. Cluny has instituted a very ambitious building programme, building the largest church in all Christendom. They hope to benefit from these offerings.'

'Aren't they rather off the route?' Beatriz asked.

'There are several roads to Compostela. One route, the *Via Podiensis* passes through Cluny, Le Puy, Conques, Cahors, Moissac. Cluny has designs on other routes too. Until recently, the papacy was in some disarray. Thirty years ago, Cluny acquired Saint Martial in Limoges on the *Via Lemovicensis*, and they have brought more and more places on the routes into their affiliation: Moissac, Saint-Gilles, then Saint Pierre des Cuisine and La Daurade in Tolosa. Ten years ago, Cluniacs from Moissac took over Saint-Sernin and sent myself and my colleagues into exile, but the papal legate excommunicated them over this presumption. Figeac Abbey, which controls Conques, was taken over by Cluny. The abbot of Conques appealed to the pope against that absorption and there has been protracted litigation. Pope Urban has ruled that Bishop Izarn, who supports the Cluniacs, must move out of Saint-Sernin, but Conques is still in contention. Abbot Frotard's abbey lies on the southern route to Compostela, passing through Saint-Gilles, Montpellier, Narbonne, Carcassona, Tolosa and Jaca in Aragon. While Pope Urban is, of course, supportive of everything Abbot Hugh desires for Cluny – he trained at Cluny himself, you know – he is concerned that everything is in good measure.'

Beatriz translated the dean's words for herself. The pope thinks Cluny is getting too big for its boots and is aiming to rein them in. Too much pilgrim silver was going to Cluny when it should be going to Rome. Imbert could have been working for that agenda in his spying. Her thoughts were interrupted.

'Like your scribe at the chateau, Gauzlin, in fact,' the dean was saying.

'Sorry,' said Beatriz, looking confused.

'Gauzlin also trained at Cluny. He was at Conques, not long ago, I understand. I think Imbert was there at the same time.'

Beatriz frowned. 'What were they both doing *there?*'

'I couldn't say.' The dean sat back in his chair and smiled at her pleasantly. 'Abbot Begon of Conques is a friend of mine and he mentioned in a letter that he had received two visitors in one week from Tolosa and how different they were in character.'

Beatriz nodded. Yes, pious, skinny little Gauzlin would certainly present a contrast with huge, gregarious, worldly, loud Imbert. Beatriz felt a wash of emotion, experiencing the finality of Imbert's absence again, but she tried to concentrate on the dean's words. What lay beneath them, just beyond her understanding?

'Sainte-Foy at Conques is also in dispute,' the dean said. 'Cluny tried to,' he coughed, 'appropriate it, but Pope Urban supported their independence. I must return to my work now, Mistress Beatriz. But I do wish you success in exonerating Anna. I cannot believe evil of that dear child. You or she will let me know if I can help you further.'

Beatriz thanked him and made her way back through the city towards the Jewish quarter.

'Hey! *Trobairitz!*' The *vectuari* Jacques was sitting outside the tavern near the Daurade. It was not a reputable place for her to stop, but she had to brave it for Anna's sake.

'Master *vectuari*,' she said in a low voice, not wanting to call attention to herself from anyone else inside or outside the tavern. He was sitting at a table alone, a large horn of ale in front of him. She sat down.

He looked momentarily surprised that she had actually joined him, but then, perhaps, he recalled the reputation Beatriz was earning for herself after the exposure of her night with Lluis. No doubt plenty of servants had overheard the scene with Raimon and the viscount in the Great Hall and had spread the news of her indiscretion far and wide. 'A mug of ale over here,' Jacques gestured to the serving woman, who set a horn in front of Beatriz, which was almost too large for her hands to encompass.

She took a sip to show willing and tried not to screw

her nose up at the strong brew. 'I would like to ask you some questions, *vectuari*.'

'Ask away!' He was drunk, but not too drunk.

'I think you told me you are conveying salt, Master Jacques.'

'That's right. White gold and tasty too.' He pantomimed licking salt from his fingertips and looked her up and down, a salacious expression on his face. Jacques' face had the reddened, patchy skin that came from hours on board ship or on the road.

'I am in mourning for my master, Imbert,' she said tartly.

'Ah yes.' He rearranged his features. 'Poor man.' He barely took a breath before adding, 'and if you're looking for a new berth, an entertainer is always welcome in my caravan.'

'That's kind, but no,' she said. 'I am in the protection of Lady Philippa of Tolosa.' She ventured a guess: 'Imbert was with you last week...'

'Yes.' Jacques looked disappointed as he took a long swig of ale.

Beatriz waited for him to set down the beaker, containing her excitement. She matched his casualness. 'You saw him …?'

'We travelled together from Aigues-Mortes back to Tolosa. It wouldn't be wise to travel that road alone and unguarded. I liked the man and welcomed him in the caravan. He was good company.'

'Yes,' Beatriz said. 'He was.'

'And he kept me in ale for a few nights to pay his way and keep his business quiet.' He tapped the side of his nose. 'What the lord doesn't know can't hurt him eh? Lord Raimon's hardly in beggary, that's for sure.'

'Do you know who Imbert met with in Aigues-Mortes or what his business was?'

Jacques shrugged. 'No clue.' He was looking for the serving woman again. 'I just met him at the tavern when he was looking for company on the road.' Beatriz detected that Jacques' former openness had evaporated and now his comments were guarded.

'Does it happen a lot?' she asked. 'Evading the count's tax on the salt.'

Jean looked around shiftily, as if Petrus' tax officers might be in the neighbourhood. 'Of course not. Now, don't go blabbing on me, girl, or you will regret it.'

'You have nothing to worry about from me.' Best to get out of there before Jacques drank too much or anyone else decided to opportune her.

She took her leave and continued towards the Jewish quarter. She turned into Rue Juzaygas and knocked on Elyas' door. It was opened by the young boy who had skinned his knee at Saint-Sernin and who recognised Beatriz. He smiled broadly and led her into a pleasant interior courtyard. 'Please sit,' he said. 'I will fetch my father.'

Elyas and his wife welcomed Beatriz and offered her a glass of aromatic tea, which helped rebalance her after the strong beer. She explained the errand that Lady Philippa had sent her on. 'My lady can offer two vineyards as surety. She asks that you attend her today to make arrangements.'

'I can walk with you now to the chateau, Mistress Beatriz, if that suits you.'

She nodded.

'Give me a moment.' He left the room and when he returned, he had two stout young men with him and, no doubt, a bag of silver attached to his belt, under a long cloak. The group walked to the chateau and Beatriz informed the guards that her companions requested entry on business for Lady Philippa. They nodded them through.

The money exchange was briefly discussed and swiftly made. Philippa set her signature to a document Elyas wrote out when they had agreed the amount required and the surety for repayment. He counted out the money in silver and a few gold coins and handed it over to Philippa, and then Elyas and his companions departed.

'I found out quite a lot on this venture into the city,' Beatriz told Philippa and Anna. Anna readied her dossier and writing materials. 'Dean Gayrard told me that Imbert and Gauzlin were in Conques recently. Jacques Sau reported that Imbert travelled back with him from Aigues-Mortes last week with the salt train.'

'Beatriz you are taking risks, going alone to taverns and in the city.'

'I can look after myself. I had to do so often enough before Imbert found me.'

'Very well. So what do we have?' Philippa asked.

Beatriz marked off the points on her fingers, and Anna checked the documents in front of her. 'The murderer might have cuts on their fingers or a pair of gloves with such marks. He was strong and right-handed. Imbert was seen arguing with Bertrand, Gauzlin and Petrus. He was spying on Raimon and Bertrand, perhaps for Duke Guillaume. He was at Aigues-Mortes stealing a bag of salt. He was at Conques the same week as Gauzlin. Both Conques and Saint-Sernin are caught up in the dispute between the pope and Cluny. Gauzlin trained at Cluny. Anything else?' When Anna and Philippa shook their heads, Beatriz added, 'It's slight, but Mafalda may be involved somehow. And Roger. Perhaps Lluis.'

They looked at each other dejected. It still amounted to saying it could have been almost anyone.

18

TRUST

Saturday 23 April, Rue Saint Rome, Tolosa

*I*t was market day in Rue Saint Rome, and Anna accompanied Beatriz and Philippa to continue their enquiries in the city. Anna put on her grey cloak and hooked her arm through the handle of a wicker basket. Roger escorted them, carrying an empty sack slung over his shoulder for larger purchases. They walked part of the way towards the market alongside the river, towards La Daurade Abbey, hoping to avoid the crowds.

Anna observed the square with the livestock market on their right. It was smelly in the extreme. Cockerels battered furiously in wooden crates. Penned goats and sheep opened and closed their mouths, and cows and oxen dropped steaming dung. Donkeys shifted from hoof to hoof. The anxiety of the murder accusation against her was constantly in Anna's head. Beatriz got too close to a sheep pen and had to retrieve the hem of her cloak from a curious black-faced sheep who was trying to pull it into its mouth. 'Give me that back!' She slapped Roger's beefy arm as he laughed at her encounter. 'It's my best cloak,' she said crossly. Anna smiled too, distracted briefly from her worry.

The crowds were unavoidable at the bridge. Each of the twelve portals of Tolosa had long queues of carts, groups on horseback and foot traffic. Vicar Regimundus' men inspected everything and everyone coming into the city, levying taxes. Another queue stretched back across the bridge, which Anna hoped could bear all that weight. Must everything she looked at be bathed in the miasma of anxiety and distress?

Loaded carts pulled by oxen and trains of donkeys burdened with long baskets passed by. Beyond the bridge was the flotilla of mills, buoyant on the river. Petrus Regimundus' bailiffs exacted tolls from the entrants based on calculations that were a mixture of the carters' statements, searches of the carts, and the bailiffs' visual evaluations. Where carters were caught out in lies, fines were added to their tolls. Others argued with the bailiffs' assessments. Anna could see an argument taking place between one young man and the armed men at the toll-gate at the bridge end. It was evident from their distorted faces and gesticulating arms that they were shouting at one another. 'What is it?' she asked Beatriz.

'The guards are claiming he and his companions are Saracens,' Beatriz said. Beatriz had the natural gift for the language of action, and Anna rarely had any difficulty in understanding her, even here, where there were so many distractions and jostlings. Beatriz spoke clearly, but she also spoke with the movements of her hands, eyes, eyebrows and her whole body.

The young man and his companion looked more like Jews than Saracens to Anna, but Saracens had to pay three *sous* each to enter and no doubt the bailiffs were keen to keep their caskets as full as possible for the sake of their own cut at the end of the day.

Anna spotted Lluis near the tax station, craning his neck to see past a cartload of livestock to someone in the queue behind.

'What are you looking out for, Lluis?' Anna asked, touching his arm.

He turned to them, surprised and smiling. He bowed to Philippa. His exchange of greetings with Beatriz was strained since she made an obvious show of being cool towards him. 'I have a cartload of marble coming in from Comminges, bound for the Saint-Sernin workshop. Not the best day for its arrival.' He grimaced. 'I can see the stone carter behind this one.' He gestured. 'He will be at the tax table next, and I have to pay his way.' He tapped the purse at his hip. 'I will be working on that marble,' he told Philippa eagerly. 'You remember my bird drawings?' he asked Beatriz, who nodded curtly.

Beatriz had told Anna about the sketch of a long row of birds in pairs, facing each other, surrounded by vine foliage. Anna would have liked to visit the workshop and see Lluis' work but, she could see Beatriz's deliberate coldness towards Lluis. Beatriz would not welcome a request to engage overmuch with him.

'Where will this marvellous bird-carved marble go in Saint-Sernin?' Philippa asked, smiling, to compensate for Beatriz's feigned disinterest.

'It's for an altar table,' Lluis said. 'Bernard Gelduinus will carve the main part, but he has given me the strip of birds to do on one side.' He raised his eyebrows happily. 'It will be my debut solo work on a very significant piece.'

'Good luck,' Philippa told him, pulling gently at Anna's arm to indicate they must move on.

'Keep off the wine for a steady hand with your chisel on that expensive marble, heh?' Roger said, making sure to position himself so that Anna could see his mouth. Anna smiled up at Roger, knitting her brows a little. That was a very long speech for him. Lluis had turned to Roger to respond. Anna noticed that Beatriz was looking down at the back of Lluis' belt, where his work gloves were looped. Anna held her breath as Beatriz surreptitiously reached for the gloves, tugging them gently, hoping to remove them without his notice, but he must have felt the movement.

'Beatriz?' Lluis twisted around, looking at her hand on the gloves in surprise.

The gloves came free and Beatriz ignored him while she inspected the insides of the fingers. Anna looked over her shoulder. There were no marks from the garrotte. Beatriz swallowed. 'Sorry, she said,' handing the gloves back to a puzzled-looking Lluis. Beatriz set off swiftly before Lluis could say anything further, and Philippa and Anna hurried to catch up with her.

They moved on towards a pungent spice stall displaying wares in small sacks, open at the neck to reveal their colourful contents. Pepper, cloves, cinnamon, ginger, nutmeg, cassia, aniseed, cumin, camphor, liquorice and galingale root were all on offer, tempting the buyers. 'Buy a small amount of nutmeg,' Philippa instructed Anna.

Anna loved the scents of the spice stall. 'God be with you,' she said, leaning in to haggle with the vendor. Servants, burghers, knights pushed around them, craning to see the best deals or pinching their noses and curling their lips at the worst. Roger was armed to the teeth, and no one could be in any doubt, looking at him, that he was well able to use the sharpened weaponry bristling on the thick leather belt he wore. With his imposing height and breadth, the fearsome tattoos on his bulging biceps, his wild hair and berserker eyes, he had no difficulty in keeping a space clear around Lady Philippa and her two companions.

They moved on up the street with the crowd trudging slowly ahead of them. Anna was even more of an object of unkind curiosity today than usual. She was used to people pointing at her and seeing the words 'idiot, stupid, dumb' on their lips. But today, they also had the word 'murder' and even a tinge of fear on the faces of some. She pushed down the roil of her emotions to concentrate on her perceptions.

Moving past a luxury goods stall, she inhaled the scents of sandalwood, myrrh, incense and musk. Philippa paused at the dye stall. Roger was carrying Philippa's purse and it would be a brave soul who would try to rob him. The dyes were a vivid display conjuring images of new gowns – scarlet grains made from crushed insects, white chalk, blue woad, red madder and indigo. Piles of bracken for mordant were set out, their greens contrasting with the other vivid colours. 'Take a small bag of cochineal and another small bag of woad,' Philippa instructed Anna. 'I need to prepare gifts to take with me if I must go to Aragon and I can order the dyeing of lengths of wool.'

Anna became aware of startled movement next to her and saw Lluis again, who had caught up with them and was speaking urgently to Beatriz. 'Beatriz, what was that?'

'Nothing.'

'Tell me!' he insisted. 'Why the cold shoulder? I had hoped …'

Beatrix interrupted him before he could express his hopes. 'I am searching for a pair of gloves, and wanted to eliminate you from the search.'

'Gloves? Why?'

Beatriz looked to Philippa for help. 'We think whoever murdered Imbert will have a pair of gloves bearing the mark of the garrotte,' Philippa admitted, 'but …' She shrugged an apology.

Lluis took this in, his expression changing rapidly and ending with a look of disgust that he threw at Beatriz. 'You thought *I* had murdered Imbert?'

Anna watched the play of emotion on his face, experiencing it as if it were her own. Her heart beat with his distress.

'There is no need to discuss this further,' Beatriz asserted and pinched the cloth of Philippa's sleeve to urge her to move on and evade further conversation with Lluis.

They found themselves in front of a fish stall bearing large trout caught in the river, nestled in salt and casting a weary eye up at the customers. Other stalls displayed salted hams and pork shoulders. Vicar Regimundus sat under an awning outside the lord's salinum. A line of mules were labouring up the ramp, taking the salt directly into the first floor of the building where it was weighed and poured through small holes in the floor down to the ground floor, where it was ground and packed into sacks for sale. The *vicar*'s inspectors roamed the market ensuring appropriate taxes had been paid, no illegal measures and weights were being used, no cheating was occurring (or none that they hadn't been paid to turn a blind eye to at any rate). The stone walls of the covered market squares dotted here and there had basin-like holes gouged into them of various sizes that were the measures for grain and salt. The holes had chutes that were plugged for the measuring, then the plug was removed and the set amount slid down the chute into the customer's sack.

Sailors and foreigners queued at the money-changers' long table, which was set up with scales and coin-testing equipment. Anna watched the face of a town crier as he called out the regulations. One of the criers stood with his finger hooked in the belt of a weeping small boy who had become separated from his father. Anna saw the distress on the boy's face. The crier called out over and over. 'Lost boy! Name of Otto! Son of Otto, merchant from Mont-pellier!' Anna was almost as relieved as the two Ottos to see a man, evidently the father, rush up to the crier and retrieve his emotional son.

Groups of Garonne boatmen who had brought in goods by river early in the morning queued at another table to put their marks to the oath that they would not damage the port and would keep it clean. They had to complete this assurance before they were allowed to make their way to the city taverns after the thirsty work of unloading. A cauldron of potage hung on chains above a fire in a stonepit outside one tavern and a maid was ladling out bowlfuls to the hungry boatmen and shoppers. Petrus Regimundus' bailiffs were evident at the taverns too, to discourage any overly drunken behaviour.

Philippa paused at a stall of animal pelts. Anna caressed the wolf, fox, rabbit and marten pelts. She glanced at Philippa, who said, 'We'll need some fur to line our hoods if we have to go into the mountains.' She pointed at the marten pelts, indicating how many she would take. She indicated a wolf pelt. 'How much? Alright, I will take that too.'

After some debating, all three girls agreed that a very handsome covering for a war horse, worked in scarlet and gold, would be a fitting gift to send to Duke Guillaume. 'It is fine work,' Anna said, fingering the material and running her thumb over the stitching.

Roger squashed the purchases into his sack and slung it back over his shoulder. At a textile stall, Philippa bought cloth, thread and needles for Anna. At another stall, she bought parchment, ink and styluses. Roger was loaded now, and they made their way back towards the chateau.

. . .

THE GIRLS WERE DISCUSSING the events of the morning in Philippa's room and the encounter with Lluis, when Roger entered and they clammed up.

'May I sit, lady?'

Philippa and Beatriz looked at Roger in astonishment because he was speaking and asking to sit, but Anna smiled a welcome.

'Of course, Roger.' Philippa was gracious.

'I fear you distrust me, lady.' When Philippa didn't respond, he was forced to continue. 'I am loyal to you.'

'Am I to take your word for it?'

'You think I killed Imbert. I could have, of course.' He stretched out his huge hand and flexed his fingers. 'But I didn't. I was with Lady Mafalda at the time. She will vouch for me if that is necessary.' Anna frowned. With Mafalda. What did he mean?

Anna read the look of shock on Philippa's face. 'At midnight, you were with …'

'Thank you, Roger. You may go now,' Beatriz interrupted.

Roger stood and left the room.

'Beatriz! It is not your place to be dismissing people here. It is my …' Philippa was furious.

'Sorry. I know, but we need to focus on what he told us. We need to know if we can trust Roger. This is for Anna's sake.' Beatriz held Philippa's glare.

'But Beatriz, what could Roger have been doing with Mafalda at that time of night? It is shocking.'

'Perhaps. Perhaps not. You need to talk with her, Philippa. She will not talk to me. I am beneath her notice. But you need to focus on what you are trying to find out.

Not whether she was committing an indiscretion, but whether she can prove that Roger is not the murderer. For Anna's sake. You must focus on that.'

Philippa considered for a moment. 'I understand. I will summon her here. You will listen concealed in Anna's room.'

'What about me?' Anna asked.

'You will stay with me and watch her responses,' Philippa said. 'She will assume you do not understand anything.'

'No doubt,' Anna said, crossly. She had had enough experience of that for one day at the market.

When Mafalda arrived, Philippa offered her a beaker of wine. She waved Roger out of the room and Anna noted that Mafalda avoided looking at him.

'Mafalda, I need to ask you something delicate.'

She raised her eyebrows.

'On the night that Imbert was murdered … were you up late that night?'

'I can't remember.'

'It's important. We are trying to ascertain everyone's whereabouts at the time of the murder to find the real murderer.'

Mafalda looked at Anna and then regarded her hands clenched in her lap.

'Anna cannot hear you,' Philippa said, squeezing Anna's hand under their skirts by way of apology.

'I was in the hall dining with everyone else that evening.'

'And later?'

'I retired to my room, of course.'

'It is … did you speak with anyone late that night?'

'Probably. No doubt.'

'It will help me if you would tell me who.'

'I spoke with Roger.' She was hesitant now.

Anna held her breath.

'He was my servant, you know. Originally. Before he became yours.'

'I know. I believe he is most loyal to you still.'

'As he is to you. You can trust him. It is I, you know, who has commanded him to always test your wine and food for poison.'

'Well, I thank you for that. Where did you speak with Roger?' Philippa persisted.

'He … he came to my room. We … spoke.' Mafalda's expression became impatient. 'Very well. You press me and I can see he has already told you. He said he might, if you did not trust him. He spent the night with me.'

Philippa took a deep breath.

'Do not judge me. I am yet a young woman. I know I can trust him. Can I trust you?'

'Of course. I will not betray you.'

'You cannot use this information. You cannot tell anyone. I would suffer greatly if it was known.'

'I will not. I swear to you, Mafalda. I simply need to know if I can trust Roger.'

'You can.' Mafalda took a deep breath. 'I was glad to tryst with a man under the nose of my former husband, you see … And God knows, I needed it!'

Anna watched the frown forming on Philippa's face and hoped she would not antagonise Mafalda with her disapproval.

'I thank you for your candour,' Philippa said coldly and rising.

Mafalda was momentarily surprised that Philippa was dismissing her, but she regained her composure and rose with dignity in her turn. 'You do not understand yet, Philippa,' she said, looking earnestly at the other woman. 'You have not felt a man's touch. You do not know what it is to long for it, to be forbidden it for the rest of your life.'

Philippa kept her head bowed and said nothing. Anna was afraid that Philippa's disapproval would be their undoing. The more Mafalda was allowed to speak, the better for them.

'Of course, I am not speaking of my former husband. I could not ever take pleasure there.' She pursed her mouth as if she had taken a bite of something disgusting. 'But I was faithful to him, nevertheless, until he decided to repudiate me, condemn me to this living death, and then, just before I was forced to the convent, I decided to lay with Roger, because I could command him to it and I knew he liked me, would do my bidding. Once I had had that one taste, I longed for more – and take it at every opportunity.'

'Have there been others?' Philippa asked. From her expression, Anna imagined there would be suppressed disapproval in Philippa's tone and that Mafalda would sense it.

Mafalda lifted her chin proudly. 'I wish it were so,' she announced brazenly, 'but I cannot trust anyone else to hold their tongue, as I can trust Roger.'

When Mafalda had left the room, Beatriz emerged from her hiding place. 'We were right to suspect Mafalda of some subterfuge then, but it wasn't the type we were looking for,' she said. 'Our investigation is likely to uncover many secrets that are not necessarily pertinent to Imbert's murder. If Mafalda and Roger are speaking the truth about being together, they are both exonerated of Imbert's murder.'

19

BERTRAND'S WEDDING

Saturday 30 April 1093, Tolosa

*P*hilippa's hand was looped through Henry's elbow. With her other hand, she raised up the gathered hem of her dark green dress, keeping it clear of the muck flowing in the central runnel of the street. Beatriz stepped carefully in Philippa's wake, protecting her blue boots. Roger brought up the rear of their small group as they made their way to Saint Etienne Cathedral for the blessing of Bertrand and Helie's marriage. Anna had chosen to remain behind in Philippa's chambers, saying she found it too heavy a burden to bear the eyes of the townspeople upon her with the murder accusation.

In the cathedral square, Beatriz's glance travelled over the assembled people: Count Raimon accompanied Bertrand, who preened and paced in his best dark blue tunic. Vicar Regimundus was in conversation with his brother, Viscount Ademar, standing close to the banquet tables set on one side of the square for the noble guests. Trestles on the other side of the square offered Raimon's munificence to the townspeople. Jugs of wine, soup tureens and fresh loaves waited expectantly. On that side of the square, Lluis and Dean Gayrard stood at the front of a crowd of masons and clerics. Beatriz rapidly shifted her gaze away from Lluis.

After a short while, the bride's group entered the square with Helie closely herded in the midst of her ladies. As the girls approached Bertrand, Helie was pushed free of her companions to stand alone. Her red brocade gown glinted with gold thread. Her childish neck was so loaded with gold necklaces, she looked like she was playing at dress up. A circlet of large yellow flowers crowned her sandy hair. Bertrand took her hand. 'Excuse me,' Henry smiled to Philippa. 'I must do my duty.' He stepped to Helie's side.

Raimon nodded to his son. 'I, Bertrand of Saint-Gilles, consent to take you, Helie of Burgundy, as my wife,' Bertrand declared loudly, sliding a gold ring onto Helie's finger.

The girl was nervous, and Beatriz wondered if she would missay the words. Helie spoke in a small voice that the crowd strained to hear. 'I, Helie of Burgundy, consent to take you, Bertrand of Saint-Gilles, as my husband.' She pushed the ring onto Bertrand's finger, and Beatriz could see the shake of her small hands. Such a swift ceremony and such a weight of matters that could go horribly wrong in the rest of her life, thought Beatriz.

Raimon and Henry broke into smiles and both clapped

Bertrand about the shoulders. Henry lifted Helie's hand to his lips and kissed the back of her fingers. The red of his mouth was sensuous amid his soft, brown beard. Bishop Izarn and Abbot Frotard approached to intone their blessings for the pair. Others in the crowd ran forward with wheat grains to throw at the cowering couple.

Henry escorted Philippa and Beatriz to a place at the trestle, and Roger took up his accustomed position behind Philippa's chair. Henry served soup and wine to Philippa and offered her a hunk of bread. Philippa's answers to Henry's attempts at conversation were mono-syllabic. Beatriz knew the lady was out of sorts because Bertrand's marriage pushed further forward her own unwanted betrothal and her disinheritance. She leant close to nudge Philippa and murmur, 'Lord Henry is trying to converse with you, lady.'

Philippa scowled, but relented. 'Henry, will you tell me something of the court of your brother, the duke of Burgundy?' she asked.

'My apologies, lady,' Henry responded. 'I can tell you very little of Burgundy as I have been a stranger there since I was seven years old. I was sent to train as a boy at the court of King Alfonso in Leon-Castile. My aunt Constance is his queen.'

'Ah yes. Well, tell me about that court instead,' Philippa said.

'It would appear very strange to you at first sight, I think.' He poured wine for Philippa and took a sip from his own beaker. 'It is hotter there, dryer. The landscape is more brown than green but still the mountains and waterfalls are very beautiful. Alfonso's court has one foot in Christian Iberia and another in a more, what would seem to you I venture to presume, exotic mix of Moor, Jew, Visigoth. I think you would find it very interesting. Alfonso spent some years in exile at the Moorish court of Al-Mamun in Toledo and has replicated some of what he enjoyed there – small pools, fountains, frogs croaking and hopping on waterlilies, colourful birds trilling.'

Philippa's green eyes glinted now with real interest. 'It sounds delightful.'

Henry smiled back. 'Yes. I am looking forward to returning.'

'You are going back there from here?'

'I am, lady. In fact, I will be travelling with you, if you will allow it that is.'

'Of course. It will be a pleasure to travel in your company. If I *should* travel in that direction,' Philippa added, returning to her former morose mood.

'Another thing you would enjoy about Alfonso's court, I am guessing, lady,' Henry persisted valiantly despite her clouded expression, 'is the learning. He values Moorish philosophers. Artists and poets too.' He leant forward to look around Philippa at Beatriz. 'You would be highly praised there, Beatriz.'

Beatriz sat up at her inclusion in the conversation. 'You think so?'

'I know so. There is a long tradition of Arabic female poets. It could be useful for your composition to meet such ladies, I believe. And I am sure the king and queen would delight in your singing and playing.'

'Then we should visit,' said Philippa. 'What about the king's family?'

'His daughter Urraca is his heir, just as you are heir here,' he ventured and glanced briefly in Raimon's direction. He allowed a pause for his statement to gain emphasis in the silence. 'Urraca is married to my cousin, Raimon of Burgundy. She is still young, only thirteen, like Helie, but she has a strong mind and spirit and will be a great queen one day. A woman who has the right to rule can be an excellent leader for her people, I believe.'

BEATRIZ AND PHILIPPA strolled back towards the chateau, with Roger a few paces behind them. 'Henry was flirting with you,' Beatriz stated.

'He was making conversation.'

'He referred to your inheritance.'

'I noticed that, but he does not have the means to confront Raimon.'

'I would not exclude him,' Beatriz said. 'He seems a resourceful man. He is a youngest son in need of a kingdom and you are a good prospect. He must be thinking about it and how he could effect it. And I think he likes you, truly.'

Philippa smiled tightly. 'That would be convenient then, for his ambitions.'

'Don't you like him?'

'Surely. What I know of him, which is very little.'

They entered the deserted chateau courtyard. Everyone was still feasting at the wedding. 'I must use the privy,' Beatriz said. 'I will rejoin you momentarily.'

On her way back to the exterior stone staircase leading up to Philippa's chambers, Beatriz passed close to the stinking midden heap. She hesitated. A triangle of greyish textile was cheek-by-jowl with vegetable peelings and eggshells. She glanced around. There was no one in sight in this dank, dark corner. Just a large piebald pink and black pig snuffling at the other side of the heap. She leant down and tugged on the triangle, which became the fingertip of a glove. Beatriz was satisfied to find herself pulling a stained grey gauntlet free of the mess. Gingerly, she pushed aside the muck one way and then the other with the toe of her boot, but she could not find the companion glove. Perhaps the hairy pig had eaten it. She held the glove beneath her cloak, so that no one would see it, and moved quickly up the steps towards Philippa's chamber.

Beatriz entered Philippa's room in excitement. 'I found this gauntlet in the midden!' she announced, brandishing it.

Philippa and Anna screwed up their noses at the stink and appearance of the glove.

'And I have begun to decipher the book!' Anna declared.

'One thing at a time,' instructed Philippa. She pointed to the table and Beatriz set the grimy glove alongside a black-ribboned scroll and Imbert's black book. The three girls contemplated the glove with interest. 'First, what is your progress with the songbook?' Philippa asked Anna.

'It is a code. The songs are codes.' Anna opened the book and pointed out her findings. 'This song has the name G-U-I-L-L-A-U-M-E as an acrostic.'

'Anna!' Philippa clapped her hands together.

'What's an acrostic?' asked Beatriz.

'The first letter of each of the lines,' she ran her finger vertically down the beginnings of the lines, 'spells out a name.'

'Clever Imbert! That is like him.' Beatriz's excited expression fell as she experienced again the wash of his utter absence.

'This one,' Anna said, turning the pages, 'has the name U-R-B-A-N. And this one,' she turned more pages, 'says R-A-I-M-O-N.'

'Brilliant!' Beatriz said. 'So these are Imbert's customers. The people he was supplying information to. I told you Pope Urban was involved,' she declared jubilantly. 'Do the songs also contain the information he was passing on?'

'Probably. The RAIMON song, for example, is all about salt. But I haven't been able to decipher more as yet.'

They exchanged satisfied smiles. 'This is some progress, Anna,' Philippa stated. 'And the gauntlet, Beatriz?'

'See here,' Beatriz turned over the glove. 'There are deep cuts on the inside of the fingers at the bend of the knuckles from the garrotte. Note the large size. We were right, the murderer was a large, strong man.' Philippa and Beatriz looked in the direction of the door, knowing Roger was standing on the other side.

'We know Roger is not the murderer,' Anna stated so loudly that Philippa felt she had to sshh her.

'The glove was discarded not long ago in the midden, which suggests the murderer is still here, is part of our usual household,' Beatriz said. 'Bertrand has a pair of grey gloves, I know. I saw him wearing them at your brother's funeral. We know Petrus and Roger have the strength to garrotte Imbert. However, Petrus is left-handed, and we know the murderer was right-handed. Roger appears to have been excluded on Mafalda's say so. I suppose it could just have been one of the men of the garrison, acting on orders from ... Raimon, Bertrand, someone.' She fizzled out, feeling a loss of momentum.

'Have you apologised to Lluis yet, Beatriz?' Philippa asked.

'Apologised for what?' Beatriz said stubbornly.

Philippa and Anna exchanged a look. 'You should,' Philippa told her. 'When you are wrong, you should admit it.'

Beatriz did not respond to the reprimand and ploughed on with her summary impatiently. 'The evidence so far seems to implicate Roger.'

'Roger is not the murderer,' Anna stated, again, speaking much too loud.

'We must deal with evidence, not belief,' Beatriz said. 'The most likely motive seems to be something to do with the salt thefts.'

'I don't see Roger involved in *that*.' Anna was adamant.

'Don't forget the letter from Guillaume of Aquitaine,' Philippa added. 'You need to go to Poitiers, to Guillaume's court.'

'But I also need to go to Aigues-Mortes, to the salt-works. They are in opposite directions.' Beatriz sighed.

Anna set about unrolling the black-ribboned scroll on the table and weighting its four corners with stones. Beatriz leant forward with interest to study the beautifully drawn and coloured map, which showed rivers, the Roman roads and the pilgrim routes.

'I got it from the chateau archive while you were at the wedding,' Anna said.

'You need an escort for your journey, Beatriz,' Philippa told her. 'I am loath to entrust you to Roger when we are unsure of him. I was thinking perhaps of Lluis.'

'We are unsure of Lluis, too,' Beatriz said. 'I will not travel with Lluis.'

'Do you think it was Roger you saw with Mafalda in the red dress?'

'It must have been, and yet I'm not sure. I'm surprised I didn't know Roger even from the back, if it was him. The man was big, but not *that* big … perhaps the floor sloped, distorting my impression of his height.'

'You are wrong about Lluis, Beatriz,' Anna said, speaking loudly again, 'and you are wrong about Roger.'

Philippa touched her arm and said gently. 'Where is this certainty coming from, Anna? And your voice is too loud.'

Anna frowned, irritated at the reprimand, and was silent for a moment. It seemed she was debating with herself what she wanted to tell them. 'It is difficult to explain. You are living in a hearing world. A world that is different from the one I live in. You,' she turned to Philippa, 'often complain of Roger's silence, of his unwillingness to talk, or his brevity. But I understand it. There are other ways to engage with what is going on around you. Roger has been immensely kind to me on our walks to and from Ademar's house.'

'He speaks to you!' Beatriz was astonished.

'Not much. It's not what he says. He is kind to me.' Anna's mouth set stubbornly. 'It's not him. I know it.'

'Is there more, Anna?' Philippa persisted.

She shook her head. 'I just know it.'

'I want to trust Roger,' Philippa said. 'I want to send him with you, Beatriz.'

Beatriz frowned. It would be useful to have Roger with her, but only if they could be certain about him.

'Trust me on this, Beatriz.' Anna touched the back of her hand.

'Anna notices things, feels things we do not,' Philippa decided. 'Wrap the gauntlet in something to stop it contaminating everything else, and hide it and Imbert's book away in your dossier, Anna.' She stood and went to the door, where she asked Roger to join them inside the chamber. Beatriz frowned with puzzlement at the sight of Roger. There was something different about him. It came to her in a rush, and she stared with consternation at Anna. Roger's dark beard was twisted into two plaits, and his hair had been combed. Only Anna could have made such plaits and wrought such change. Anna smiled to herself, studying her hands in her lap.

'Roger, I am sending Beatriz on a journey, and I would like you to accompany her. You are to go to the court of Duke Guillaume of Aquitaine in Poiters.'

Roger's usual impassive expression shifted mildly to something that could be read as alarm. 'Anna?' he said.

'You know I will take good care of Anna while you are gone. The viscountess has invited me to stay with them for several weeks so that Anna does not need to go to and fro every day. Viscount Ademar will take care of us both in your absence.'

Anna nodded at Roger. He held her gaze and then gave one nod back in turn to Philippa. There was no certainty, yet Beatriz suddenly felt certain that Anna *was* right about Roger.

'It will be a long journey,' Beatriz warned him. 'I want to stop at Uzès on the way back from Poitiers. It's where Imbert is from,' she turned to explain to Philippa and Anna. 'I think he had a house there. Perhaps there is something useful to be found. And we will also go to Conques, and Aigues-Mortes – I know he was at both places recently. There are questions I need to pursue in all these places.'

Beatriz began to plot their journey on the map with her finger. She had moved along some of these routes and roads before with Imbert. 'We can take the river as far as Bordeaux,' Beatriz said, 'and then take the pilgrim road north to Poitiers.' Anna and Philippa watched the journey of Beatriz's finger on the parchment. 'I wish I could travel with you,' Philippa said. Philippa traced her finger on the map in the opposite direction – the road to the south, over the Pyrenees and on to Jaca and Sancho Ramírez. She screwed up her nose. 'I would rather go *your* road,' she said, reversing the direction of her finger on the map back towards Tolosa and on to Poitiers.

Philippa lifted her hand away and Beatriz resumed the finger journey from Tolosa. Roger nodded his agreement at Beatriz's suggestions or shook his head, tracing an alternative route. They agreed they would head first to Moissac on the river, then Agen, then Marmande, where they would continue on horseback. Beatriz looked at Roger's chunky fingers, each one at least twice the size of her own. Could they have so delicately unlaced the red dress? They matched the gauntlet, for sure.

'Roger,' Philippa instructed, 'ensure you are well armed and provisioned for the journey. I will write another letter to Duke Guillaume to introduce you, Beatriz. And I will give you silver for the expenses of your journey and the gift to give to the duke.'

'I will sew the silver into your undertunic,' Anna told her, smiling. 'I will miss you, Beatriz. Hurry back!' Her eyes filled with tears.

Roger took one more look at Anna and left to put together his arsenal and arrange their passage on a boat to Moissac. Beatriz wondered what she should take with her: a selection of instruments, some fine clothes that Philippa could lend her. Performing at the court of Duke Guillaume, who was renowned for his own poetry, would greatly aid her purpose of uncovering whatever it was Imbert had been up to.

A maid knocked, entered and curtseyed to Philippa. 'There's a man come from Viscount Ademar, lady. He says he's to escort you and Mistress Anna to his house. And there's a messenger here with an important letter.'

'Show the messenger in. Tell the viscount's man we will be ready shortly. Send him up to collect my baggage.' Anna stood to check the contents of Philippa's chest and fasten the straps around her dossier, which would go to the viscount's house with her.

'I will walk back with you into the city,' Beatriz said. 'I'm going to ask Dean Gayrard to give me a letter of introduction as well, a letter to the abbot of Sainte-Foy in Conques. It might help me find out why Imbert and Gauzlin were there. And will you ask the viscount something for me?'

Philippa nodded.

'Ask him if he has Imbert's satchel that was found in the undercroft with him and, if so, what the contents were. Have a look at them, if you can.'

'We will do that. How will you get back alone after dark? Should Roger …'

'No,' Beatriz interrupted. 'Don't worry. I can manage.' She remembered nights in Sort when she had not only been on her own in the dark, but had slept alone outside for weeks before Imbert came across her.

The messenger was at the door, and Philippa instructed him to hand over the letter and leave. Anna and Beatriz looked with curiosity at the packet in Philippa's hands. It was sealed with the red wax seal of her father, Count Guilhem. Philippa cut the seal with her knife and unfolded the parchment. Expressions flitted across her face as she read: surprise, sorrow, a frown.

Eventually, Beatriz could stand the suspense no longer. 'What does it say?'

'My father writes from Jerusalem and tells me something of that holy place. He says he is feeling better – healed there, and will join my mother in Jaca to meet me shortly. He asks me to be reconciled to the marriage to the king of Aragon. He argues it is the best course for my future. He says he knows nothing of the agreement that Frotard and my uncle showed me after my brother's burial!' She looked up at them, her eyes wide.

'The agreement is a forgery,' Anna stated.

'So it seems. But he advises, nevertheless, that resistance against my uncle would be unwise. My father says he is too strong and too favoured by the populace. My father still counsels me to the Aragon marriage.'

PART III

May–September 1093

2 0

THE RUNNING STAG IN HIS LAIR

May 1093, On the road and Poitiers

*T*he river barge made the transfer from the Garonne to the Tarn and the town of Moissac, and its abbey was soon in view on the left bank. Vineyards stretched as far as Beatriz could see on the right bank. They had made good time on this first part of the journey, but Michaelmas loomed large in her mind. Four months *seemed* ample time, but she knew the journeying would be slow and prayed it would be worthwhile, that she could discover something about Imbert and, therefore, about his murderer that would be incontrovertible proof and set Anna free and cleaned of the charge of murder.

Roger, so far, had been as Beatriz had expected – an entirely taciturn companion, but one who created a welcome wide berth around her and her belongings.

Beatriz felt loaded with things. Nervous at the thought of performing for Duke Guillaume, she had settled on two main instruments – the *vielle* and Imbert's *oud*, plus a tambourine and a flute – but even these few needed careful handling in the dampness of the river and open air. The three robes Philippa had loaned and Anna had adjusted were carefully wrapped in one casket, and the horse trapping gift for Duke Guillaume was in another. Then Roger had his bundled possessions, which consisted entirely of weaponry as far as Beatriz could ascertain, apart from the ivory comb that Anna had given him to redress his hair and beard when they arrived at the Poitiers court. Beatriz observed that he certainly wasn't using the comb at the moment. The more berserker he looked for the journey, the better.

Having spent that year a while back, living on the street, with nothing but the clothes she stood in (and those slowly eroding upon her), she was not used to being encumbered with all this baggage. Her motto had been that she shouldn't carry anything she couldn't run with. Imbert had 'refurbished' her, as he put it, and added a cloak and a *vielle* to her burden, but her possessions were still few. She had left her songs on their parchments and the drawing of her father in Anna's keeping. Roger and two of the chateau servants had handed their baggage onto the barge as Philippa and Anna stood on the rickety pier, taking a tearful leave of Beatriz. It was the intangible materials she carried that weighed heavier on her: relentless anxiety for Anna gnawed at her; fury for gone Imbert; sadness still for her abandoned father far away in the Pyrenees, his face receding in her dimming memories;

some unnameable, unknown knot of emotion concerning Lluis; and concern for Philippa and her fate and, in turn, Beatriz's own. A great deal was riding on this visit to Poitiers. If Duke Guillaume would marry Philippa, Beatriz would find herself living between the courts of Poitiers and Tolosa. If he would not, then Philippa and Beatriz would be travelling to Sancho Ramírez's court in Aragon.

It was a relief to step off the barge onto the bank at Moissac. Too much free time, inactive, watching river water swilling around them, had made her morose. They left their baggage on the barge under guard and walked up the main street towards the abbey to ask accommodation for the night. At the guesthouse of Saint Pierre Abbey, Beatriz showed a letter Philippa had scribed, stating Beatriz of Farrera and Roger of Scopello, the holders, were about the business of Lady Philippa of Tolosa and to give them gentle dealings.

Roger and Beatriz were housed separately in the men's and women's guest quarters. The abbey, like Saint-Sernin, had building work going on and the air was full of stone dust. It was expanding to an impressive size. Shadows of overhanging yew branches swayed on the emerald square of grass in the huge cloister. After taking refreshment in the refectory, Beatriz made her way to a welcome sleep, pausing to talk with the fat guesthouse master on the way. 'Do you know Brother Gauzlin, late of here?' she asked.

'I know him,' he responded, a clear note of unenthusiasm in his tone.

'I ask because he is at the Tolosa court where I am living.'

'So I heard.'

'I see him on a more or less daily basis.'

'Nice for you.'

'You didn't like him when he was here, then?'

'It's a long time ago.'

Beatriz waited, urging her tongue to be still. She had led him enough. Either he would say more or not.

'I'm not surprised to hear he is at the Tolosa court. He is ambitious.'

'His ambition, then, is poorly served,' Beatriz said, aiming to create her own thread of curiosity for him to pull on.

'How do you mean?'

'He is clerk to Count Bertrand, who is mostly at dice and drinking.'

The guesthouse master smirked without mirth. 'Gauzlin won't be enjoying that, no. He thought he would be the righteous prior of Saint-Sernin by now.'

'He did?'

'Aye, that's what he thought when he elbowed and clamoured his way into the group that went there, for all the good it did him. Must be rankling.'

'I imagine.'

She had dropped Gauzlin's name at dinner too, but received no further information. The monks had eyed Roger's tattoos askance, and Beatriz suspected that, beneath his impassive, stony stare, he was rather enjoying their trepidation at his appearance.

In the morning, they were up early. A wreathing morning mist tumbled lazily above the river surface. Roger handed Beatriz up the plank. She settled back into her accustomed place, where she could watch the passing brown waters, waiting for their next stop in Agen. The confluence of the two rivers, the Tarn and the Garonne, was just up ahead. The barge rejoined the Garonne and continued on.

After their night in Agen, they were on the river again for a while until they reached Marmande, where they slept another night, and Roger used some of Philippa's silver in the morning to gain them horses and a pack mule.

They rode towards Sainte-Foy-la-Grande. Everywhere they went, they encountered herds of sheep and goats moving up to higher ground, which slowed them considerably as they waited for the road to clear. A family of herders with several children and two dogs stood at the side of the road, watching them pass. Just before lunch, their horses were chased by a gaggle of honking geese. Beatriz laughed at the look of alarm on Roger's face as the geese nagged loudly close behind him. Yellow gorse flourished on the hillside. Large daisies and honeysuckle were in the hedges. White jasmine scented the nights. At Sainte-Foy-la-Grande, they found a busy port, loading bottles of wine destined for England, and they paid more of their silver for a room and stabling for their animals. Roger slept on the floor, his sword at his side.

Early in the morning, they set off on a long day's ride towards Angouleme. At noon, they took shelter in the shade of a tree to break fast on the bread and cheese they had bought at a stall in Sainte-Foy. Beatriz decided to paddle in the river. She was enjoying the cold, clear water on her bare toes when she heard a commotion behind her, and Roger shouted, 'Beatriz!' Turning to his voice, she saw Roger had moved behind a fence on her right and three men and a woman were running, then scrambling and being hauled over the fence. She turned to look at what was alarming them. A huge white bull with a ferocious set of horns was heading straight for her at a lick, a frayed rope dangling at his neck, near tangling under his front feet.

'Beatriz!' Roger shouted again, gesturing her towards the fence. She ran, and he hauled her over. The small crowd of people sheltering there hastily stepped back as the bull thudded against the wood behind her, frustrated. 'His dander's up, alright,' said one of the peasants.

'It be Arnaut's bull,' another man told her, 'escaped again.'

'Does it escape often?'

'Oh aye, most days. He'll settle down in a while and stroll on back home.'

Beatriz looked at Roger with her own frustration. How long was a while? But Roger was pointing and laughing. Beatriz turned to see the bull had decided to stand on the boots she had set aside to paddle in the water. She blew through her nose, much like the bull. 'My boots!' she wailed. Luckily, they were not her best blue ones. She glanced in the direction of their abandoned picnic, where their horses and mule were tethered. 'Our baggage and horses, Roger?'

'He's not interested in them,' the peasant told her. 'Sure likes your boots, though. They be goners.'

The bull was trampling her boots good and proper.

They would be useless. 'We can't wait here forever. Can't you shoo him off, Roger?'

He pointed at his chest and shook his shaggy head, laughing, even white teeth in his brown beard.

'Best not to rile him, that beast,' the helpful peasant asserted.

Beatriz paced up and down, and the bull trampled back and forth across her boots, took a great draught of water at the river's edge and returned to stand on her boots.

At last, two more peasants came into view, running and carrying long sticks and ropes. 'That's Arnaut, I presume,' said Beatriz. It took them a while to recapture the bull, dancing around his horns and his lowered great head, but eventually they had him secured and dragged him off. Roger opened the gate. Beatriz paused to look down at her ruined boots. There was no point in picking them up. She was loath to wear her blue ones and ruin them on the journey too, but she would have to. Perhaps she could pick up replacements at the next market they passed through.

'We won't make Angouleme, now,' Roger said.

Beatriz called out to the talkative peasant, who was trudging past them. 'Do you know someone who might sell me boots and give us room for the night?'

'You're in luck!' the peasant declared.

She resigned herself to losing an extra day on the journey. The peasant's hut was comfortable enough; his wife's potage was edible and her best boots were the right fit for Beatriz and adequate to travel in.

The next day's riding was going well, and they were

close to the city of Angouleme, but the sky was darkening almost to night. The hailstorm came on suddenly. Huge ice balls shredded leaves and thundered on barn roofs. They were soon soaked through and wrestling to control their frightened horses and mule. The convent of Saint Ausonius was just up ahead, and they rode hard for the gate, clamouring to be let in. An old nun ushered them through the portal in the great gates and slammed it behind them on the wet and wind. She had a fire going in the gatehouse, where she was ensconced with a cat and a prayer book. 'Get warm and dry.' She flapped them towards the fire. Roger's unkempt appearance was even worse for a dousing, but Beatriz had found the storm exhilarating, cleansing. They stamped their feet in front of the fire and shook the rain from their hair and cloaks.

'Are you staying the night?' the nun asked.

'Please,' Beatriz said. 'It will be a while before the heavens give us leave to get back to our road.'

Roger had a sheepish look about him at the meal in the refectory as a group of young nuns nudged each other, studying him surreptitiously over the rims of their beakers.

'You are in the service of Lady Philippa of Tolosa?' the abbess asked Beatriz, giving the giggling nuns a reproving glance.

'Yes, abbess. She sends me on a mission to the duke in Poitiers.'

Beatriz gave the abbess what news of Tolosa she could, and she recounted their escapade with the bull. The abbess, in her turn, told Beatriz that the duke was in residence in Poitiers and hosted the count of Anjou there.

'There is a negotiation going forward, I believe, for a marriage to the count's daughter,' the abbess said. Perhaps Beatriz would be too late in her mission on Philippa's behalf then. 'The duke is a young man much in need of a wife,' the abbess went on, her tone implying some disapproval. The abbess made several unsuccessful attempts to draw Roger in conversation. 'I would like to see Sicily,' she said. 'I hear it is very beautiful.'

Roger nodded.

'Tolosa must have been a great change for you.'

Roger nodded again and took in a large mouthful of stew.

Looking around the wimpled faces at the table, Beatriz saw Roger was cause for excitement and curiosity for some of the older nuns, as well as the novices.

'Does he speak at all?' the abbess whispered to Beatriz.

'Only if he has to.'

AFTER A FINAL STOP overnighting in Civray, the duke's city of Poitiers was at last in sight. They stated their business to the gatekeeper and rode through the massive gate in the walls and up the main street. The duke's palace was a rectangular keep with a square tower at each of its corners built from pale grey brick, very different from the pink bricks of Tolosa.

They arrived late in the day, exhausted. Beatriz was glad to step down from the saddle, her legs wobbling, struggling to find their new mode. She presented her now dog-eared letter of introduction at the palace gate. After a wait, the steward came out to greet them and took them into the courtyard, where two servants unloaded and carried their baggage and a groom led their horses towards the stables. The steward showed them to a corner of the undercroft, where he told them they could unfurl their bedrolls and take ease. 'I will speak with you about your business in the morning.'

Beatriz was relieved to be able to sleep and, tomorrow, dress in her finery before an audience with the duke. Remembering the duke's character from her last visit, she knew she needed to be on best form, with her wits about her.

Early the next morning, she opened her eyes on the rather fearsome sight of Roger's head looming close over her. 'What?' She sat up fast, clutching her shift around herself. Roger advanced Anna's ivory comb towards her as if it were a knife. Slowly coming to and gaining his meaning, she shook her head. 'I don't do hairdressing, and besides, I think it will please the duke to encounter you in your natural state.' Roger frowned and reluctantly put the comb away in his saddlebag. 'Save your grooming for Anna's hands,' Beatriz said. She made a mental note to herself that if Roger should be moved to kill anyone on this trip, she would not attempt to get in between them.

In the great hall, the court appeared to be hungover. The huge space was littered with half-dressed men and maids moving slowly, tidying. The fire was smouldering low. A few cloaked humps huddled close to the embers were men still sleeping. The duke himself lolled in a great chair on the dais, his eyes closed, one leg slung over the arm, looking as if he had slept the night there. A finely dressed young lady who Beatriz presumed to be the daughter of the count of Anjou was sitting next to the duke, whispering in his ear. Keeping his eyes shut, he flapped his hand at his ear as if she were a mosquito.

The steward mounted the two steps to the dais and approached them. He spoke in a low voice. The duke opened one quizzical eye and looked at Beatriz and Roger. He sat up slowly, and the steward handed over Philippa's letter of introduction. The duke read and then waved them forward. He seemed as impressed and amused by Roger's appearance as Beatriz had hoped, as was the young lady, who was eyeing Roger from his unkempt head to his tattooed neck, across his bulging biceps and down his huge torso and thighs.

'From Tolosa?' the duke asked, switching easily from the few words of *langue d'oil* he had spoken with the steward to use Occitan to address Beatriz. The language of his court was *langue d'oil*, but most of his lands were in the Occitan-speaking territories.

'Yes, lord. I am *trobairitz* to Lady Philippa of Tolosa and bring you greetings from her.' She gave her best flourishing bow, like a man, which made him smile.

'Excellent.' He drew the word out slowly. 'I would hear Lady Philippa's *trobairitz* play at the feast later today.'

'Gladly. And my companion is Roger of Scopello, guard to Lady Philippa.'

The young lady was still looking Roger over as if he were a horse, her face flushed. Beatriz noticed that although she was pretty, her two eyes did not quite look in the same direction. It was disconcerting. Beatriz did not know which of the eyes to focus upon, and it was making her feel boss-eyed herself to try.

'Your purpose here?' said the duke, regaining Beatriz's straying attention.

'I bring a letter and gift for you from Lady Philippa.'

'The morning fair hums with delight!'

The young lady was not so delighted and scowled at the mention of Philippa's name. Beatriz nodded to Roger, who lumbered forward and placed the casket with the horse trapping on the table in front of the pair. Beatriz tried to imagine if Philippa would be glad to marry this man or not for his own sake, regardless of his great wealth and ability to safeguard hers. But it seemed the skew-eyed young lady was staking a claim, and Philippa might be too late in the game.

Beatriz had only seen the duke from afar on her previous visit to Poitiers with Imbert. Up this close, she saw a handsome man with large brown eyes and dark shoulder-length hair that was almost black. His hair was very straight and thick, tucked behind his ears. Beatriz was intrigued to see that he wore a small gold hoop with a sapphire in one ear, despite the Church's recent pronouncement against such decorations for men. The light glinting on parts of his hair hinted at deep reds. His mobile face conveyed intelligence. He wore a green cloak and a blue, long-sleeved tunic embroidered with gold thread. Small pearl buttons stepped up the sleeves of his tunic, and silver brooches clasped his cloak to his shoulders. The duke stood to open the casket. Beatriz saw now he was quite short, petite almost, but he was well-formed, nonetheless. His hands were small, like a woman's.

He exclaimed with pleasure at the gift. 'Very fine work and colour.' He smoothed his palm over the textile.

The young lady rose, revealing herself to be several willowy inches taller than the duke. Philippa would be taller than him too, Beatriz thought. The young lady stamped her way from the dais and the hall. The duke shrugged with amusement after her, turning back to Beatriz. 'Lady Ermengarde of Anjou,' he told Beatriz. 'The daughter of Count Fulk. Rather moody,' he confided.

'There is also this letter and enclosure from my lady to you, sire.' Beatriz watched him extract the small portrait of Philippa that Lluis had painted – a second portrait for his view. The duke's lively eyebrows rose and fell. 'She *is* a beauty, your lady.'

Beatriz bit her lip, wondering how much pandering was her responsibility. Roger glanced at her impassively, but his very impassivity seemed to accuse her of being remiss.

'She has hair the colour of honey and eyes the colour of the greenwood,' Beatriz blurted. 'She is fair of voice and countenance and body.'

The duke smiled at Beatriz. 'Of course she is.' He resumed his seat and bent his head to read the letter. 'Well,' he said, folding it up and setting it atop the horse trapping in the casket. 'Well.' He left his palm upon the folded letter.

He was cryptic, Beatriz felt, but perhaps the mooted betrothal to Lady Ermengarde was not quite concluded yet. 'I would speak with you, sire, on another matter.'

'Tomorrow …' he sighed. 'I am feeling rather jaded today.'

'Sire, I am sorry to press. I am aware that you are a

busy man. But my business is a matter of some great urgency.'

He frowned. 'Very well. My steward will call you to me again later, when I have a free moment.'

'You may want to know of this now,' she persisted. Beatriz carefully withdrew the burnt letter from her satchel and placed it on the table in front of him. The duke leant forward to look at it. 'What is this?' He pointed at the ravaged parchment.

'I believe it was a letter from you to my lady.'

He moved it closer with the tip of his stylus. 'Yes,' he said, 'it could be. She did not read it?'

'No, sire.'

'The lady disapproved of my proposal *that* much that she must burn it down?' he asked with a wry smile.

'My lady had no opportunity to approve or disap- prove. The letter was intercepted by Count Bertrand, and Count Raimon burnt it.'

His left eyebrow raised. 'I see. And how do you come by it ruins?'

'I witnessed the burning, covert-like. I saw Imbert rescue the remains.'

'Ah! Dear Imbert! It is true he is gone?'

Beatriz nodded solemnly.

'I can hardly believe it. He seemed like the type to live forever.'

'You may remember we visited here together a few years back. I was with him for four years and am sore aggrieved at the manner of his passing and feel his lack every day.'

The duke's jovial expression sobered. 'I have a copy of

this letter, of course. I will ask my scribe to copy it out, and perhaps you would be so good as to give it to your lady directly for me?'

'I will gladly do so, sire.'

He pressed the tips of his fingers together several times, contemplating his own thoughts, then looked up at Beatriz again suddenly. 'What other news of Tolosa?'

'Lord Bertrand is lately wed to Helie of Burgundy. Count Raimon intends to marry my lady to King Sancho of Aragon, but she is not minded to that match.'

'And Imbert's death?'

'I was at first accused.'

'You?'

'The murderer planted one weapon among my possessions and the second in the room of my lady's maid, Anna.'

'Two murder weapons? Some excess!'

'Yes. A brooch belonging to my lady with long sharp pins that was used to stab Imbert in the neck and an instrument string used to garrotte him.'

The duke grimaced, picturing the scene in his mind. 'My dear, dear Imbert.'

'It was widely known that Imbert intended to marry me,' Beatriz went on, 'and that I was not minded to that match. I was exonerated, however, by the evidence of a friend.'

'The maid still stands accused?'

'Yes, but she is innocent, and the guilty party saunters free. I would have them. Perhaps you have some piece of information about Imbert that can help me.'

'Garrotting is an unlikely act for a woman. Is she burly, meaty?'

'No, sire. She is not. And she is, for certain, innocent.'

'I wish you success in your quest. Imbert was an excellent poet, and we spent many a joyful evening together composing.'

Beatriz approached the dais more closely and dropped her voice. 'Was he more than a poet for you, sire?' she ventured.

'Poetry isn't enough, *Trobairitz?*'

She said nothing, and he contemplated her with a gravity that had not been in his demeanour before.

'I believe Imbert was working for you?' she prompted.

His expression became guarded. 'He wrote poems for me.'

'I believe he did more than that, sire. I was in Imbert's employ for four years. We travelled together. I would have been his wife if he had not been murdered. I believe he was assisting you with … information.'

The duke took a long breath in through his nose. He waved at Beatriz to dismiss her with one hand and beckoned to his steward at the far end of the hall with his other. 'We will speak of this later, after the feast, after you perform.'

THE LIAR

May 1093, Poitiers

The steward showed Roger and Beatriz to a guest chamber. It was good to have their own comfortable place to be after the rigours of their journey, but she barely noticed. Beatriz was thrown into a mess of anxiety about her performance for the duke at the coming feast. Roger, seeing her increasingly frantic rearrangements of instruments and her pacing and talking to herself, decided to leave her to work out her performance in isolation.

Beatriz fixed on delivering a version of her *vida*, to repeat the *stampida* she had performed at the Tolosa Easter Court, where it had been well received, and to play a complicated instrumental piece on the *oud* that Imbert had taught her and made her practice over and over. But she wanted to compose something new for the duke, something of her own. She wanted to impress him, surprise him. Perhaps he would consider being her patron. No. That would be disloyal to Philippa and yet, that lady's future was uncertain. His was solid, and a *trobador* or *trobairitz* could not find a better court as their berth.

Beatriz strummed the *vielle* and composed a song aloud.

> *I loved you dear and you betrayed me,*
> *Sold me in marriage to an old man*
> *When I was still a child, your child.*
>
> *I had no choice but to leave you,*
> *Live as a frightened beggar.*
> *Do you long for me now?*
> *Do you cry for me now?*

No. She did not want to expose her pain to the duke and his court, to all these strangers. She sounded a few more notes on the *vielle* and cleared her throat.

> *Zephyr arises gently*
> *and the warm Sun proceeds;*
> *Earth lays bare her bosom,*
> *melting with her sweets.*
>
> *Spring enters, dressed in crimson,*
> *puts on her finery,*
> *scattering flowers on the earth,*
> *leaves on every tree.*

Animals build their lairs now
and the sweet birds their nests:
among the flowering branches
they sing their happiness.

Your golden curls, your smiles.
Your fingers strong and skilled
stroke stone, play my body's
agony and pleasure.

Lure for the falcon.
My lover or my liar?
My strutting Catalan,
Are you strangling song?

I send my sorrys.
Go swift to Tolosa
Where my sweet love lies.

Yes, this was on the way now. It was yet more of her pain on display, but it was at least concealed. Nobody here knew Lluis or knew her history with him. Why did she suspect him so much? Because she was afraid to trust or love someone after her father's betrayal? Yes, she could admit that to herself now. Because she could not remember, and there was too much coincidence in that on the night that Imbert died? But it was *more* than that. Because Lluis was a compatriot of Bertrand? Because there was something shifty in his demeanour! Suddenly, Beatriz realised. She *had* seen. She *had* sensed that. She *wasn't* wrong, as Philippa and Anna had insisted. There was something there!

She must find someone to write to Anna about Lluis, what she had sensed, and see if they could find something out. But she was procrastinating, distracting herself. She had to focus on the song, on the coming performance.

Just before the feast was due to begin, Roger returned to the room, having (somehow, given how close-mouthed he was) made fast friends with a number of the kitchen maids. He told Beatriz the duke's mother wished him to wed Ermengarde of Anjou, but the duke was prevaricating.

Beatriz stood in the hall, tuning her instruments as the tables were set around her. A well-dressed, grey-haired man passed her on his way to the dais with Ermengarde on his arm. He must be Fulk, the count of Anjou.

'Mistress.'

Beatriz turned to a woman's voice beside her. It was Guillaume's mother, the Dowager Duchess Audearde, a fine-boned woman in her forties.

'I believe you are lately from the court at Tolosa?'

'Yes, lady.'

'How does my nephew Henry and my niece Helie?'

'They are well, lady. I was at Helie's wedding to Count Bertrand.'

'Good. Good. Henry travels soon to Spain, I believe?'

'Yes, I believe that is his intent.'

She turned as if to leave Beatriz, but then turned back to her. 'And the monk Gauzlin of Cluny is also at Tolosa, I understand.'

Beatriz frowned, perplexed at Audearde's interest in Gauzlin. 'Yes, lady, he is. He is clerk to Bertrand.'

'Yes.' Beatriz saw Audearde reading the confusion on her face. 'He was my scribe for a while, when I was still an unwed girl at the court of Burgundy.'

'Ah, I see. He is well.'

'Thank you.' She picked up her skirts and swept on her way to the high table where her son handed her to one seat beside him and Ermengarde to the other side.

Guillaume had inherited the county and the duchy at the age of sixteen, and his mother had steered his rule for the first few years, but Beatriz saw no sign that he was still in thrall to his mother. Audearde had been separated from his father for ten years. When the former duke died, she returned to Poitiers to support her son in his inheritance. Guillaume was very much the master here now, though he wore his command lightly, almost humorously, so confident in it was he.

There were other skilled musicians and minstrels performing before Beatriz, and her nervousness grew to a pitch, and she could not eat a morsel of food. When it came her turn, she worked through her prepared repertoire: the *vida*, the *stampida*, the instrumental on the *oud*. These were well received, and, since they were well known to her, she gradually relaxed. Finally, she performed her new (Lluis) song, which was still a little rough at the edges, she explained. At the completion of her performance, the court fair resonated with applause. Guillaume even rose to his feet to clap. Struggling to control her glee, smiling as modestly as she could to herself, she sat down and contemplated her boots for a moment. She looked up to see Roger watching her, entranced and proud.

'Beatriz!' The duke gestured to her. 'Come and sit here beside me. I would speak with you.'

She stepped up and was embarrassed to have to shift Ermengarde from her seat. The steward rose from his place at the end of the table, and everyone else shifted along to make room for her at the duke's insistence. Ermengarde's face was pointedly turned away, her mouth set in a serious pout. Guillaume's brother Hugh and his young sister Beatrix completed the party on the dais, and all congratulated her on her song.

'That was truly marvellous, Beatriz. Your lady Philippa shows great taste in appointing you as her *trobairitz*.'

Again, at the mention of Philippa, Ermengarde rose in high dudgeon and made her way from the dais, knocking away her father's hand as he reached for her. She moved swiftly from the hall.

'Really, Guillaume,' his mother whispered across Beatriz. 'If you will not have her, could you at least be civil about it.'

He shook his head and blew out between his lips. 'I'm being as civil as I am able. Where do you draw your material, Beatriz?' he asked quickly, before his mother could say more on Ermengarde.

'Imbert schooled me in Ovid.'

'Of course.'

'And we studied Arab song together, the *muwashsha* and the *kharja*.'

'Ah!' The duke was nodding his head, and Beatriz was gratified to see he really did know what she was talking about. She had not met any other who did. 'Do you know Baudri's poetry?' he asked.

Now it was her turn to nod. 'Indeed. He is my Lady Philippa's favourite.'

'Really!' His eyes were alight, looking in her face.

'Imbert and I looked at *winileodas* and the *chansons de toile*.'

'Oh, Beatriz! We have *too* much to talk on.'

Beatriz dropped her voice to a whisper that even his mother on his far side would not hear. 'Might I trouble you for some conversation on Imbert and his murder and speak with you of poetry later? There is urgency to my quest.'

He frowned. 'Yes, but that is not conversation for here. Come to my chamber, tomorrow morning. My steward will fetch you.'

Beatriz acquiesced. She raised her voice to a normal tone again. 'I am tired now, lord. Might I beg leave to take rest?'

'Of course, of course, you must be tired after that superlative performance. Was it not a superlative performance, Mother?' He leant forward to look around Beatriz to his mother.

'Yes, superlative, Beatriz,' she told her graciously. 'Let the poor girl get some sleep now, Guillaume. You can be avid for Ovid together tomorrow.'

They smiled at her jest. 'Indeed,' the duke said, 'I will allow the uncompromising but highly talented Mistress Beatriz to seek her pillow and refresh herself for more poetry tomorrow.'

She rose and made her way to the bedchamber with Roger in her wake.

IN THE MORNING, Beatriz rolled over in the great bed and looked at Roger lying on the floor, a cushion under his head, his eyes open and contemplating the ceiling. She smiled to herself, remembering how she had been a great success the night before. Soon after she and Roger were dressed, the steward tapped on the door and guided them to the duke's chambers. Roger took up silent station just inside the door, and the duke glanced at him with amusement. He pointed to a seat across a low table from him. 'Well, Beatriz of Farrera, what can I tell you about Imbert?'

She decided she had best cut to the chase. 'He was giving you information, lord?'

The duke nodded. 'From time to time. He was well informed.'

'Yes, and I believe that is why he was murdered.'

The duke frowned. 'Who do you accuse then?'

'I am still unsure, but it would help if you would give me testimony that Imbert did write to you from time to time with information.'

'I cannot incriminate myself, my dear. You knew Imbert well, I think, Beatriz. He had many talents. Knowledge was one of them. Gathering information.'

Beatriz nodded. 'His information-gathering seems likely the cause of his murder.'

'That seems possible. But the information he gathered for me was the sum of what you already know. He kept me informed on the court of Tolosa and anything else he gleaned on his travels that he thought might be of use to me.'

'Would you give me written testimony to that effect, sire? It would help my defence of Anna. She did not commit the crime. An injustice will prevail, and the murderer will go free if you cannot help me.'

Again, he contemplated Beatriz with a serious expression that was not his habitual mode. 'Perhaps I can give you something. I would like to see his murderer brought to justice.' He shifted his expression to open a new topic. 'Can I tempt you to remain here with me, Beatriz? You are a songstress, not a sheriff! I would speak with you more, compose with you. Your man, Roger, can carry letters to Lady Philippa in your stead.'

'I thank you.' It was a tempting offer. She took a swallow of the beaker of wine he poured for her to give herself time to contemplate it. He was right. She could stay at the court in Poitiers and send Roger back to Tolosa with the letters. She owed Philippa and Anna nothing, really.

She shook her head at herself, knowing already what her answer would be. If she did not go on with her investigations on this journey, if she did not go back to Tolosa with more than she had at the moment, Anna would hang and Philippa would be loaded in grief onto a pack horse bound for the old king in Aragon. Imbert's corpse would fester on the injustice of it all. There was no clarity at all about who had stabbed and garrotted him. If Beatriz gave in to the temptation of the duke's invitation, Philippa would not get her stag.

She smiled to herself and saw her smile responded to on the duke's face. Yes, he would do for Philippa, no doubt. Beatriz sighed. She would go on. Perhaps she would return to Poitiers one day, perhaps with Lady Philippa as duchess. If she took the easy route and acquiesced to the duke's request, harsh fates for Anna and Philippa would follow as day follows night.

'Most reluctantly, I must leave and go on with my task of exonerating Anna. I am bound to make enquiries in Conques and Uzès. I hope to return, and am truly glad of the honour you do me with your invitation,' she said.

'Hmm, well I am sorry for that.' His expression was petulant, but he quickly recovered. He handed Beatriz a wadded packet. 'This is the copy of my burnt letter and a new letter from me. My letter assures Lady Philippa I will attend the Michaelmas Assembly. I will do what I can then to help you in the matter of the murderer.'

She thanked him and took her leave swiftly, so that he had no more time to inveigle her further to change her mind, and to ensure that she did not succumb.

Roger checked their saddles and secured their baggage to the mule in the courtyard. Beatriz patted her satchel and tied it to her saddle hilt. She assumed one or both of the letters contained an offer of marriage to Philippa, but it was frustrating not to know for certain.

WORDS LET LOOSE

June 1093, Conques

It took Beatriz and Roger near three weeks to ride from Poitiers to Conques, staying in monasteries and inns on the route and occasionally sleeping on the hard ground, wrapped in their cloaks and close to a fire. Time was passing and Michaelmas was coming on. If they had reduced their baggage and sold the mule, they could have made better speed, but Beatriz's good clothes and instruments had proven their worth so far, and Beatriz would never willingly give up the instruments. She suspected Roger felt the same way about his weaponry. They would reach Conques tomorrow, if all went smoothly with the final day's ride, and, this night, they were ensconced in a comfortable inn.

Beatriz felt the need to explain her strategy to Roger, even though he hadn't asked her to. She suspected he had already overheard or pieced together a lot for himself, but she found talking things out aloud was helpful in any case.

'We knew Raimon and Bertrand had intercepted a letter from Duke Guillaume to Philippa and burnt it and that Imbert picked it up.'

Roger gestured at the salt cellar and Beatriz passed it to him.

'We guessed the letter might be an offer of marriage to Philippa, which would be a serious threat to Raimon's hold on Tolosa, you see.'

Roger said nothing, but his eyes were on her face.

'That's one possible reason for Imbert's murder. But there are others and I'm hoping this journey will shake the right one and the murderer from the mix.'

Roger nodded.

'Another possibility is something to do with the conflict between the monastery of Cluny and the pope over the pilgrim routes. There was conflict over Saint-Sernin in Tolosa and Gauzlin was mixed up in that. I think he is working on behalf of Cluny. The Burgundy family, Henry of Burgundy, are close with Cluny too, and I saw Gauzlin and Henry talking surreptitiously. There is something underhand going forward and I daresay Imbert had sniffed that out too.'

Roger had finished eating and sat back in his chair, beaker in hand. Beatriz continued her summary.

'Dean Gayrard at Saint-Sernin told me Conques is part of this conflict over the pilgrim routes and that both Imbert and Gauzlin were in Conques a month ago. If I can find out more about that, it may be enlightening. By finding out about Imbert, walking in his shoes, we may discover why someone felt they had to murder him. Another possible motive for Imbert's murder is the salt thefts. I found evidence Imbert was investigating that too.' Beatriz was mildly frustrated that she could not gain much in the way of response from Roger, but she was growing to accept this was his way. He was simply there.

Conques seemed an out of the way place, hidden on the cliff-face of a deep wooded valley, and yet it was crowded with visitors. She threaded her horse slowly up the main street, through the throngs of pilgrims on their way towards the tomb of Saint James in distant Galicia. The abbey of Sainte-Foy faced Beatriz and Roger, head on, at the end of the thoroughfare. A few paces before the abbey, two inns vied for the pilgrims' business.

Beatriz dismounted to make enquiries. 'You'll not find room at the abbey guesthouse,' the innkeeper told her. 'Always rammed full there. I can fit you in, Mistress.'

'And our beasts?' Beatriz gestured to where Roger sat on his horse, holding the reins of her mount and the mule.

The innkeeper eyed Roger. 'Aye. I've got stable room for the horses and mule round the back.'

After a negotiation and payment of the price for a night's rest, a stableboy came to show Roger where to take the horses, and Beatriz sat outside the inn in the sunshine, clearing the dust from her throat with a welcome beaker of ale. Roger returned, carrying their baggage, which he took inside, and then joined her at the table. The innkeeper set a large beaker for him and Roger downed it in one rapid gulp. 'You needed that,' Beatriz remarked. He nodded. She had noticed that she was supplying articulation for him.

On the next table, a group of pilgrims were also recuperating from their journey and looking around themselves at the abbey, the town, the milling people. 'Where have you come from?' one woman called over, addressing Roger.

'We've come from Poitiers,' Beatriz answered, knowing Roger would not respond.

'Ah! We're on the pilgrims' route. Started in Clermont-Ferrand and came through Le Puy. Already need new boots,' the woman said, laughing and holding up her feet to view.

'You will head next towards Moissac?' Beatriz asked, and the woman nodded her agreement.

'God bless you and your journey,' the woman said.

After the ale, they washed and changed their clothes and went to seek audience with Abbot Begon in his house adjacent to the abbey. Dean Gayrard's letter of introduction soon got them through the door and ushered into the abbot's presence. He was a large, solid man with a shock of blond hair going white around his tonsure. His eyebrows were bushy and white too and gave him something of the look of a cat about him. 'Mistress Beatriz and …' The abbot gestured towards Roger.

'Yes, I am Beatriz de Farrera and this is Roger of Scopello. We are in the service of Lady Philippa of Tolosa.'

'Please, sit.' The abbot gestured to two small benches set before his desk. His desk was piled with scrolls and writing materials. The room was small but comfortable, with glass in the windows that looked out onto the abbey. A quantity of colourful cushions, crucifixes and small statues of the Virgin decorated the walls and niches. 'The

Dean has told me something of your quest and enquiry in his letter.' The abbot tapped the letter.

'I believe you received two visitors here a while back: a monk named Gauzlin and Imbert the *trobador*, who was recently murdered,' Beatriz said.

'I heard of his murder. A terrible business. I enjoyed Imbert's company. He was a truly gifted musician. And Gauzlin? The monk from Moissac?'

'Yes, Gauzlin is working as a scribe for Count Bertrand in Tolosa at present. Dean Gayrard said Imbert and Gauzlin were here at the same time?'

'Yes. They were here just over two months ago.'

'What was their business here?'

'They had no particular business with me – not that either of them made plain, at any rate. I assumed they were travelling on their way to business elsewhere.'

'Presumably, they were not travelling together, and Gauzlin was unaware of Imbert's presence?'

'Oh no. They were travelling together.'

Beatriz knit her brows. 'I thought Imbert was likely spying on Gauzlin,' she admitted.

'Ah.'

'I am searching for the reason for Imbert's murder and I am sure he was spying and this may have been the cause. You said they did not make their business plain. What did you mean?'

'I shared a meal with Imbert and, as I said, found him fine company. As for Gauzlin …'

Beatriz waited.

'I had no doubt he was here as a spy for Cluny. You are perhaps aware of the recent conflicts?'

'Dean Gayrard told me something of it.'

'During the time of the two popes and Pope Urban's exile from Rome, the monastery of Cluny increased in importance and sought to capitalise on their network across southern France and into the Iberian peninsula. The Cluniacs are, of course, held in great esteem in Iberia.'

'May I ask, Father, do you know why the Castilian royal family is so close to Cluny? Castile is distant from Cluny, unlike the court of Burgundy.'

'Indeed. It is a good question. During the pope's exile, Cluny was instrumental in negotiating the release of Alfonso, now King Alfonso of Castile, from his brother Sancho's prison after he rebelled. If it hadn't been for Cluny's intervention, Alfonso would likely have been executed. Instead, he was freed.'

'And Sancho was murdered soon after,' Beatriz added.

'Yes, God rest his soul. I see your time with Imbert has given you worldly wisdom, Beatriz.'

'Why is Conques caught up in this matter?'

'Like Saint-Sernin in Tolosa, Conques is an important stopping point on the pilgrim route to Compostela. You see how busy we are,' he said laughing and gesturing towards the window. 'Cluny would like to control us, just as they sought and failed to control Saint-Sernin.'

This sounded interesting, but the abbot's account was tantalisingly incomplete. Beatriz waited to see if he would say more. She had found that sometimes her silence was more enticing than posing questions. Begon rummaged through a pile of parchments on his table, found one, and contemplated it. Beatriz felt frustration again at her exclusion from all these words scrawled on parchments.

'Cluny has added Saint Martial in Limoges, Moissac and Saint-Gilles to its network, giving it a toehold on at least two of the pilgrim paths to Compostela. Happily, the papal legate refused them control of Saint-Sernin and excommunicated those Cluniac monks squatting there, including Gauzlin.'

'And Conques?' Beatriz asked quietly.

'The conflicts began with your lady's father, I'm afraid.'

'Count Guilhem of Tolosa?'

The abbot nodded. 'Yes. He is a supporter of Cluny. It was he who originally gave Saint-Sernin to them and he tried to do the same with us. If Cluny were to acquire these last two, Tolosa and Conques, they would dominate several of the pilgrim routes entirely. He transferred Figeac Abbey, our mother house, to Cluny some ten years ago and my predecessor, Abbot Stephen, appealed against this to Gregory, who was then pope. We are still waiting for a final ruling.'

'So you think Gauzlin was here, assessing the situation? Reporting back to Cluny?'

'Without a doubt.'

'You caught him out somehow?'

'Well, it was Imbert, in fact, who did the catching.'

'The parchment in your hand, Father. How it is related to this?'

The abbot looked up at her under his white, bushy brows. 'It is a letter from Gauzlin to Cluny. I intend to send it on to Rome as evidence in our case. It was Imbert who gave it to me.'

'So, Imbert took it from Gauzlin. What does it say? Can you read it to me?'

The abbot frowned. 'These matters are not for you, I think, Child.'

Roger shifted in his seat, leaning forward and putting his hands on his knees, reminding the abbot of his presence.

'Abbot, you have a letter there from Lady Philippa and another from your friend, Dean Gayrard, which are surety that you can trust me and I am about the serious business of finding Imbert's murderer.'

Roger sat back again, each movement putting his tattoos and bulging muscles on display, punctuating Beatriz's exchange with the abbot.

The abbot's expression continued sceptical for a moment. He looked over Dean Gayrard's letter a second time. 'Hmm. Hmm. Very well.' He put that down and picked up Gauzlin's letter again. 'Gauzlin writes to Abbot Hugh at Cluny.'

'Will you read it to me?' Beatriz interrupted. 'A small detail may be an important clue.'

The abbot cleared his throat. 'To venerated Abbot Hugh of Cluny, from your brother Gauzlin, in service to you in the south, greetings.'

Beatriz was excited by what she heard. Gauzlin stated plainly in the letter that he was in service, that is spying, for Cluny.

The abbot continued to read: 'Cluny continues in great esteem with the Castilian royal family. I have this from Henry of Burgundy who is visiting the Tolosa court at present for the marriage of his niece to Bertrand de Tolosa.' The abbot decided to switch back to summary of the letter, after glancing at Beatriz again with a doubtful expression. 'Gauzlin confirms that he has arranged for Henry of Burgundy to carry a prayerbook from Cluny as a gift to Alfonso's sister Urraca.'

Beatriz's excitement rose another notch. Here was proof, too, that Henry of Burgundy was involved with Cluny. It was an explanation of the secret conversation between Gauzlin and Henry that Beatriz had seen in Tolosa.

The abbot interrupted her thoughts. 'And then Gauzlin describes the situation with Figeac and the appeal to the pope, just as I have told to you.'

'Father, may I ask for a copy of this letter?'

'No, no. I won't do that.'

'Father. I believe this letter is important evidence for Imbert's murder.'

The abbot's face showed his consternation. 'Yes,' he said slowly, thinking it through. 'I can see that. What would you do with a copy?'

'I would give it to my lady Philippa, who will share it with Viscount Ademar, who is sitting in justice on the case.'

The abbot took some time to think, and Beatriz waited anxiously. Roger shifted forward again. The abbot glanced at him and back to her. 'Very well. I will get a copy made for you. I believe you are right, although I had not realised before now that it could relate to this awful murder. I suppose Imbert had already taken his own copy. You think Brother Gauzlin committed this crime?'

'It seems one possibility.'

Beatriz made a mental note to ask Philippa and Anna what they had found in Imbert's satchel. Although it was likely the murderer – could it have been Gauzlin? – had removed any document incriminating him and that may have been the purpose of the murder, that and to silence Imbert. But was this reason enough – spying for Cluny against the pope – to commit murder? Imbert might well have wanted to relay that information to the pope, but could puny Gauzlin really have done the killing?

'I do not understand how Imbert was travelling with Gauzlin on the one hand and spying on him on the other,' Beatriz said.

'Ah, Imbert was a complex man.'

'Thank you for this information, Abbot. It brings some clarity. Will it be possible to collect the copy of Gauzlin's letter from you tomorrow? We will be back on the road then.'

The abbot agreed that would be possible.

'I wonder if I might ask another favour. Is there someone who could scribe a letter for me?'

'Yes, the same monk who will copy this for you.' He wafted the parchment he was holding, Gauzlin's letter. I will introduce you now.'

He led them through the cloister. In one of the scriptorium alcoves that looked out over the grass square, the abbot left them with a young monk named Omer.

'The matter I have requires discretion,' Beatriz told him.

Omer nodded, his large brown eyes solemnly holding her gaze.

'First, can you read these letters to us?' Beatriz handed over Duke Guillaume's two letters. Beatriz had already broken the seal and taken the letters out of their packet.

Omer perused the letters and looked up at Beatriz, an expression of doubt on his face.

'We are in the service of Lady Philippa of Tolosa,' Beatriz said and thrust her battered letter of introduction at him to reassure him.

Omer studied the documents before him some more, glanced up at Beatriz and Roger again when he had finished reading. He nodded. 'I think this letter comes first.' He read out:

> To the beauteous and wise Lady Philippa of Tolosa, greetings from Guillaume, count of Poitiers and duke of all Aquitaine. Lady, you do me great honour with your communication. Princess Mafalda has also communicated with me on this matter. A joining between us could be mutually beneficial. You will see me as soon as I am able and we will judge how well we might like each other. Farewell.

Not a proposal of marriage then, but not a refusal, Beatriz thought. And it meant Raimon and Bertrand knew about the role of cupid Mafalda had played between the duke and Philippa. 'And the second letter?'

Omer read again, hesitating and stumbling here and there at the words on the parchment:

> To Philippa, the most beautiful lady of

Tolosa, from Guillaume, count of Poitiers and duke of all Aquitaine. Thank you for your gift. It is a marvel of craftsmanship and a constant reminder to me that I must ride to you, for you, mayhap upon you.

Beatriz saw that Omer's ears had turned quite scarlet at the duke's innuendo.

Omer recovered himself and continued:

Your trobairitz shone here in Poitiers. She is a rare talent. She is your most eloquent ambassador, showing me your delightful portrait and telling me of your pleasure at Baudri's poetry. I might say with him, you suggest my song to me. You will give breath to my pen and I would give life to you beyond the stars. You compel the taciturn to speak. Let your naked finger touch my naked parchment. Place my letter beneath your breast. I would create a silken nest for you in my poetry, where you might lay out your body.

Omer shifted in discomfort on his stool.

'Carry on!' Beatriz commanded impatiently. 'The duke is saucy, for sure.'

Omer compressed his lips in response but continued:

You surpass all other women in your appreciation of poetry and your knowledge of books. You reward the merits of poets, so look on your most affectionate bard and give me my reward. Look at me for just a moment with your serene brow; a simple glance would be sufficient. I will come to your Michaelmas court in Tolosa, carrying a gift for you, hidden about my person, and we will skirmish together for you to uncover it. Until that promised bliss, farewell.

'Quite flattering and … ambiguous,' Beatriz remarked.

'I would say so,' Omer said. 'Does he mean marriage to your lady? I hope so, if he speaks in such terms …'

Philippa, for sure, would not like some of his words. 'He says nothing else? Nothing concerning Imbert?'

'I have read the whole letter to you, Mistress.'

Beatriz frowned. The duke had reneged on his promise to write something about Imbert spying for him. 'Thank you for reading these letters. You will not speak of them to anyone. Murder has been committed for less,' Beatriz told him ominously. 'So, I would keep your silence, if I were you.'

'I will,' Omer said.

'Now, I need you to scribe a letter for me.' Beatriz dictated a letter to Philippa and Anna, reporting on her progress so far.

To Lady Philippa of Tolosa, from Beatriz de Farrera, trobairitz in your service. I hope you and Anna fare well. We have heard much of Gauzlin on this journey - from the guest-house master at Moissac who told me Gauzlin was ambitious to be prior of Saint-Sernin and from Abbot Begon, who has given me a letter he intercepted from Gauzlin, proof that he was spying for Cluny concerning the pilgrim paths.

Omer paused with his scratching and glanced up at Beatriz.

'I have this information from your abbot,' Beatriz told him.

'A scribe must be discreet, always,' he said. 'You need not fear I will gossip on any of this.'

Beatriz did fear that, but she had no choice. She had to trust someone. She continued on:

Even Dowager Duchess Audearde in Poitiers asked after Gauzlin. We know the Burgundy family are Cluny supporters. It seems Henry of Burgundy is involved with Gauzlin.

Beatriz had been anxious to warn Philippa of this, since Henry had shown her attention and she was, perhaps, warming to him.

Gauzlin appeared to be travelling with Imbert in Conques, which is strange and there is more to unravel there. We are going next to Uzès to examine Imbert's house. Duke Guillaume told me Imbert was spying for him. I have positive letters from the duke for you on your other matters of the heart. My performance at Poitiers was well received, and the duke would have had me stay with him, but, of course, I would not.

Did you search Imbert's satchel? Was there anything of interest? It's likely Imbert was carrying a copy of this letter from Gauzlin to Cluny. Of course, that parchment could have been removed from the satchel by the murderer.

I have another commission for you and Anna. I realised I noted something shifty about Lluis. I know he has done something wrong. Perhaps not the murder of Imbert, yet something. I saw it in his face as far back as your brother's burial at Saint-Pons-de-Thomières. I saw it again whenever I spoke to him of you or Bertrand. There was always a small hesitation. Please don't assume I am wrong about him. I am not. Now, I can see *clearly, past the embarrassment and guilt I felt at failing to remember that night with him.*

She glanced at Omer and saw he was red as a beetroot in the face again; even his tonsure was rosy. He kept his eyes averted from Beatriz. His fingers were stained with the brown ink, and he had made a great splutter of it on the parchment, which he blotted carefully with a cloth. She completed her dictation:

Try to find a way to probe Lluis. What is he guilty about? Farewell.

23

SANCTUM

Uzès, June 1093

*T*he sun had become a tyrant. Beatriz and Roger rode under blue skies that sang against the red soil and the iridescent green of endless vineyards. Summer storms frequently boiled up the clouds with sudden darkenings, downpours, thunder and lightning that came on rapidly and disappeared as quickly. They sheltered from the showers in dripping caves and rocky overhangs. Lizards darted in the daytime, cicadas filled the nights. The town of Uzès was visible beyond the rocky *garrigues* just ahead of them. They paused to let their horses and the mule drink from a stream, and Beatriz looked out across the prospect.

The town was built into a steep cliff and seeped down from that rocky promontory to spread into the valley below, clustering towards the bank of the Eure river. A tall, round, fenestrated belltower rose high above the town. In her head, Beatriz honoured Uzès as the home of the great writer Dhuoda. It was here, two hundred years ago, that Dhuoda had written her book to her son William, who was a hostage at the court of King Charles the Bald. Beatriz had sat one day and listened to Imbert reading the complete text. It was Dhuoda's book that had first inspired Beatriz to think that she, too, could compose poetry. Imbert had told her about Uzès and his house here, but she had never been invited to visit. He always left her waiting behind in another town when he made his infrequent visits to his house.

They rode through the town walls and on past the impressive Duché palace, the fortified seat of the de Cressol family, and past the bishop's palace and garden. They rode through dense alleys into the heart of the town. At a pleasant-looking inn that Beatriz thought Imbert might have liked, she climbed down from the saddle to ask directions.

'I'm looking for the house of Imbert, the *trobador*.'

'Poor bugger's dead.'

'Yes. I was at the court of Tolosa when it happened. Do you know which is his house?'

'Not … sure. It's somewhere over in the quarter near the Place aux Herbes. Somewhere over there.' He gestured vaguely.

'Thank you.' She gave the innkeeper a coin for his trouble and ordered two small ales for herself and Roger, gesturing to Roger to tie up the horses and join her at a table for a short respite. After the refreshment, they walked the horses round to Place aux Herbes, which was in the throes of a busy market, with venders selling multi-coloured vegetables from carefully arranged baskets, and others selling noisy oxen and pigs. Beatriz asked again after Imbert's house at the bakery on the corner of the square.

'Oh ah, oh poor Imbert! We all miss him! We can't believe we'll never see him again. Murdered by a deaf and dumb girl, we heard. What wickedness.'

Beatriz allowed the young woman to run out her lament and made no comment on her misinformation. 'Do you know which is his house?'

'It's just around the corner somewhere. I'll fetch my son. He sometimes delivered pies to Imbert when he was staying here. Niles, Niles!'

A young, gangly boy, around twelve, appeared in the doorway. 'Maman?'

'This girl is looking for Imbert the *trobador*'s house. You know it I think?'

But the boy had been struck speechless at the sight of Roger. His mouth hung open, and he was oblivious to his mother's question. 'Niles!' She flapped a cloth at his face to wake him from his trance.

He swallowed and looked away from Roger. 'Yes, it's nearby. I can show you, mistress.'

They followed the boy, who glanced back at Roger often. 'He's just big,' Beatriz told him. 'He doesn't bite.' She looked at Roger, who remained silent as usual. 'Well, not to my knowledge.'

'It's this one, mademoiselle.' The boy pointed to a nondescript door of unpainted wood, looped with cobwebs. Beatriz looked up at the single-storey house with its thatched roof.

'Are the servants still within?'

'May …. be. May be not. Haven't seen them.'

Beatriz rolled her eyes, and Roger took his cue, thumping on the door fit to break it.

'If there is anyone in there, they just died from an apoplexy,' Beatriz remarked. Roger ignored her.

They were about to give up when they heard noises coming from the other side of the door. Scraping, boots on tiles, then the latch being pulled back. 'Yes?' an old voice quavered from behind the door.

'I am Beatriz, Imbert's *jograresa*,' she called out. 'Step to the side,' she said quietly to Roger, 'we don't want you to be the first thing she sees.' Roger obeyed. The boy was still standing with them, curious and wanting to see the outcome of their enquiries. The elderly woman who opened the door a sliver was wearing an apron that swamped her and her eyes were milky.

'Who?' she asked. Perhaps she was hard of hearing, too.

Beatriz explained who they were again in a loud, clear voice. 'May we come in? We mean you no harm.'

'I don't know you.' She began to close the door, but Roger put a boot into the gap and wrenched the edge of the door from her grip. 'Hold the horses,' Beatriz instructed the baker's boy, pressing a coin into his palm. 'Be gentle, Roger,' Beatriz called out, as Roger bodily lifted the old woman up by her upper arms and shifted her out of his way. Beatriz followed him into the house, with the woman squawking her protests.

Inside the house, Beatriz was assaulted with the smells of smoke and animal dung.

'Amelie! Amelie!' the old woman shrieked. 'Robbers!'

Beatriz tried to calm her. 'We mean you no harm, truly. I am a friend of Imbert's. We need to search the house for information that might lead us to his murderer.'

When the woman continued to try to block their further entry, Roger spun her around and prodded her gently but relentlessly down the passage ahead of them. The passage had a packed earth floor, and a few sheep and goats were housed in a byre to one side with a kitchen and cooking pit on the other side. Here, more pleasant smells of herbs and cooking meat vied for the attention of Beatriz's nose.

The woman proceeded them into a comfortable long chamber with a large table, benches, cushions, a couple of tapestries on the walls. The chamber was spotlessly clean. Beatriz could almost see Imbert in here, with his *oud*, laughing at his own jokes, trying out a line or two of lyric.

'Are you … Imbert's mother?' Beatriz tried.

The woman didn't answer at first. Beatriz sat her down gently on a bench. 'What's your name?'

'Yselda,' she conceded.

Beatriz sat beside her and stroked the back of her shaking hand. 'Yselda, please believe me. We are not robbers. We are friends of Imbert. I know Roger looks a bit fearsome, but he's a gentle giant, really.' She must see something from those milky eyes, but not a great deal, Beatriz guessed.

She glanced over at Roger and back to Beatriz's face. 'I'm not Imbert's mother. I'm his housekeeper. For many,

many years now. I couldn't say where his mother went. Maybe died in a ditch. Left him on a church doorstep. You are his *jograresa*, you say? He never mentioned you.'

'I am. We were together for four years.'

'Do you sing, play music?'

'I do. Would you like me to play for you?'

'Oh yes!' Her face lit up and the shaking in her hands now was more a palsy of old age than fear.

'I would be happy to.'

'I would love to hear a little music. Imbert was always singing and playing and I do miss him so.'

'Me too,' Beatriz said, gesturing for Roger to sit down. He would be less threatening then. 'Imbert was my teacher. We are come from the court in Tolosa,' she explained. 'It has been a long journey and we would thank you for some refreshment.'

There was still doubt in the woman's face, but it seemed in contest with her hospitable instincts. She left the room and Beatriz could hear frantic whispering in the kitchen.

The old woman returned with a young girl, around fifteen, carrying a tray with bread and a gaily patterned jug and beakers, which she set on the table. So, the woman had help with the cleaning and cooking. 'This is my granddaughter, Amelie,' the woman told Beatriz proudly. 'This lady is a friend of the master. Musical like him,' she told the girl.

Beatriz nodded her head formally to them both. 'I am Beatriz de Farrera, *trobaritz*, and I was at the court of Tolosa with Imbert. He taught me how to sing and play.'

'Do you know what's to become of us, of the house?' Yselda asked.

'It depends whether Imbert left a will, I imagine. Did he have any family?'

'None that we ever met. But he may have left a will in his private room. We can't read, mistress, but I'm sure you can. You can decipher his papers. We're not allowed in there. We've never set foot in there, have we, Amelie?' The girl shook her brown head.

'My instruments are in our packs,' Beatriz said. 'Might Roger fetch them in? Might we rest the horses and ourselves here for the night, Yselda? We can pay for our victuals.' Beatriz spread ten silver coins on the table, which amounted to a great deal more than the cost of some bread and wine. Yselda and Amelie exchanged glances and Beatriz saw Amelie give a small nod. Yselda swept the coins into her apron with a smooth movement and held a gnarled hand around the lump they made there.

'I'll show the boy where to take the horses and bring in your instruments and packs. You can sleep in here tonight.' She gestured to a corner where a couple of straw pallets were stacked.

'Roger will help the boy with our packs; they are heavy,' Beatriz said. Roger went back out into the passage.

When Roger returned, Beatriz tuned the *vielle* and sang her 'Lluis' song for them. Yselda, Amelie, and even Roger were wreathed with smiles, and the old woman was full of praise for her playing and singing.

'You say Imbert has a private room?'

'It's locked.' Yselda set her mouth defensively again.

'It is where he would keep a will, if he left one.'

'I don't have the key. Show them,' she instructed her granddaughter.

Amelie led Beatriz and Roger to the tapestry at the far end of the chamber. She lifted the tapestry, revealing a closed door. It was sealed with a thick metal band across the door jamb and a heavy padlock. Beatriz frowned. Why all the secrecy? She'd never known Imbert to be fussily private. He had lived his life in the full blaze of companionship – singing, gambling, arguing, discoursing – sleeping and eating in crowded halls.

'You don't have the key or any idea where Imbert kept it?' she asked Amelie, who shook her head.

'The master composed his music in there. He didn't like to be disturbed or to have his parchments moved around. We never went in or cleaned in there. Master Imbert made us solemnly promise.'

Beatriz looked at Roger. 'We need to get in there.'

He flipped his hand at the two girls to encourage them to move to the side. He braced one arm with the other and began thumping his shoulder and hip against the door. Eventually, the wood began to splinter and give way. Yselda had come running at the noise and stood wringing her hands.

'We'll be accused of causing this damage!' she said to Amelie, her face aghast.

Roger had made sufficient progress with his shoulder to resort to kicking the rest of the door out of his way. He pulled the ruins of the door out of their path and gestured to Beatriz to precede him into the small room beyond – Imbert's bedroom and study.

'I hope you can find a will,' Amelie said, backing away and pulling at her grandmother's sleeve.

Beatriz walked to the long, floor-length shutters and threw them open onto a lovely, colourful garden, buzzing with bees and other insects. An olive tree stood in the middle of the garden, with a square of herbs flourishing at its foot.

She turned back to the room and walked to the desk. Perhaps a will would have a seal on it. Perhaps it would have flourishing signatures and look more official than the other scrolls in this room, of which there were very many. One wall had shelves full of scrolls and a few books. The desk had a replica set of the writing materials, inkpots and styluses, tablets and parchments weighted with stones, that Beatriz was used to seeing Imbert working with. The wall opposite the books was a veritable gallery – filled edge to edge with hundreds of drawings. She had never known Imbert to draw.

Stepping closer, she saw the drawings were all of young men, made with brown ink on sheets of parchment. Many of the faces were painfully beautiful – just come to manhood. A young man with his dog. A man with a loaf of bread and a big grin. A young man, his long hair parted in the middle. A man with straggling hair blowing in the wind. Two young men, sitting together with scrolls and styluses before them. A man, staring up at the ceiling in a daydream. A young man, looking back over his shoulder and pointing at the artist capturing his image.

Beatriz's eyes slowed across the blizzard of drawings. She recognised Lluis' face in one picture – drawn by his own hand perhaps, using a polished mirror maybe, and there was another of Bertrand that was definitely drawn by Lluis. She recognised his signature on the bottom right corner. Roger was moving beside Beatriz, ahead of her, also looking at the drawings. 'Lluis,' she said pointing, 'and Bertrand.' As they approached the window, the wall turned at a right angle, creating a small alcove with yet more drawings.

'*Trobairitz*.'

'Roger?' He was looking at the walls of the alcove. She followed his gaze. The wall was covered again with drawings of young men, but this time they were naked and aroused.

'This is not for your eyes, *Trobairitz*,' Roger said quietly. He placed his large hands over some of the erect penises in the images, but there were too many for him to cover them all.

'I am no innocent, Roger.' She pulled his arms away and took in the images. 'I don't understand though. Imbert was not an artist. These are not from his hand.' She understood the drawings, however. Suddenly, Imbert made sense to her. His lack of lasciviousness, for instance. If he had married her, she would have been his cover, perhaps. She had never guessed at this. Imbert had given no hint. But now she thought back with this new knowledge, she saw Imbert's glances at Lluis and Bertrand. She saw what she had blithely not seen before.

Roger reached for one of the drawings and pulled it from the wall, brought it closer to her face, pointing at a mark in the corner. It was not a signature. It was more like the mason's marks she had seen Lluis and others use on bricks and sculptures.

'I can't decipher it. Can you?' she asked.

He shook his head. He searched the first wall for a drawing with the same mark in which the model was wearing clothes, comparing the one in his hand. Eventually, he found one. 'Same artist,' he told Beatriz.

Beatriz took the clothed drawing and found Yselda and Amelie in the kitchen, chopping vegetables and feeding the cooking fire.

'Yselda, do you know who made these drawings?' She showed the parchment to them both.

Yselda shook her head. 'I can't see much these days. Imbert had a lot of friends coming in and out, playing music.'

Beatriz nodded. 'He was a sociable man. But was one of these friends an artist?'

'There was one – always with charcoal or paint on his hands and boots. I was worried about him making a mess. His name was Davello. It could be him.'

Beatriz conveyed the information and the clothed drawing to Roger, who went out in search of Davello. She turned back to the room. There were so many documents here, but Beatriz could not read a one. She was loath to expose Imbert's private sanctum to any other curious eyes. She would have to collect it all up and take it to Anna. She began to take the naked drawings from the wall and the others too, creating a neat pile.

Roger returned an hour later with a young man in tow. The man had long dark hair and ink-stained hands. Beatriz poked her head into the kitchen to ask Amelie to give her a jug of wine and beakers. 'Have you found a will?' Yselda asked.

'Not yet.'

Beatriz returned to Imbert's study and dropped the tapestry behind her. She examined the young man's face, wondering if he was one of the models from the drawings, but she could not discern a likeness to any she had seen. She poured wine for them all.

The young man was nervous. 'Davello at your service, lady. Out of Italy and the workshops of the masters.'

'Glad to meet you, Davello.'

He spoke rapidly. 'You are wanting to commission a portrait, Mistress? You have an exquisite face, may I say. You would make a fantastic model for a portrait. I would be glad to do it … Your man waved this drawing at me and was quite mysterious about what you wanted. Is he mute?' He smiled anxiously at Roger.

Beatriz shook her head. 'Just spare with his words.'

Davello was glancing around the room. He, no doubt, knew about the drawings that had been on the wall and in the niche, which were now stowed in Beatriz's satchel.

'I *am* looking for an artist,' she said.

'You have found one!'

'I am looking for the artist who drew this.' She selected and withdrew one of the naked drawings from the satchel. 'This is your mark.'

'I …,' he began a denial, but Roger stepped towards him, looming. 'Yes, yes, alright,' he said testily. 'What of it? Master Imbert had me make these drawings and paid me well. The models he found and the poses he decided on. I don't know who they are. Except for the monk, of course.'

'The monk?'

He was silent.

'What monk? What was his name?'

He shook his head. 'I don't know.'

Roger took him by the shoulders of his tunic and lifted him off his feet with ease.

'I can't tell you anything more, I swear it,' he squeaked. 'I am not one of his catamites. I don't want to be caught up in Imbert's dealings. I'll be hanged or worse.'

'Put him down, Roger, and hold him fast. We will visit your lodgings,' Beatriz decided.

'My …' Davello spluttered. 'There's nothing to see there.'

Roger hauled Davello through the tapestry, into the main room.

'We will be back in time for dinner,' Beatriz called out to Yselda as they hurried past the kitchen. She could feel Amelie's eyes on their backs but did not turn around.

Roger kept a tight hold on the squirming artist as they walked to a ramshackle house near the ramparts. A wooden sign displaying an artist's pallet and brush was swinging above the door. Inside Davello's small studio, there was an unfinished picture of the Virgin on an easel. Pots of brushes and pigments and stacked canvases and rolled parchments filled the room.

'Where is the drawing of the monk?' Beatriz asked.

'I gave it to Imbert, so I don't know,' Davello responded sulkily.

Roger exchanged a glance with Beatriz. She nodded her head, and he began searching the room, with no regard or care for Davello's work.

'Stop! You're ruining everything! Stop!'

Roger smashed a few jars of precious pigment.

'If you want him to stop, you need to tell us where the drawing of the monk is.'

'I don't …'

'Yes!' Roger held a parchment aloft. Beatriz could only see the back of it. 'Gauzlin,' Roger told her.

'Really!' She stepped around to look at the drawing. The unfinished portrait showed a naked Gauzlin. 'Well!' Beatriz exclaimed.

Beatriz rolled the portrait and placed it in her satchel.

Davello was a mixture of fearful and sulky now. He began to bend to tidy up the mess Roger had created. 'Will you report me and Imbert to the authorities? It's not me who… It's Imbert.'

'I won't report you. I'm not interested in what men want to do in bed together. It is their own business. And I can't report Imbert since he has been murdered.'

Beatriz took another look around the studio, but was sure they had what they needed.

Back in Imbert's house, Beatriz and Roger sat behind the tapestry covering the ruined doorway of the study again. 'So, how does this work?' Beatriz mused aloud. 'Imbert used himself as a blackmail trap for Gauzlin, perhaps? To get him to hand over the letter to Cluny or … Roger, I need you to speak,' Beatriz said impatiently. 'It helps me divine the truth if I can speak about it with another.'

Roger grunted and then, in response to Beatriz's cross expression, said, 'Maybe.'

'Or perhaps, the relationship between them was one of genuine affection.'

Roger pursed his lips and tipped his head to one side, which Beatriz interpreted as another maybe.

'It's not clear what this discovery means. If Imbert had exposed the drawing of Gauzlin, he would have been at risk of charges of sodomy himself, so ... but it does mean that Gauzlin must be under suspicion for the murder. There was some covert relationship. Is it enough to clear Anna?'

They passed the night on the straw mattresses in the main room and, in the morning, explained to Yselda they were taking Imbert's documents with them to be looked over by a lawyer. Beatriz told the old woman and her granddaughter they should continue to keep the house well, as they had for so long and she would be in touch with them again. The door closed behind them and Beatriz stood on the street, waiting for Roger to finish strapping their baggage onto the mule. She looked up at the house that had held so much, concealed so much of Imbert. Did she have enough evidence now to return to Tolosa?

THE SALT MARKET

July 1093, Aigues-Mortes

'We will go on to Aigues-Mortes,' Beatriz told Roger, as they turned their horses from the main street in Uzès onto the road to the south and the coast. 'Maybe I have enough to cast doubt on the accusation against Anna, to show that Gauzlin was likely the murderer, and yet … I'm not fully sure.' She paused.

Roger said nothing.

'There is still the salt. Imbert was involved too, somehow, in the stolen salt. For answers on that, we have to go to the salt lakes. There is still time to get back to Tolosa after that, well before the Michaelmas Assembly.'

Despairing of gaining any response from her companion, Beatriz fixed her eyes on the horizon and sought through her memories of what Jacques, the salt merchant, had told her about Aigues-Mortes and what Simo, the stableboy, and the cook at Chateau Narbonnais had revealed about Imbert and the salt bag.

They rode past many mills along the river and brilliant yellow fields of blooming sunflowers. They rode past the spectacular remains of the Roman viaduct that had carried water to Nimes. The land flattened out as they neared the coast. It was four more days' slow riding with their plodding mule before they reached the marshes just west of the delta of the great Rhone river.

Watery inlets and islets began to appear. Great flocks of water birds wheeled, screeched, stood at the edges of streams. Small orchards and vineyards dotted the swampy fields. Clusters of white horses lifted their heads from the grass as they passed. The marshlands buzzed with clouds of mosquitos that Roger batted away from his face. Their horses blinked at flies crowding their eyes and swished their tails, occasionally skittering from a mosquito bite. Miles of pink lakes came into view with hundreds of neat, conical mounds of white salt on the land between the lakes. These long lines of little salt mountains drying in the sun were everywhere amid the checkerboard of the salt pans.

A wide stone tower rose high above a settlement of thatched huts where the workers and merchants lived. Lines of workers trudged past with baskets filled with salt. The baskets, which had one long handle, were balanced on the back of the men's necks and shoulders, making them look like turtles that had sprouted long legs and arms. The baskets sat on padded cloths to protect the workers' necks, and the men wore cloth caps with long earflaps to shade them from the sun. Their faces and hands were burnt red from sun and salt, the skin on their noses peeling. Other workers wielded long-handled wooden shovels, moving the salt into the mounds or scraping it into sacks.

Aigues-Mortes meant stagnant waters. The colouration all around them was shockingly alien – the usual greens and browns replaced by stark contrasts of pink, white and blue. As they approached one of the lakes, Beatriz leant from the saddle to look at the salt crystals forming on the surface of the shallow water. In the waters of the lakes, large pink birds with long bent beaks waded on spindly red legs. Some stood on one leg, grunting and honking.

'Hello,' Beatriz called to a passing worker. He stopped, lifted the basket from his neck with the handle, and placed it carefully on the ground.

'Mistress?' As usual, the worker was glancing with a mixture of curiosity and alarm at Roger and not focusing on her.

'I'm looking for the merchant Jacques Sau. Do you know where I might find him?'

He brought his gaze back to Beatriz and pointed towards the tower. 'The merchants' hall is close by the tower. You'll probably find him there or in the market place.'

She thanked him and they rode towards the tower. Jacques saw them before her eyes found him. '*Trobairitz!*' he called out in a delighted tone from where he stood on the steps of the merchants' hall. She smiled back and dismounted to greet him. Roger stayed on his horse, surveying the situation. 'What do you here, Mistress Beatriz? Come to sing us some songs?'

'I could do that. I came looking for you. I have some questions.'

'Ah! More questions!'

'And we will need a place to stay the night and rest our beasts. Can you recommend somewhere?'

'Of course. I'll show you to the best inn, close by the market place. Come along. And then I can treat you and,' he jerked his head towards Roger, 'him to dinner tonight.'

Beatriz smiled. 'And I can repay you with a few songs.'

'It's a deal!'

The market place had the usual produce on one side – vegetables, fruit, fish. The other side was given over entirely to salt. The vendors measured out sacks of salt, which were loaded onto the merchants' donkeys to take to the waiting ships. The salt belonged to the count of Tolosa – in effect to Philippa, Raimon and Bertrand. It was the salt and the labour of these lines of burdened men, the skin of their faces and hands dried and salted like cured hams, that flooded silver into the count's coffers and paid for the building of Saint-Sernin or Bertrand's castle at Najac – or at least, that was a large part of their income. But someone was somehow siphoning off substantial quantities of the white gold.

Beatriz and Roger stabled their horses and secured a room at the inn. They sat outside in the sun, looking at the market. 'At what stage in the process is the theft occurring?' Beatriz said to Roger, not expecting an answer. 'It could be stolen out on the salt flats we saw? From the mounds? Or here in the market place, short-changing the merchants? But the market is carefully supervised, the weights and measures overseen. Or could it be where the sacks are loaded onto the ships or the donkey trains going inland? That seems the most likely. I will go and look at these two places.'

Roger gestured that he was staying where he was, at the cafe next to the market place.

Beatriz frowned at him. 'It has been a long journey, I know, but you are getting lazy, Roger.'

He took no notice of her and signalled for more ale to the boy waiting at the tables.

Beatriz reclaimed her horse and sought out the main hub for the donkey trains. The donkeys had sacks tied to their buttocks to collect their dung and avoid dirtying the street and contaminating the washed salt. They were roped together in long lines and loaded with sacks and led off by the merchants who took the land routes north. Beatriz watched the comings and goings for several hours, but was none the wiser.

Jacques appeared at her shoulder. 'Any joy?' he asked, knowing her task. She shook her head, frustrated. 'I'm going to the port,' Jacques told her, 'to supervise the loading for my ship bound for Genoa. Do you want to come with me?' They rode the few miles to the edge of the sea, where four merchant ships sat at anchor.

All around her, Beatriz heard the alien Genoese tongue spoken by the sailors. 'Which ship is yours?' she asked.

Jacques pointed to the nearest one. They watched the loaded donkeys being cajoled along the pier where the sacks were transferred into small boats and taken out to the ship riding at anchor. He kissed two fingers and thumb with a loud smack of his mouth. 'The salty seawater is evaporating, and the salt drying all through the winter and into early summer, and then the salt can be collected from August to October, and then that's where I come in!' He beamed at her.

She turned to him, smiling. 'It's good to see a man who loves his work.'

'I'm shipping last year's salt at the moment and will return for more after this year's harvest. She can take a great load,' he told her, pointing again at the ship. 'The sacks are counted onto the donkeys and counted again onto the ship.'

Beatriz considered there seemed little room for purloining the salt in this process.

'Imbert had an idea the theft was occurring here, in Aigues-Mortes,' Jacques said. 'He was trying to find out how or who. He asked questions, skulked around. But the workers, the Aigues-Mortais, they are a tight, close community. He didn't get much out of them, I wager. Would you like to go aboard?'

Beatriz breathed in the salty, invigorating air. 'I would!'

The train of donkeys halted for a few minutes to allow Beatriz and Jacques to walk along the wooden pier and step into one of the small boats that was already loaded with salt, allowing just enough room for them to sit. The boatman sculled out to the ship, the salty sea slapping at the sides of their small boat and occasionally spraying them and making them laugh. Beatriz's black hair whipped at her face.

The boatman held the boat to the netting slung over the side of the ship and Beatriz climbed up, helped over the gunwale at the top, with Jacques swarming up close behind her. He showed her around the ship and introduced her to the captain and some of the crew – they were all Genoese so communication was limited to showing her their teeth in wide grins and creasing their eyes, where they already had white streaks ingrained into their faces from squinting at the sun.

Beatriz breathed in deeply, looking out at the endless ocean and sky. An ungainly flock of flamingoes flew overhead, on their way inland to the pink lakes. 'I have a proposition for you, Beatriz.' She brought her attention back to Jacques.

'Your talent would be much appreciated in Genoa. I sail tonight at the tide. Come with me. I have a very comfortable townhouse in Genoa and I could introduce you at the duke's court there. It is a city that outshines even Tolosa.'

Beatriz laughed.

'I'm serious!' he exclaimed. 'I know the princes of Genoa would reward you well for your song. You would be feted all over Italy.'

'I have been to Italy before,' she said, 'with Imbert.'

'So, come again, and let me lead you to fame and fortune!'

Beatriz sat on a mound of salt sacks behind her and studied him. It wasn't a very comfortable seat, but it could be a comfortable berth with him. He was an astute and energetic merchant. She didn't doubt that it would be beneficial to her to answer him positively. She had enjoyed her brief time in Italy before. She sighed and kept him waiting, looking out to sea.

'Imbert, Philippa, Anna,' she said at last, turning back to his expectant face. 'These are the three reasons I cannot come with you at the turning of the tide, Jacques. I have obligations to them. Wrongs I must right. Perhaps next year, when the tide turns, I will join you on an adventure, but not this year.'

Jacques sighed. 'Are you sure? Perhaps next year I will be in another port with another *trobairitz?*'

Beatriz laughed loudly at that. 'We are not so many that you will easily find another.'

'And I am not so many either,' Jacques said, his eyebrows raised at her with his final hope. 'You will not get many such offers.'

'I appreciate it. I do. But I cannot.'

Beatriz was rowed back to the pier, leaving Jacques onboard his ship, and she returned to Roger and the inn, feeling frustrated. If Imbert had discovered something here, she could not see how or what. Roger was sitting in exactly the same place she had left him, sipping at his ale, shaded by a tree. He raised his eyebrows.

'I saw the donkey trains and the salt ships, but I can't see how or where the thefts might be occurring,' Beatriz reported. She thumped down onto the bench.

Roger smiled.

'Why is that occasion to grin?' Beatriz asked crossly. 'I've had a wasted day, and we have had a wasted journey here.' Had she made a mistake turning down Jacques' offer?

Roger shook his head and tapped the side of his nose with a chunky index finger.

Beatriz sat up again, looking at him with hope. 'You've seen something?'

He nodded his head once and stood up, stretching after his long vigil. Beatriz had to move out of the way of one of his long arms reaching out. When he had sufficiently reorganised his muscles, he walked slowly towards the covered market with Beatriz on his heel. She knew better than to throw questions at him. He would show her what he had discovered.

Markets had the same system everywhere for measuring out produce – whether it was wheat or salt. All around the low stone wall of the roofed market square were basins carved into the wall of varying sizes – to measure out *litrons* (a sixteenth of a *boisseaux*), quarts (a quarter of a *boisseaux*) and *boisseaux*. Sixteen *boisseaux* made up a *setier*. The measuring basins were bunged with flat wooden plugs that fitted snugly in the basin's hole. The plug was on a string. The basin was filled with salt. The purchaser held a sack beneath a chute, below the basin, on the outside of the market wall. The plug was pulled, and the salt spilled into the waiting sack. The only way to cheat was not to fill the basin properly or to have inaccurately carved basins, both of which seemed unlikely, with the market overseers patrolling and watching carefully.

Roger was looking at these basins.

'How?' she whispered to him.

One of the overseers who checked that all measures

were fair was passing, inspecting procedures, and Roger looked at him.

'Is he crooked?' Beatriz whispered.

Roger shook his head. He plucked Beatriz by the sleeve and stepped to the overseer, bringing her with him. He nodded to Beatriz.

'We beg your attention,' she said, guessing and looking at Roger.

'How can I help you, Mistress?'

Roger pointed at the back of a tall man wearing a long apron. The overseer stepped closer to him. The man sensed their presence and looked back over his shoulder. 'Overseer,' the man greeted him in a friendly but uncertain tone.

Beatriz and the overseer both looked at Roger for an explanation. He pulled her closer and pointed at a sack between the man's legs. 'String,' he said.

The overseer put his hand on the man's arm and pulled him away from the full basin. The merchant, with his sack on the other side of the low wall, was looking at the group in confusion. 'What's going on?'

Beatriz reached past the man in the apron for the plug string and pulled on it. Salt spilled through the chute into the waiting sack. Beatriz looked with astonishment at the contraption in her hand. The plug had a wooden tube fitted to it that was full of salt. She saw how the man now shaking in the grip of the overseer could empty this fifth of the measure into the sack between his legs. If he did that all day, he would end up with a purloined sack of his own. If he did it all week, all year, the count's coffers would be significantly light.

'I have never seen this ruse before!' declared the overseer. 'I thank you, both. We will question this thief.'

'I would like to listen in,' Beatriz said, handing over the plug contraption. To prove theft was one thing, but what she needed to know was who was behind it. Did Imbert know about the contraption and had he figured out who was pulling the strings – so to speak?

The overseer shrugged his agreement as he gestured to his colleague and they led the quivering man away towards the merchants' hall. Under a harsh interrogation and facing certain hanging and eternal judgement, the man soon confessed he had been siphoning off the salt for over a year, and the man he answered to with the purloined salt was Vicar Petrus Regimundus.

REUNION

August 1093, Chateau Narbonnais

*R*oger and Beatriz reached Tolosa late in the evening and Roger had to rouse the guard to open the city gate for them. They led their horses and mule through the portal and were relieved to hand them over to a stableboy who had been woken from his slumber by the late-night commotion. Roger unloaded their baggage and carried it up to Philippa's chambers, setting it down outside the door. 'I suppose Philippa is asleep,' Beatriz whispered. Roger nodded and unrolled his bedroll outside the door. Beatriz followed suit and soon fell into the sleep of the truly exhausted.

She opened her eyes on an upside-down view of Philippa's face, wearing a frown. 'What are you doing on the floor? Why didn't you come in?'

Beatriz struggled to consciousness. 'It was very late. I didn't want to wake you.'

'Well, now I must wake you. I'm desperate to know your news. Thank god you are here! But only just in time!'

Beatriz looked over to Roger's bedroll and saw he had already vacated it and packed it away. Their baggage had been taken into Philippa's chambers. Beatriz struggled upright and pushed the covering from her. Roger came around the corner with a basket of delicious-smelling fresh bread.

'Come on!' Philippa held out a hand and heaved Beatriz to her feet.

Seated once more at Philippa's familiar table, Beatriz tucked hungrily into the breadrolls. 'Why only just in time? We've weeks yet before Michaelmas. Where's Anna?'

Philippa's face fell.

'At Ademar's?' Beatriz said, but she could already see in Philippa's expression that Anna was not at the viscount's house.

'My uncle has seen fit to remove Anna from the viscount's custody and place her in a cell at Saint-Sernin.'

Roger banged down his beaker in consternation. 'What?' Beatriz voiced loudly for both of them.

'It happened a few days ago. Raimon said it was necessary because he has decided to bring the trial forward. It will be in a few days' time. She is in the custody of Dean Gayrard and as you know, he is a fair man. I've been to visit her. She *is* alright,' she said, addressing Roger, whose frown could have brought on an eclipse.

'Why has the trial been brought forward?' Beatriz asked.

'My uncle was suspicious about your absence and Roger's. He kept asking me where you were and I kept spinning lies. But I think he had word that you were in Poitiers. He has his own spies, of course. I think he has guessed that the duke might come at Michaelmas and offer for me. He means to preempt that by bringing forward the trial and sending me off to Aragon straight afterwards.'

'Did you receive my letter?' Beatriz asked, reaching for her bulging satchel.

'Yes,' Philippa said. 'You have letters from the duke for me and you have uncovered evidence that *must* throw doubt on Anna's guilt?'

'I hope so,' Beatriz said. 'I hope it is enough.'

She handed the duke's two letters over first. Philippa's eyebrows rose and fell repeatedly as she read the second, saucy letter. 'Well, he is ambiguous, flirtatious, rude.'

'I think he means to offer you marriage, lady. His mother was negotiating for Ermengarde of Anjou, who was at his court when we visited, but I am sure he did not like the match. He seemed captivated by your portrait and the report I gave of your poetic inclinations and love of Baudri's work.'

'Well, he had best get here soon. He is cutting it too fine. And what of the murderer? Have you uncovered him? Do we have enough to go to the viscount?'

'We uncovered much, lady.' Beatriz took a gulp of wine to marshal her thoughts. 'Before we left, we had the evidence of the stab wounds on the body – seen in Lluis' drawing – that the murderer was right-handed. We have the glove with the marks of the garrotte – the glove is clearly too large for Anna's hand. We had Imbert's code book on his spying for Duke Guillaume and Pope Urban and his salt investigation.'

'I have more on that,' Philippa interrupted, 'but continue for now with your news and then I will add my own.'

Beatriz nodded. 'Also before we left, we had evidence (from Simo, Jacques Sau and the cook) that Imbert was tracking down the salt thief. The new evidence is this. At Moissac, we heard from the guesthouse master that Gauzlin was ambitious to be prior of Saint-Sernin, and so disappointed in that ambition. When we reached Conques, Abbot Begon confirmed that Gauzlin was spying on behalf of Cluny in the dispute over the pilgrim routes.' Beatriz handed over the copy of Gauzlin's letter with a covering letter from Abbot Begon.

Philippa read slowly through the documents, nodded her head and added them to the pile on the table before them.

'It was in Uzès, at Imbert's house, that we made an even bigger discovery,' Beatriz said, looking toward Roger.

Philippa waited eagerly for her to continue.

'We were surprised in Conques that Imbert and Gauzlin had been travelling together. In Uzès, we found a collection of drawings of young men, many naked and displayed in Imbert's private room.'

'What!'

Beatriz handed over the drawings and Philippa began

to shuffle quickly through them, pausing when she reached the likenesses of Bertrand and Lluis.

'This, in itself, means nothing certain for our investigation,' Beatriz said. 'It shows that Imbert's desire was for men.'

'This is shocking,' Philippa stuttered. She pointed at the drawings of Bertrand's and Lluis' faces. 'What does this mean?'

'It means nothing,' Beatriz said. 'It means that Imbert admired them. He wanted to look at their faces. I think the drawings were made by Lluis. He probably had no idea of the reason why Imbert wanted the drawings. It is not unusual for men to be close friends or for friends to exchange portraits. You had to see the drawings all displayed together in his house to see it was more than that for Imbert.'

Philippa nodded slowly. 'But you think Imbert's unnatural desires could have been cause for his murder?'

'Possibly.' Beatriz handed over the naked drawing of Gauzlin and Philippa gasped.

'It seems there was a ... relationship,' Beatriz said. 'That could be cause for murder. Gauzlin's ambitions would be destroyed completely if he was accused of sodomy. He would have been excommunicated and mutilated.'

Philippa was looking at Roger and then Beatriz, a little dazed now.

'Yes,' Beatriz said (falling into her habit from the journey of articulating for others), 'we were not expecting this.'

'Surely this is enough to persuade the viscount that Anna is wrongly accused,' Philippa declared.

'We also found evidence in Aigues-Mortes that the salt thefts were controlled by Vicar Petrus Regimundus.'

'Petrus! But this must be a separate matter, then? Not related to the murder. And we know that Petrus is left-handed too.'

Beatriz shrugged. 'Did you search Imbert's satchel?'

'Yes. There were only a few poems and notes of gambling debts in it.'

Beatriz smiled wryly at the summary of Imbert's life: poetry and debt. 'I suppose that is to be expected. If there was anything incriminating, the murderer would have taken it.'

'I just … find it hard to believe that Gauzlin could have the strength to garrotte Imbert, who was so much bigger.'

'I know. Did you pursue enquiries concerning Lluis?'

Philippa shook her head. 'Anna and I discussed it but we could not see a way to broach it.'

Beatriz reached into her satchel for the final pile of documents they had collected from Imbert's sanctum. 'Then there is all this, but we could not read any of it so I brought it back for Anna to sift through. You said you had found more on the code book?'

'Only that Anna has deciphered the whole code and book, and it confirms our previous guesses. It records Imbert's spying on Raimon and Bertrand for Duke Guillaume. It confirms that Imbert sent word to Pope Urban of Gauzlin and Henry of Burgundy's contact with Cluny. It documents his enquiries concerning the salt thefts. But he had not solved that crime, as you and Roger have.'

'It was Roger who saw it, figured out how they were stealing the salt and then the overseers terrified Petrus' name from the man he was employing in Aigues-Mortes,' Beatriz said. 'Did the coded book tell you anything else?'

'There is much in it. Imbert recorded everything he overheard and spied on. I suppose he wasn't sure what would be of import, so he simply collected everything.'

'And?'

'This part is interesting.' She turned to the middle of the book. 'He writes here that Abbot Frotard took a bribe from my other uncle, Count Berenguer of Barcelona, to give him absolution for the murder of his twin brother, Count Ramon. The bribe given to Abbot Frotard was control and proceeds from the Catalan monastery of Saint-Cugat. He also copied out a letter from Abbot Frotard to the pope where he writes, "we must wrestle control of the pilgrim routes from Cluny, especially in Iberia, at any cost".'

'Yes, I can't imagine Abbot Frotard would like the pope hearing of his bribe in Barcelona. But, like the salt and Petrus, this seems perhaps a side issue, not related to Imbert's murder?'

'Most likely.' Philippa pondered their position for a moment. 'I will call the viscount to us to listen to what we have. But we must get Imbert's papers to Anna to sift through – it will take a considerable amount of time. It will do her good to have something to do before the trial. Can you go to Saint-Sernin with them, Beatriz?'

'Yes, of course.'

They carefully packed away their evidence all together in one dossier, except Imbert's papers, which Philippa packed into a separate satchel. She added in parchment, a small bottle of ink and a stylus for Anna to make notes and handed this second package to Beatriz.

MASS WAS in progress in Saint-Sernin. Beatriz slipped in and looked around at the congregation and visiting pilgrims. She spotted the girl she knew who was in the service of the dean. The girl turned to leave while the rest of the crowd lingered in the church.

Beatriz moved through the throng to follow her. She caught up with the girl in the shadow of an arched doorway. 'Friend!' The girl turned. 'Do you know where Anna is kept?' The serving girl looked perplexed. 'The deaf girl who Raimon de Saint-Gilles has accused of murder. She is being kept here until her trial.'

'I don't know.' The girl's expression and tone were impatient. She probably had a long list of chores to complete that weighed heavy on her mind. 'Maybe in the cell adjacent to the beggar's hospital.'

'Thank you,' Beatriz said, but the girl had already turned and was taking the stone steps leading up into the building two at a time.

Beatriz asked her way to the beggar's hospital and entered, clamping a hand to her nose at the stench of sickness. There was a fat monk making his way amidst the crippled and needy lying on the ground on rough blankets. The lower part of the monk's face was covered with a thick cloth. Beatriz pulled her neckscarf up around her mouth and nose and made her way towards him, stepping carefully around and over outstretched limbs.

'Brother.' He looked up. 'I am seeking the deaf girl, the prisoner. Is she here?' She looked around at the sick people, gulping, hoping Anna was not here. There seemed to be contagion almost visible in the air.

The monk nodded and gestured to a studded door. There was another monk outside the door, a guard, she supposed. He was sitting at a small wooden table, writing with a stylus on parchment. 'Brother,' Beatriz stood before the table and addressed the guard. 'I would like to bring food and a prayer book to the prisoner.'

He frowned and shook his head.

'She is a Christian like you and I, and has the right to Christian solace, surely?'

He frowned again. 'No visitors.' He waved her off with the stylus. There was a small, brown wine jug and beaker on the table along with his parchment, where he was inscribing a list of some sort.

Beatriz retreated to the shadows at the edge of the cloister and watched the scene. Quite close to where she lurked, there was a table of medicines that the fat monk, every now and then, dispensed to one of his poor patients. She watched as he prepared a concoction from several small bottles and soaked a sponge in it. She knew what this was. Back home in Farrera, her father had many roles in the tiny village. His main trade was blacksmithing, but in the remote Pyrenees he had limited work and often supplemented their meagre income with occasional mining work when he could find it, and with performing small surgeries for the villagers. He would pull rotten teeth, sew up deep cuts and even amputate a finger, or worse, when that was necessary.

Beatriz turned her memories away from her father and focused back on the immediate scene before her. The monk took the sponge over to an old woman and held it to her nose and began to cut at a large pustule on her leg. She did not move or scream in pain. Beatriz grimaced, watching the operation and, eventually, had to turn away in disgust, although she usually prided herself on her lack of squeamishness. The monk carried the sponge back to the table and set it down. Beatriz contemplated taking hold of the sponge and drugging the guard at Anna's door, but she was fearful she might accidentally kill him.

She was still pondering this option when she was surprised to see the monk gesture to the guard who stood up and unlocked the door of Anna's cell. Anna herself emerged and watched the monk's lips for instructions and then began ministering to the sick people lying there. The fat monk left the room, and the guard went back to totting up his laundry list.

Beatriz slipped quietly from the shadows. 'Oh, Anna!' The girls embraced. Beatriz peered into Anna's cell. There was a small grilled window, a long stone shelf with blankets and Anna had a book, Beatriz was pleased to see. 'This is not too bad!'

She glanced at the seated guard, who relented, shrugged and waved Beatriz in to speak with Anna as long as they left the door open.

'Am I exonerated? Have you come to get me out?'

Beatriz shook her head and spoke slowing, enunciating clearly as she looked Anna in the face. 'I'm sorry no, not yet, but we have compiled a lot of evidence that should prove you innocent. Philippa has summoned the viscount to lay it before him. Are you warm enough? Have you food?'

Anna nodded. 'Yes, but I am not free, and I will hang.'

'No!' Beatriz exclaimed. 'We will not allow that. We will prove your innocence. Are you being treated kindly?'

'The monks were sceptical, at first, that I was truly deaf. They had me sit still while they blew horns in my ears over and over again to see if I would startle. I could feel the heat of their breath on my ear, but heard nothing. They have convinced themselves now, I am glad to say, and they find I can be some help to them with the poor sick people here.'

'I have scrolls I took from Imbert's house in Uzès, and we wondered if you could sift through them, see if there is anything of significance here.'

Anna took the satchel and placed it on the stone shelf.

'I need to tell you what we have found out, Anna, so that you can understand if you do find something of significance.' Beatriz summarised the findings that she had recently told to Philippa.

'But, Beatriz, this information would see Gauzlin punished for loving somebody … for loving Imbert, and that is unfair.'

'No,' Beatriz asserted. 'Gauzlin will not be punished for loving Imbert. He will be punished for killing him. I had better go,' she said, glancing at the guard who was peering in and frowning at her now. She dropped her voice. 'There is a serving girl, here, who I know. I will bribe her to send messages to you. And, through her, you can write to us if anything urgent comes up.'

Anna tried to smile, but looked desolate as Beatriz

readied to depart.

Beatriz gripped her hand for one last consolatory squeeze. She slipped out, resisting the urge to look back at Anna.

Beatriz sought out the serving girl and gave her two silver coins to arrange that she would be the one to take Anna her tray of food of drink and secretly collect any messages Anna might have for Beatriz. 'If you perform this well,' Beatriz said, 'there will be two more silver coins.' The girl's expression was avid. Four silver coins were a fortune for her.

WHEN BEATRIZ REGAINED Philippa's chambers, there was a visitor: a young man. 'This is Jaufre. He is a lawyer, and he tells me he has found a way to save Anna,' Philippa exclaimed.

'The young lady is deaf, correct?' the lawyer said, perhaps recapping, for Beatriz's benefit, a conversation he had already begun with Philippa.

'Yes.'

'Then I will put forward the idiot's defence.'

Beatriz and Philippa stared at him in confusion.

'A deaf person,' he explained, 'cannot fully participate in oral legal transactions. They cannot be expected to adequately defend themselves in judicial proceedings. The law has to treat them as minors. I will sue for this.'

'I do not think Anna will approve of this, Philippa,' Beatriz warned her.

'I know, but if all else fails, it may be all we have to stop her from being hanged.'

JUMPING

August 1093, The Garonne, Tolosa

*B*eatriz woke to a commotion. She had slept on Anna's pallet in the small closet adjacent to Philippa's bedchamber, and the noise was coming from Philippa's room.

'Roger, go and get Jaufre *now*!' Beatriz heard panic in Philippa's voice.

Beatriz stepped into the room in her nightshift. Philippa was rapidly dressing herself. 'What's happening?'

'My uncle has decided to try Anna *today*! I am rushing to Saint-Sernin to get there before the guards and reassure her. Roger has just gone in search of Jaufre. My uncle has ordered that the trial take place at the viscount's hall. The viscount sent me word his knee pain renders him unable to walk. He can do no more than see me this morning at the trial. Will you bring the dossier of evidence as soon as you are dressed and wait for me there?' Philippa's face was racked with anxiety.

'Of course.' The girls exchanged a brief embrace and Beatriz worked to show Philippa an encouraging expression, which did not accurately reflect her own fears.

Philippa left, and Beatriz pulled on her clothes and boots. She took a swift look through the dossier of evidence to ensure it was all there, in a good order and to rehearse what she would say about it. The memory of Anna yesterday, telling her miserably that she would hang, was vivid in Beatriz's thoughts. She set off towards the viscount's hall with the dossier under her arm.

She stepped through the chateau gateway heading north, but she had not gone far before she felt a prickling between her shoulder blades. Was someone following her? She strained her ears to listen for footsteps. She hefted the dossier more tightly under her arm. She twisted to look over her shoulder and took in a few people behind her on the street, one wearing a big hood that covered his face. Perhaps she was imagining it. She glanced back again and saw only the hooded man now. She crossed to the other side of the street and looked back. He had also crossed and was gaining on her. She broke into a run and heard him follow suit behind her. There was no one else on the street. She ducked left into an alley that she knew was a shortcut to the Comminges Gate. She picked up the pace. Whoever he was, he was a big man and would soon outrun her.

Through the gate, the pier to the floating mills was dead ahead and near the platform for unloading materials and goods coming by the river, south of the city. At this early hour, the riverside was deserted.

Three mills were moored in a row extending out into the river. The mills were boats with a thundering water wheel on one side that harnessed the water's power and drove the millstones. Four sets of ladders led up from the boat deck to a roofed hut where the wheat was poured into a funnel to fall onto the millstones. The three mills were roped to each other and to the pier. If Beatriz could get to one of the mills before the hooded man saw her, she could hide.

She ran along the short pier and swung herself across to the deck of the first mill, ducking down behind the criss-crossing mesh of ladders. She could glimpse out and could not be seen.

The hooded man emerged from the alley, slowing his momentum, looking left and right, wondering where she had disappeared to. Her heart thundered in her chest and she tried to control her panicked breathing. The mill structure swayed and banged in the furious flow of the river. The sound of the rushing water was loud and relentless in her ears.

The man stepped left to look around the corner in that direction, came back again, stepped right, doing the same for that direction. Came back again. The man was not Gauzlin, but he could have paid someone to chase her down. The man was advancing up the pier.

Beatriz fled up one of the ladders into the roofed hut. The mill creaked with the weight of the man stepping onto it. If only the miller would arrive, but perhaps it was too early in the morning yet. She couldn't stay here. He would soon be upon her. She stood at the doorway, looking out to the second mill.

The water wheel was just below her, churning piti-lessly. Could she make the leap across to the second mill? If she failed and fell into the wheel's mechanism, she would be horribly mangled. The gap between the two mills closed and widened erratically as the structures heaved and tossed with the current. The dark green mirror of the river surface was agitated and transformed, roaring in the teeth of the wheel mechanism, chewed into white froth, rushing to escape the inexorable roll.

She could hear the man coming up the ladder behind her. She had to jump. She wedged the dossier firmly into her belt, stretched her arms out to grip the door frame on either side, swung herself backwards and forwards a couple of times to gain momentum, and leaped.

Her boots hit squarely on the floury wooden floor of the second mill. She checked the security of the dossier in her belt and sped across to the doorway facing the third mill. Would the man follow her and make the leap? Perhaps he would fall into the wheel's thrashing blades.

She looked down at the second water wheel, saying a prayer, swearing to the Virgin that she would adjure wine and men forever if only she would keep her safe. She swung herself in the doorway and leaped again.

Only one foot found the solid floor of the third mill and she had to use the forward momentum of her body and grapple for a handhold on a flour sack to keep herself from falling back into the wheel. The mill tipped and the flour sack she was desperately gripping began to slide towards the doorway and the wheel. It wedged in the doorway. Beatriz hauled herself up and over the sack.

Would he follow her? There was nowhere left for her to go. Could she secrete the dossier somewhere? She moved silently behind the biggest pile of flour sacks. The mills banged and swayed against each other in the river's powerful flow. She felt the dip of the third mill, her hiding place, as the man's weight landed. He had made the two jumps. He was in the room. Beatriz held her breath. A billhook leant against the wall, close to her. If he came nearer, she would make a grab for that. Quietly, she pushed the dossier under the nearest flour sack. She heard a scraping sound that she could not identify at first and then realised, when she smelled smoke, that the man had been striking a fire flint.

She peeked around the sacks and immediately felt the wash of heat on her face. The man was gone, but the flour was ablaze and fire was spreading rapidly around the hut. The floor, everything, was covered in a sprinkling of fine white flour dust. The fire was licking it up greedily, lapping at flour spills, consuming bulging sacks, hungrily claiming the wooden walls, climbing up corners towards the roof, making its own cracking sound that drowned out the river.

Beatriz was convulsed with a hacking cough, and her eyes streamed. She was afraid he had set the fire to flush her out. If she ran for the doorway, he would be waiting for her. Sweat ran in rivulets down her face and neck. She had to get out before it was too late. She could hear shouts outside – people had realised and would start throwing buckets of water to put out the blaze. If there were people around, he could not kill her in front of them.

She pulled the dossier out from beneath the flour sack, which would soon catch fire, and started for the doorway, but the smoke was thick in her vision and thick in her lungs. She was losing control of her legs. She could not make the leaps back above the raging wheels. Her vision was dimming. She could just make out the doorway in the billowing smoke and a figure standing there. Her knees gave way, and she sank to the floor, the dossier spilling beside her, fodder for the rampaging flames.

THE IDIOT'S DEFENCE

16 August 1093, The Viscount's House, Tolosa

*A*nna's nausea was awful. Her hands were shaking, and she knew the blood had drained from her face. Her stomach roiled. Philippa gripped her hand tightly as the guards escorted them to the viscount's hall. Curious faces lined their route, pointing fingers at her. She averted her eyes from what they were saying.

In the hall, Viscount Ademar and Count Raimon were seated at the high table. At first, all Anna could see was a blur of faces. Her emotions and sickness overwhelmed her. She had to get a grip on herself. She recognised the kindly and concerned face of the viscountess. She saw Bertrand frowning at her, but she could not tell if he frowned with concern or disgust. Mafalda was there, Abbot Frotard, Bishop Izarn and Gauzlin – all in their black robes like so many crows in a graveyard. Henry of Burgundy sat on the bench close to the dais and gestured to Lady Philippa that she should sit with him.

When Philippa let go of Anna's hand, Anna felt she might fall down. She was alone in a sea of others. A stool was placed dead centre before Raimon and Ademar. A guard pushed her down onto it.

She looked up at Count Raimon and saw his mouth was moving, but his head was bowed over a parchment before him on the table. He was reading, but she could not see the words on his lips.

'Stop!' She rose to her feet.

The guard was about to push her back down roughly, but Philippa echoed, 'Stop! Anna's lawyer is on the way. You must wait for his arrival. *Please*, wait,' she added.

Anna struggled to shift her gaze quickly enough between the faces to see what they were saying. The viscount spoke to Count Raimon, but she was still in such a state of turmoil that she could not settle enough to understand what was said.

'Stop!' she called out again.

Raimon and Ademar looked at her. 'Why do you shout out?' Raimon said, and she could see his mouth now. 'It is not for you to order us!'

'I say stop because it is for me to know what is said in a trial for my life. I cannot know what is said if you do not look at me when you speak.'

Anna saw Raimon was about to shout her down, but Ademar spoke. 'We can certainly do this, Count. We can speak so that Anna can understand.'

Raimon took a breath, his expression reluctant and impatient. 'Very well, we will address the deaf woman so that she can see our lips moving on our words.'

'Thank you, lord,' Anna said. She took a deep breath. Calm was beginning to befriend her.

Raimon and Ademar looked up past her to something happening at the back of the hall. She turned to follow their gaze. Roger was coming in with a young red-haired man at his side.

'Stop!' called out the young man.

Anna looked back at Count Raimon to see his eyebrows rising at all these upstarts telling him to stop.

She turned to look again at the back of the hall. Petrus Regimundus was close behind Roger and the young man. 'I am this young woman's lawyer,' said the man, who she had never seen before. 'These proceedings must stop on the basis of the idiot's defence.'

Anna turned back to the dais just in time to see Count Raimon say, 'The what?'

The young man moved to a position where Anna could see his face, but he could also address the judges. Philippa must have instructed him in this. 'Since the woman is deaf, she cannot fully participate in these oral proceedings. She must be granted the rights of a minor to a no trial.'

Raimon's expression was sour and Ademar was speaking in his ear. The lawyer placed a scroll on the table before them and handed a copy to Anna, who read through it as Raimon and Ademar were doing the same.

Anna rose to her feet again and addressed the count

and viscount. 'I am sorry, but I cannot accept such nonsense. I am not incompetent. I am not a minor. I am able to read and write and have intelligent thought like the rest of you.' She looked around the room at each of the faces. 'But I am not a murderer. I am innocent of this crime.'

Count Raimon leapt on Anna's statement. 'The woman says she is competent and so she sounds. The idiot's defence is denied.'

Anna saw Philippa put her face in her hands. She sat down, mustering her dignity. 'Please continue to speak so that I can see you,' she said to the lawyer and to the judges. Where was Beatriz with their evidence? Where was Lluis?

Count Raimon recounted the evidence of the stab wound and the brooch found in Beatriz's possessions and the lute string used to garrotte him. 'The lute with the missing string was in the possession of this young woman, the maid Anna. There are several witnesses to this effect, including my niece, Lady Philippa of Tolosa.'

Philippa looked up at Anna, her face a picture of misery.

Raimon continued. 'The *trobairitz* Beatriz of Farrera was exonerated by Lluis of Pedret, a sculptor at Saint-Sernin. She had been in his bed all night. The deaf girl must have concealed the brooch to incriminate her so-called friend.'

'Where are Beatriz and Lluis?' the viscount asked. 'They should be here to give testimony.'

Raimon shrugged. 'Enough of us heard that evidence.

Saw the sculptor swear it on a prayer book. Perhaps they have absconded. We cannot wait for them.'

'Might we beg a small break,' Jaufre said, 'to locate them? Beatriz of Farrera is carrying important evidence for the case in support of the accused.'

Raimon looked displeased but declared, 'Very well. We will take a break. Secure the prisoner. We will resume when the candle burns down.' Gauzlin placed a short candle on the table before the two judges. Raimon stood and left the hall. Ademar moved his painful knee to a different position and massaged it. The guard bent to tie Anna's hands and then to tie her ankles to the stool. 'This is not necessary,' Philippa approached and remonstrated with him.

'Sorry, lady. It was the count's orders.'

Anna wriggled uncomfortably in her restraints and watched the candle burning relentlessly down. Philippa brought a beaker of water to her lips and made her drink. 'Beatriz will be here soon,' she mouthed. But Beatriz did not come. The candle reached its remnants and fizzled out.

'We will resume and conclude these proceedings,' declared Count Raimon as he shifted the bench to resume his seat. 'I have other business to attend to today.'

'Please untie Anna,' Philippa said angrily. 'There is no need to keep her bound like a pig at market. She needs to be able to move, to see fully what is going on.'

Count Raimon jerked his head to the guard, who set about undoing the knots. Anna rubbed her wrists as the blood flowed back in.

Count Raimon was speaking again and pointed at Anna. 'The evidence shows clearly that this …' He stopped, his mouth open, staring at the back of the hall.

Anna swivelled on her stool to see what he was looking at. Lluis was in the doorway, supporting Beatriz, who had one arm slung around his neck and the other hanging limp at her side. He part-carried her into the hall to sit alongside Anna, hooking one foot around another stool and dragging it over, carefully lowering Beatriz onto it. Anna saw streaks of soot on Beatriz's face and smelled the strong scent of smoke upon her. Beatriz wobbled on the stool as if she would fall, and Lluis supported her back.

'What is this?' demanded Raimon.

'I found Beatriz on one of the floating mills. Someone had set fire to the flour and tried to kill her.'

Philippa went to Beatriz. She gestured to a maid for a beaker of wine for her. She knelt and took Beatriz's hands. 'Are you alright?'

'I will be.'

'You look …' Philippa searched Beatriz's face. 'You have no eyebrows!'

'No, nor any hair on my arms!' Beatriz held out one of her arms.

'If you have other evidence, present it,' Raimon said. 'If not, I'm ready to pronounce sentence.'

Beatriz got shakily to her feet, pushing down hard on Lluis' arm to help her rise. 'Lord, I have uncovered evidence against Gauzlin and evidence against Petrus Regimundus.'

Anna saw commotion, mouths opening and closing as

people shouted in consternation. Petrus was at the back of the hall and would have left if the people there had not stopped him. Abbot Frotard took hold of Gauzlin's wrist. Bertrand's expression was avid. She turned back to the dais to look at Raimon.

'What evidence do you have?' Raimon demanded.

Anna struggled to keep swivelling between speakers and following what was happening in the hall.

'I have a sworn statement from the overseers and a man they interrogated in Aigues-Mortes that Vicar Regimundus is behind the recent salt thefts.'

Jaufre helped Beatriz sort through the materials in the dossier Lluis had carried in for her, and he found the relevant one. He passed it to Raimon and Ademar.

'Well, Vicar?' demanded the count, looking down the length of the hall.

Anna watched Petrus' face. 'This is a lie, lord, I swear it.'

Raimon must have gestured to the guards because they took hold of Petrus.

Anna screwed up her nose as the guards pulled Petrus towards the dais. 'He smells strongly of smoke,' Anna said, 'like Beatriz.'

Viscount Ademar was looking at his brother with horror. 'You are a thief and a would-be murderer?'

'It's all untrue,' Petrus declared. 'You believe the word of this slattern over me.' He was pointing at Beatriz, his expression incredulous.

Raimon wafted the letter from the overseers at Aigues-Mortes. 'I believe this. Take him away and secure him for questioning.'

Petrus was marched from the hall, and Anna watched him throw a sign to Mafalda as he passed her. One of the monks' signs. *Get me free.* She turned back to the dais to see Raimon say, 'I see no connection to Imbert's murder, however.'

'Imbert was investigating the salt theft. We have proof in this book, which is in code.' Beatriz waved the book. 'Anna has broken the code and can explain it to you.'

'You also accused Gauzlin.' The count and everyone there looked over at Gauzlin where he stood in the grip of Abbot Frotard. 'So, which is it?' Count Raimon asked. 'Do you accuse Petrus or Gauzlin or Imbert's murder?'

'Gauzlin was spying for Cluny. I have proof of that here, too.' She handed up the copy of the letter from Abbot Begon. 'Imbert, in turn, was spying for the pope against Cluny.' Beatriz looked down at the naked drawing of Gauzlin in her dossier. She would hold it in reserve if the rest was not enough to free Anna.

'You have been very busy, *Trobairitz.*' Count Raimon's expression was almost humorous. 'Perhaps I should employ you as my new vicar.' He swivelled to face Ademar but by bending, Anna could just catch his words. 'It seems we have more work to do, Ademar.' He turned back and addressed the hall. 'We will assess the import of this evidence and make further enquiries. The maid Anna is released into your custody, Philippa, for now.'

Relief coursed through Anna. Again, she felt she might collapse, but with happiness this time. Beatriz and Philippa pulled her to her feet and took her into an embrace.

'You smell so bad, Beatriz!' laughed Anna.

'She does,' agreed Philippa.

Beatriz just laughed and put her two smoky hands on Anna's cheeks. Roger, Lluis and Henry stood nearby smiling and waiting to escort them back to Chateau Narbonnais.

FUGITIVES

Michaelmas 1093, Tolosa

*T*he court reconvened the following day in the viscount's hall, but the configuration of people had changed subtly. Count Raimon and Viscount Ademar sat on the dais as before, but Gauzlin sat on the stool in front of them. Anna was seated protectively on the side bench between Philippa and Beatriz. Beatriz searched the faces of the people crowded into the hall but could find no trace of Petrus or Mafalda.

'We have interrogated this cleric,' Count Raimon declared with distaste, 'and he has confessed to his crime.'

A rumble of gasps and whispers flowed around the crowded hall. Gauzlin's head was bowed, his hands clasped in prayer and his lips moving in silent penance.

'More copies of spying letters he had sent to Cluny

were discovered among his possessions. The letters described events in Tolosa, at Saint-Sernin, at my court, at Saint-Pons-de-Thomières. You have betrayed my court,' Raimon fair thundered his final statement at the quivering monk. 'Furthermore, this man, Gauzlin, priest of Cluny and Moissac, has confessed to stabbing Imbert. Do you have anything to say in your defence?'

Gauzlin mumbled and could not meet the eyes of the count.

'Speak up!' Raimon instructed impatiently.

The guard pulled the monk to his feet and shook his arm hard. Gauzlin swallowed and looked up to Count Raimon and Viscount Ademar. 'I stabbed Imbert with the brooch. I admit it,' Gauzlin quavered. 'He tricked me. I thought he was my friend, but he was blackmailing me. He … he was making my life a misery of anxiety. I couldn't stand it anymore.' His account was gaining in volume. 'But, lords, I swear he was alive when I left him in the undercroft. He would have recovered from that wound. The brooch was still in his neck when I left him there.' He gasped down bile at his own memory of the scene. 'Lords, please believe me. I did not pull the brooch out of his neck and put it in Beatriz's belongings. I swear to that on the Bible. Someone else must have done that, must have killed him!' His final sentence was desperately voiced.

Raimon waved an impatient hand. 'You have confessed to the assault on Imbert. We have no reason to listen to your excuses and further lies. I find you guilty of murdering Imbert and betraying my court.'

Bishop Izarn stood hurriedly. 'Brother Gauzlin is a cleric and subject to my justice, my lord!'

Raimon considered the bishop and Gauzlin with displeasure. He conferred with Ademar in a low voice. 'Very well. The scribe Gauzlin is handed over to the ecclesiastical court who will decide on his fate.'

Beatriz stood hurriedly. 'What of Petrus Regimundus? Where is he? He certainly committed theft against you, lord, and he tried to kill me. Is it not more likely his hand that wielded the garrotte? You saw the evidence of the glove, my lords.' Were they trying to cover it up? Making Gauzlin now the scapegoat for it all. Was Viscount Ademar covering for his brother? She stared angrily at him.

'Petrus has disappeared,' the viscount said mildly, eyeing Beatriz and knowing what she was implying. 'He managed to slip his guards and cannot be found anywhere in Tolosa.'

'The nun Mafalda is also missing,' added Abbot Frotard.

'We will find Petrus, and … the nun if she is involved,' Count Raimon declared. 'The maid Anna is exonerated and released.'

Gauzlin was taken away by soldiers to be held in the bishop's dungeon and sentenced by the ecclesiastical court. Anna and Philippa stood and embraced.

Raimon's voice interrupted their ecstasy. 'Niece!'

Philippa passed an emotional Anna to Beatriz. 'Uncle?'

'You will prepare to travel into the mountains. You will leave tomorrow.'

'Tomorrow …' Philippa drew herself up, readying for an argument.

'There has been enough delay. We received news today of the death of my aunt, Countess Lucia de la Marca. You and Bertrand will go first to Pallars Sobira and represent the family at the burial. Then you will travel on to Jaca to meet your mother and your husband, King Sancho. Bertrand will accompany you.'

'I can take Beatriz with me, as well as Anna?'

Raimon glanced at Beatriz and turned back to Philippa, nodding, disinterested. 'The *trobairitz* is no use to Imbert now. Henry of Burgundy is returning to King Alfonso's court at Sahagun and will also travel with you, and Abbot Frotard. You will be well protected. Some of the artists and masons from Saint-Sernin are travelling with your party too, on their way to Compostela. You should organise your possessions. You have little time. God speed to you, Niece.'

Philippa held her uncle's gaze for a long moment, her expression inscrutable. She gestured for Beatriz and Anna to follow her from the hall.

In her own chambers, her composure dissolved. 'My fate is sealed! Duke Guillaume has not fulfilled his promise. I will be queen in Aragon then, and my uncle steals my inheritance.' She hung her head and glumly contemplated her clasped hands in her lap. After a moment, she rallied. 'But we must celebrate Anna's release. Between the three of us, we have saved Anna and solved the mystery of Imbert's murder!'

Beatriz frowned. 'Actually, we have saved Anna and partly solved the mystery.'

'What do you mean, Beatriz?' asked Anna.

'Gauzlin confessed to stabbing Imbert. He was motivated by his need to regain the evidence Imbert had against him of his spying for Cluny and he feared exposure of his sin of sodomy.'

'Yes,' said Philippa. 'He has confessed.' Impatience was growing in her expression and Beatriz glimpsed, for a moment, the family resemblance between Philippa and her uncle Raimon.

'But he did not confess to garrotting Imbert. Do you really think he had the strength to do that? The brooch injured Imbert. Gauzlin certainly committed that injury. But it was the garrotte that killed Imbert.'

'What are you saying, Beatriz?' asked Anna. 'That the murderer was Petrus?'

'Yes. If it was him who chased me onto the floating mill, his attempt to kill me seems to prove his guilt, although I suppose he could have just been trying to destroy the evidence of his salt theft. The person who garrotted Imbert, the actual killer, could be right or left-handed.'

'It must be Petrus,' stated Philippa.

'Lluis was on the mill, in the fire,' said Beatriz. 'I didn't see Petrus.'

'Your delusion concerning Lluis, again!' Philippa exclaimed. 'Remember the prophecy of the Holy Lots, Beatriz? You will be deceived by your faults.'

'That's meaningless!'

'Not so. One of your faults is to distrust men. Lluis saved you!'

'I suppose so,' Beatriz said grudgingly.

'Don't ignore the evidence of my nose, Beatriz,' Anna told her. 'Petrus definitely set that fire. I could smell it on him, just as I smelled it on you and Lluis. Do you think Mafalda has run away with Petrus? Do you think she was involved in the murder, after all?'

'Mafalda was desperate to escape her nun's habit,' Philippa said. 'She has dallied with Roger, but that was only lust by her own word. He could not help her escape. Perhaps she believed Petrus would. He is of noble blood and he was amassing a fortune from his thievery. Her only other option was Henry.'

'Henry?' Beatriz asked, astonished.

'While you were away, we observed Mafalda and Henry speaking close together on several occasions. But Henry could not afford to liberate Mafalda. She would bring him no dowry or kingdom.'

'Beatriz, there is something else you should know,' Anna gained her attention, pulling at her arm. 'I looked through those papers you gave me from Imbert's house. He did leave a will, and he left his house and instruments to you. I suppose there was nothing else because of his gambling.'

Beatriz exclaimed in surprise. 'Well ... that's ... that's extraordinary! Thank you, Imbert.' She cast her eyes to the ceiling, as if Imbert were up there. 'So now I own a house!'

Philippa looked worried. 'Oh, don't leave me, Beatriz, please. I need you now.'

'Of course not. I never thought to do that. We must travel into the Pyrenees, find out about Petrus and Mafalda, find a way out of this marriage for you.'

Philippa smiled her relief at Beatriz's response but said, 'There is no way out. The duke has reneged, or perhaps never intended to offer marriage to me.'

Beatriz sighed. There was no use in trying to guess at the twists and turns of the duke's mind. 'Will you write to Yselda and Amelie in Uzès for me, Anna?' she asked. 'I must tell them about Imbert's will and instruct them to continue taking care of the house. I suppose I have to send them some money, but I don't ...'

'I will send money and a messenger for you with the letter Anna will write,' Philippa said. 'The messenger can read the letter to your new servants.' She smiled at Beatriz's astonished expression.

'Thank you.' Beatriz dictated the note to Anna and watched Anna folding and sealing the parchment. Eventually, she voiced what had been on her mind since Count Raimon's mention of his aunt's funeral in the Pyrenees. 'Pallars Sobira is close to my home, to Farrera.'

'You should visit your father,' Anna said, and Philippa nodded her agreement.

'Perhaps so.'

THE MORNING CAME on relentless and there was no sign of the duke, nor any clue concerning the whereabouts of Mafalda or Petrus. The hall buzzed with the news that the ecclesiastical court and Bishop Izarn had decided to send Gauzlin back to Cluny to do penance as a murderer.

The travel party began to assemble in the courtyard with Count Raimon and Viscount Ademar standing on the hall steps to see them off. Bertrand took a perfunctory leave of Helie and a more lingering farewell with his hound, Bragge.

Henry took leave of Helie, kissing the back of her hand and passing it to Raimon. He mounted his horse and took up a place at the head of the cavalcade alongside Philippa. Henry was as colourfully dressed as the first time Beatriz had seen him. His overtunic was a vivid green and gold and contrasted with his longer undertunic of brown and white, which matched his cloak. He settled the fabrics around himself carefully in the saddle. Philippa's expression was closed and Beatriz guessed she was struggling to conceal the emotion she felt at leaving her home and her birthright.

Behind Henry and Philippa, rode Bertrand and Abbot Frotard, who would not be comfortable travel companions. 'The Christian advances in Iberia have slipped away again, I hear,' Bertrand said, baiting the abbot, who pursed his lips, preparing a retort.

Lluis approached Bertrand's horse. Bertrand leant down from the saddle and the two men spoke quietly together so that the abbot could not overhear. Concluding his conversation with Bertrand, Lluis mounted the horse a servant held for him and steered the horse alongside Beatriz. His greeting was tentative.

'You go to work on the cathedral at Compostela?' she asked. She searched his face in vain for any clue concerning the vestiges of her suspicions over the night of Imbert's murder, which she could not remember, and the fire on the floating mill, which was similarly obscured from her penetration by a haze of smoke and the noise of water thundering in the mill wheels and fire cracking through flour sacks.

'Yes,' Lluis responded, 'but I will ride with you to Pallars Sobira on the way. I will see my father who is working on a chapel fresco there. And you? Will you see your father? Farrera is nearby.'

Beatriz shrugged. 'I doubt we will go that way.' She turned her face away, intent on having no further friendly conversation with him. She could not trust him. She did not know where his loyalties were anchored. After a while, she glanced sidelong at his face, saw him frowning at her coolness. He urged his horse forward to ride alongside Bertrand.

Beatriz looked over her shoulder to see Roger ride up behind her, and Anna took up a position alongside him on her own horse. Roger and Anna exchanged a sunny and silent greeting with each other.

The group were accompanied by six men-at-arms and several servants hauling a string of mules, laden with their baggage, including Beatriz's instruments. A cart pulled by two oxen held the belongings Philippa had chosen to take with her into Aragon, including the princess chest, her own chests of robes and jewels, her bed, her books, her cat constrained in a wicker cage. Adimante walked alongside Philippa's horse. Bertrand's Bragge whined from the stable where a groom held him fast.

The Holy Lots had failed Philippa. Duke Guillaume had given her only lies and empty flattery. Would the Holy Lots be equally unkind to Beatriz? What path would she find and were there more serpents on her route? Was she safe now, or were her faults still deceiving her? She looked at Lluis' back. His fair hair glinted in the sun. He was happy to be going to a new artistic challenge, to be on the road. But she did not know his mind. As they rode through the gate, into the city, Beatriz swivelled in the saddle to look back for a final view of the pink walls of Chateau Narbonnais.

TROBAIRITZ SLEUTH SERIES

Book 2 coming soon

In Book 2 of this series, Beatriz, Anna and Philippa travel into the Pyrenees and the Iberian kingdoms.

Become a free subscriber to my quarterly newsletter, *Just Meandering*, to receive news on the publication date of the next book in the series.

https://justmeandering.substack.com

HISTORICAL NOTE

Preconceptions about the long period of the Middle Ages need to be nuanced by knowledge of specific times and specific places. In the eleventh century, France was simply the region around Paris. The territory to the south had a different language (Occitan), a different culture, and different laws from the north and had close ties to the Iberian kingdoms across the Pyrenees. Occitania was invaded in the thirteenth century by the northern French in the Albigensian Crusade, which was ostensibly a military campaign against the Cathar heresy, but which was also an attack against many of the Occitan lords. The south was subsumed into the French kingdom and the Occitan language and culture were suppressed.

At the end of the nineteenth century, children speaking Occitan at school were punished in the *vergonha* (the shaming). There have been efforts to revive Occitan since the early 20th century. There are an estimated 600,000 fluent Occitan speakers and the language continues to regain impetus. Occitan is an official language in Catalonia and Italy, but it is still not officially recognised in France. In 2016, after a public vote, the name Occitanie was adopted for a large administrative area of southern France.

All the noble characters in this novel were real historical people and the key events in their lives recounted here are based on historical evidence (see the genealogies on my blog https://traceywarrwriting.com/loves-knife-genealogies/). Nevertheless, this is a historical novel rather than a history. Beatriz, Anna, Lluis and Imbert are fictional, although there were real female troubadours (*trobairitz*) in Occitania (see Bogin, 1980; Bruckner, 2000; Dronke, 1984).

In depicting Anna, I have drawn on my childhood relationship with my deaf grandfather. Due to malnutrition, accidents, war, disease and the status of medieval medicine, a high proportion of people in the Middle Ages lived with some form of disability. This period had no notion of ableism or many other forms of discrimination. I have aimed to avoid gratuitous ableism, but some of my characters (such as Raimon and Bertrand) reflect common pejorative attitudes of the time towards disabilities. In a society where the majority of people were not literate, in a still largely oral society, the ears were viewed as the best means of gaining understanding. A disabled person was often seen as childlike or subhuman and they were assumed to be mentally impaired. It was often assumed that a deaf person was mute. They might be regarded as a 'holy fool', or closer to God, or their disability might be seen as a punishment for sin. The deaf were usually precluded from inheriting and were viewed as having limited legal agency.

This novel takes place before the invention of any complete sign language and before the emergence of deaf communities. There are a few examples of first-person accounts by medieval deaf people, including Chaucer's fictional account of the Wife of Bath (Hajduk, 2018; Sayers, 2010); Rixendis of Rayensa (Kuuliala, 2016: 253); and Teresa of Cartagena's *Arboleda de los enfermos*, written in fifteenth-century Castile, which expressed the solitude of her deafness (Cartagena, 1998). The *Love's Knife* extended bibliography on my website includes additional sources on deafness in eleventh- and twelfth-century Europe (https://traceywarrwriting.com/loves-knife-extended-bibliography/).

My Substack, 'Love's Knife and its Bread', https://traceywarr.substack.com has posts on a range of topics I researched for this book, such as Toulouse's floating mills, the pilgrim routes, monks' sign language, the medieval salt trade, troubadours and *trobairitz*, female inheritance, and the Witham Pins brooch. These posts are also listed in the extended bibliography.

Medieval attitudes towards sexuality ranged through a negative and repressive stance to an earthier and lustier picture. The Church taught that the purpose of sex was procreation. Sex between men, or 'sodomy', as it was termed, was reviled because it was nonreproductive. In the early medieval period, sodomy was tolerated as long as it did not become publicly notorious, but intolerance gradually increased. Around 1051, Peter Damian wrote his *Book of Gomorrah* on 'the sin against nature' among the clergy. Sodomy was outlawed from the twelfth century and the death penalty was introduced in the thirteenth century (Karras & Pierpont, 2023).

Guillaume of Aquitaine was the first recorded troubadour and a fine poet. The troubadour poetry of the eleventh to thirteenth centuries was the first poetry in medieval Western Europe to be composed in the vernacular language – in Occitan – rather than in Latin (Bond, 1995). Poitiers in Aquitaine was bilingual, on the border of Occitania and France. Guillaume of Aquitaine spoke both *langue d'oil*, the language of the north and *lenga d'oc*, the language of the south, of Occitania, of *trobador* poetry. I have given his name in *langue d'oil*.

Troubadour poetry was created for an audience of connoisseurs who could appreciate its difficult forms, complex rhymes, and literary references. Beatriz and Guillaume refer to the influence of Arabic poetic forms from Andalusia (the *muwashsha* and *kharja*). The troubadours were listening and singing to each other, responding to and reinventing each other's songs. The court game of *trobar* began in southern France, in Occitania, and spread across Europe to Spain, northern France, England, Germany, Italy.

The troubadours composed their own music and poetry and were not, on the whole, wandering entertainers (Egan, 2018). Many troubadours were noblemen and women, such as Guillaume IX, duke of Aquitaine; Jaufre Rudel, prince of Blaye; Richard the Lionheart, king of England; Count Raimbaut d'Aurenga; and the Comtesse de Dia. Some troubadours were less exalted and travelled from court to court, seeking patronage. An example is Bernart de Ventadorn, who was probably the son of a baker. Some troubadour poems were bawdy, some were political, but the majority were love songs (Blackburn, 1978; Bogin, 1980; Dronke, 1968; Goldin, 1973).

A significant number of poems by women have survived. There are around twenty-one named *trobairitz* with poems preserved in the manuscripts. That compares to some four hundred named male troubadours. Between twenty-six and forty-six songs have been attributed to women. A further seventeen *trobairitz* are mentioned in other texts, but none of their work survives. Only one poem by a woman has survived with its musical notation – 'A chantar m'er' by the Comtesse de Dia. The majority of *trobairitz* were well-educated women of the court. The term *trobairitz* comes from *Flamenca*, the only surviving medieval novel in verse in Occitan (Bruckner, 2000).

The laws in Occitania were based on Visigothic rather than Roman traditions and afforded women more status than women in other regions. An assessment of the surviving charters from the eleventh and twelfth centuries shows 10–12% of the southern lords or vassals were women acting in their own right (Debax, 2013). A few women ruled in their own right as heiresses, when there was no surviving male heir (see, for example, Cheyette, 2001, on Ermengard of Narbonne). Many women became regents when their husbands died and their sons were still children. Examples of Occitan *domnas* (female lords) include Ermessende of Carcassonne, who ruled Barcelona for at least sixteen years; Almodis de La Marche, who was countess of Toulouse and then co-ruled

Barcelona with her husband (see my novel, *Almodis: The Peaceweaver*); Almodis' sister Lucia de La Marca, who was regent in Pallars Sobira in the Pyrenees; Marie of Montpellier; Ermengard of Carcassonne; Ermengard of Narbonne; and Eleanor of Aquitaine.

By the twelfth century, matrimonial and inheritance customs were gradually changing, concentrating inheritance in the oldest son. The rate of this change in the south was gradual, happening over a couple of centuries, and varying from family to family. The division of the domain of Toulouse between the two brothers, Guilhem IV of Tolosa and Raimon IV of Saint-Gilles, is an example of 'partition', based on Visigothic practices, but the brothers' agreement that Raimon (as the surviving male kin) would inherit rather than Philippa is based on Roman practices (see Mundy, 1954). Gradually, cognate inheritance (with ancestry traced through the male or female line) was shifting to agnate inheritance (brothers inherited first, before sons), and then, eventually, to patrilineal inheritance (through the first-born male line).

BIBLIOGRAPHY

Blackburn, P. (1978). *Proensa: An anthology of troubadour poetry*. New York Review of Books.

Bogin, M. (1980). *The women troubadours*. W. W. Norton.

Bond, G. A. (1995). *The loving subject: Desire, eloquence, and power in Romanesque France*. University of Pennsylvania Press.

The British Museum (n.d.). *The Witham Pins*. The British Museum. https://www.britishmuseum.org/collection/object/H_1858-1116-4

Bruckner, M., Shephard, L. & White, S. (2000). *Songs of the women troubadours*. Routledge.

de Cartagena, T. (1998). *The writings of Teresa de Cartagena: Translated with introduction, notes, and interpretive essay* (Dayle Seidenspinner-Núñez, Trans.). D.S. Brewer.

Catalo, J. (2007). Pérennité des lieux de pouvoir: Le château Narbonnais de Toulouse, porte monumentale antique transformée en forteresse. *Archéopages*, 19, August.

Cheyette, F. L. (2001). *Ermengard of Narbonne and the world of the troubadours*. Cornell University Press.

Débax, H. (2013). Le lien d'homme à homme au féminin: Femmes et féodalité en Languedoc et en Catalogne (XIe–XIIe siècles). *Etudes Roussillonnaises: Les Femmes Dans L'Espace Nord-Méditerranéen*, 25, 71–82.

Dillon, H. (2016). *Walking the Middle Ages on the Camino de Santiago: The history behind The Way*. Self-published.

Dronke, P. (1968). *The medieval lyric*. D. S. Brewer.

Egan, M. (2018). *The vidas of the troubadours*. Routledge.

Goldin, F. (1973). *Lyrics of the troubadours and trouveres*. Doubleday.

Henriet, P. (2017). Cluny and Spain before Alfonso VI: Remarks and propositions. *Journal of Medieval Iberian Studies*, *9*(2), 206–219.

Hill, J. H. & Hill, L. L. (1959). *Raymond IV of Saint-Gilles*. Edouard Privât.

Hajduk, M. L. (2018). *I can't hear you: Queering and hearing in the wife of Bath's prologue and tale*. [Doctoral dissertation, Seton Hall University] https://scholarship.shu.edu/dissertations/2545

Institute National de Recherches Archéologiques Préventives (2016). *La redecouverte du Chateau Narbonnais a Toulouse.* https://www.inrap.fr/la-redecouverte-du-chateau-narbonnais-toulouse-11887

Karras, R. M. & Pierpont, K. E. (2023). *Sexuality in medieval Europe: Doing unto others* (4th edn.). Routledge.

Kurlansky, M. (2003). *Salt.* Vintage.

Kuuliala, J. (2016). *Childhood disability and social integration in the Middle Ages.* Brepols.

Metzler, I. (2006). *Disability in medieval Europe: Thinking about physical impairment in the High Middle Ages c. 1100–c. 1400.* Routledge.

Mortimer, I. (2024). *Medieval horizons.* RosettaBooks.

Wikipedia (n.d.). *Moulins de Château Narbonnais.* Wikipedia. https://fr.wikipedia.org/wiki/Moulins_du_Château-Narbonnais

Mundy, J. H. (1954). *Liberty and political power in Toulouse 1050–1230.* Columbia University Press.

Paterson, L. M. (1993). The world of the troubadours: Medieval Occitan society, c. 1100–c. 1300. Cambridge University Press.

Picard, M. (1952). *The world of silence.* Gateway.

Rée, J. (2000). *I see a voice: A philosophical history of language, deafness and the senses.* Flamingo.

Sayers, E. E. (2010). Experience, authority, and the mediation of deafness: Chaucer's wife of Bath. *Disability in the Middle Ages: Reconsiderations and reverberations,* (pp. 81–92). Ashgate.

Le Studio Différemment (2016). De la porte au château, *Patrimoine,* Feb–Mar, 60–63. http://www.studiodifferemment.com/telechargement/PDF/toulouseb42portenarbonnaise.pdf

Werckmeister, O. K. (1988). Cluny III and the pilgrimage to Santiago de Compostela. *Gesta, 27*(1/2), 103–112.

Wright, S. K. (2017). The salting down of Gertrude: Transgression and preservation in three early German carnival plays. *Early Theatre, 20*(2), 11–30.

ACKNOWLEDGEMENTS

Beatriz de Farrera was 'born' during a residency I undertook at the Centre d'Art i Natura in Farrera in the Catalan Pyrenees. Immense thanks to Lluis, Ceske and Arnau Llobet for their hospitality and inspiring conversations in Farrera. In conjuring up Beatriz, I used Whistler's portrait of Alice Butt.

A map of early medieval Toulouse given to me by Musée des Augustins inspired me to find out about water mills on the River Garonne. A speculative image of Chateau Narbonnais by François Brosse (Le Studio Différemment, 2016) helped me imagine the characters moving around in the chateau. The remains of the count's palace were recently discovered beneath the contemporary Palais de Justice in Toulouse and have been explored in archaeological digs (see https://traceywarr.substack.com/p/the-medieval-palace-of-the-counts).

The poem in Chapter 6 is an extract from 'The winter that comes to me' by Bernart de Ventadorn (Goldin, 1973, p. 131). 'A knight once lay beside' in Chapter 8 is an extract from a song by Gaucelm Faidit (Blackburn, 1978, p. 195). 'Time comes, and turns, and goes' in Chapter 8 is an extract from a song by Bernart de Ventadorn (Goldin, 1973, p. 155). The poem in Chapter 10 is an extract from 'Of things I'd rather keep in silence I must sing' by

Comtesse de Dia (Bogin, 1980, p. 83). The poem in Chapter 21 is an extract from 'Zephyr arises gently', an anonymous Latin *winileod* from the early eleventh century (Dronke, 1968, pp. 92–93). In his letter to Philippa in Chapter 22, Duke Guillaume is quoting from Baudri of Bourgueil (Bond, 1995).

Bertrand's tale of salting virgins derives (anachronistically) from fifteenth-century Bavarian carnival manuscripts, which are discussed in an article by Wright (2017). A 1557 engraving in the Bibliotheque Nationale in Paris shows women 'salting' their husbands' genitalia to increase their libido.

Thanks to Bob Smillie, my muse who keeps me company through the ups and downs of writing and life in general. My daughter Lola Warr is an inspiration when writing about strong women and brilliant mothers. Countless thanks to all my supportive family and friends.

I am grateful to my friend Jane Swingler, who accompanied me on research trips to Toulouse and Aigues-Mortes and who has been an inspiration in so many ways, since we were eleven-year-olds together.

Thank you to Anne Mylan for filling me in on Easter rituals and Black Saturday; to my brilliant cover designer, Jessica Bell; and to my authenticity reader, Michelle Swinea. I have presented on the *trobairitz* in the Occitan University in Laguépie in France for the last two years. This informed my understanding of the *trobairitz* through the researched lectures and hands-on workshops I ran. Thank you to my collaborator Amandine Rey for her glorious singing of the *trobairitz* songs and to the valiant participants in my *trobairitz* workshop: Tiffany Black,

Veronique Gaumont, Christine Hopps, Anne Mylan and Florence Poret. Thanks also to the Occitan University organisers, Sylvain Lamur and Arne d'Avignon.

I am grateful to my early readers, especially Dianne Bonnet, Rob La Frenais, Orlando Hill, Sara Perry, Danae Penn, Marieke Ponsteen, Jack Turley and Julie Turley. Above all, I am grateful to the Laguépie Writers, who have been such good critical friends and who keep me writing: Gary Amphlett, Madeleine Hall, Ann Hebert, Peggy Lee and Tim Smith.

ABOUT THE AUTHOR

Tracey Warr was born in London, lived in southwest Wales and now lives in southern France. The castles and landscapes of Wales and France inspire her historical fiction. Her historical novels are set in medieval Europe and centred on strong female leads. She draws on old maps, chronicles, poems and objects to create fictional worlds for readers to step into. Her writing awards include an Author's Foundation Award, a Literature Wales Writer's Bursary, the Rome Film Festival Book Initiative and a Santander Research Award. Before becoming a full-time writer, she worked as a contemporary art curator and art history academic.

Sign up for the author's quarterly newsletter, *Just Meandering*, at https://justmeandering.substack.com

Follow her blog at https://traceywarrwriting.com

Publisher's website: https://meandabooks.com

facebook.com/traceywarrhistoricalwriting

ALSO BY TRACEY WARR

HISTORICAL FICTION

CONQUEST I: Daughter of the Last King
CONQUEST II: The Drowned Court
CONQUEST III: The Anarchy

HOUSE OF LA MARCHE I: The Viking Hostage
HOUSE OF LA MARCHE II: Almodis the Peaceweaver

FUTURE FICTION

The Water Age and Other Fictions
Meanda (French)

NON-FICTION

Writing in the Vicinity of Art Vol 1
The Water Age Art and Writing Workshops
The Water Age Children's Art and Writing Workshops

www.ingramcontent.com/pod-product-compliance
Ingram Content Group UK Ltd.
Pitfield, Milton Keynes, MK11 3LW, UK
UKHW030648100225
454893UK00004B/81

9 781739 425777